THE SAFEGUARDED HEART

THE SAFEGUARDED HEART SERIES BOOK ONE

MELANIE A. SMITH

WICKED DREAMS PUBLISHING

Published by
WICKED DREAMS PUBLISHING
info@wickeddreamspublishing.com
Boise, ID USA

Edited by Jennifer Gardner

Cover design by Wicked Dreams Publishing

Formatting by Wicked Dreams Publishing

eBook (K) ISBN: 978-1-7323900-0-3
eBook ISBN: 978-1-7328154-6-9
Paperback ISBN: 978-1-7323900-1-0
Hardback ISBN: 978-1-952121-02-9

CONTENTS

PROLOGUE

The threat of imminent death fills my senses, my brain clouded with pain and terror. I can't help but wonder if, knowing where it would lead, I would do anything differently. Knowing myself, likely not. My stubbornness knows no bounds, and my natural ability to persevere is what got me here in the first place.

In any case I know it's pointless to speculate, and this journey has been ten years in the making. And just as it seems like it will end in suffering and horror, so did it start, when I was only nineteen years old and broken to my core. My mind tears through memories, struggling to make sense of it all, taking me back to the time when, the pain of loss fresh once again, I turned to my grandparents. Remembering how they took me in and gave me comfort, wisdom, and direction as I climbed out of my pit of despair to finish my business degree.

My grandfather, especially, gave me so much more. His cheerful, round, and wrinkled face flashes across my memory, and warmth spreads through me, my emotions mixing in a confusing swirl. A wealthy real estate tycoon since well before I was born, Grandpa was also a patient teacher. At his side I learned about the power of cash flow, how to negotiate from a position of strength with the simple ability to say "no" and mean it, and how to build a team that would start me down the same path he had walked more than four decades ago.

I made my fair share of mistakes in those early years, and he was there to see me through them all. Those small defeats had pushed me to grow, to adapt, and at the time had seemed like natural discomforts that I needed to endure to find my way. But looking back at the costs, I lament my thick skin, my acceptance of what "came with the territory."

Because, as the moment of my demise approaches, I realize with startling clarity that the real estate business, with its many facets and complexities, is ultimately about people. It's so easy to forget, amid the drive to succeed, that people's lives are in your hands.

My strength has always been in facts and figures, the bones on which the industry operates and grows. Learning how to handle people was always the most difficult part for me. So I used the same tactic I'd applied to everything else. I compartmentalized, quantified, and planned for it. Emotion and empathy were enemies to reason and logic.

And I realize only now that approach was an illusion. A

coping mechanism for my ruined ability to care deeply. To trust. To love. Perhaps the lack of those abilities is what led me here.

But that wasn't something my grandfather could teach me, and I had to learn this lesson myself.

And while my grandfather lived to proudly see me start my own business at twenty-five, I'm suddenly thankful he wasn't here to see me learn this lesson too late.

My gut wrenches at the thought of his disappointment. And at the thought of disappointing my nearly four dozen employees, who helped me build a full-service real estate investing support company. It was a niche I'd long hoped to carve, and it had just begun to bear real fruit.

As if it were a sign, in early February on nearly the anniversary of my grandfather's passing, we acquired two new major clients: The first, a large company looking for centralized property management. The second, another young but rising company that had moved into the Seattle area from San Francisco only a couple of months prior.

But nothing could have prepared me for what came next. For meeting Alessandro Giordano, the company's owner. Unspeakably handsome, with a thick Italian accent and a disarmingly charming demeanor. At least, at first.

As past events continue to spin through my frantic brain, I can't help but try to cling to the memories of those early months. The countless meetings, site visits, and rejected proposals that often brought us head-to-head in heated exchanges about almost everything. He is one of the most challenging people I've ever met. As stubborn and intelligent as he is handsome.

I remember, also, shutting down his flirtations from the start, noticing the appreciative glances from nearly every female in the office, and how frequently he returned them. It was clear from the beginning that he was a man who lusted voraciously after what he wanted and was used to getting it. I overestimated my ability to keep that part of me shut down. Or perhaps I merely underestimated his persistence.

Tears fill my eyes, and I wonder if I'll have another chance to tell him how I feel one last time. And that I forgive him.

ONE

As I ride the elevator up to my company's suite on the 30th floor, I breathe deeply, steeling myself for another challenging day. Another day of arguing with Buone Case, with Alessandro Giordano. I can't decide if I'm exhausted or thrilled by the prospect. Probably a bit of both. But, as it's Friday, there is a light at the end of the tunnel.

The elevator doors open, and I get the same small thrill I do every morning to see my company's name, Evans Realty Services, over the entryway of our reception area.

Though it's well before her usual start time, our reception-ist, Lucy Drummond, has already arrived. Just, from the looks of it, as she removes her coat and starts her computer.

"Good morning, Lucy," I offer as I enter.

She looks up, momentarily surprised, her dark eyes jumping

to meet mine. "Oh, Ms. Evans," she responds, "good morning. I didn't hear the elevator."

I smile warmly. "Sorry if I startled you," I apologize. "Why are you in so early?"

"I have to leave after lunch for a doctor's appointment," she explains, then adds in a dry tone, "Don't worry, there will be someone else in this afternoon to cover the phones."

Lucy has always been a bit mouthy for the year or so she's worked here, but I frankly find it kind of refreshing. And far preferable to the fake deference so many people show me.

"I have no doubt you have everything under control, as usual, Lucy," I reassure her. "I'll be in my office." Secretly, I do doubt it, as I doubt everything, but as the company grows I've had to learn to let go of micromanaging every dimension.

As usual, I don't see anyone else as I head to my office. Besides my general feeling that as the boss I should be here first, I like to be in before everyone else to have some quiet time to get ready for the day. I set my bag on my desk and hang my coat on the back of my office door, glancing at the dull, misty Seattle skyline out the window before taking a seat.

After sending a few emails, I review the latest briefing I've assembled for our weekly tag-up meeting with Buone Case. It's a summary of the relevant regulations governing build size based on property zoning. I'm hoping to use it to convince Mr. Giordano to scale back his plans or increase his budget. But the real trick will be convincing him he can't have both.

At first, I chalked up his insistence on waiting for perfection to a cultural difference — perhaps Italian real estate development is easier, more adaptable to the developer. But with several years of developing in the San Francisco Bay Area under his belt, and his clear shrewdness and business acumen, it's become clear that it's merely stubbornness. In a way I admire his tenacity, but it's bordering on being a nuisance, and in any case is impeding our ability to move forward.

A few minutes before the meeting I hear a small knock on my door. I look up, expecting to find my assistant, Maggie, checking in to remind me of the meeting, but instead am startled to see Mr. Giordano.

His dark brown hair carefully mussed, he looks more like a male model than a real estate developer leaning casually against my door frame. His fitted, tan slacks and black buttoned shirt open at the neck would be fitting for a casual Friday if they weren't clearly designer and impeccably tailored to his tall, slim frame.

"*Buongiorno*," he greets me, and as usual I must suppress a shiver of enjoyment at his deep, lilting accent. "Do you have a minute?"

"*Buongiorno*," I respond, glancing at the clock. "Of course. We have a few minutes before the meeting. Let's head to the conference room and we can talk."

I rise, bringing my laptop and folio. His appraising glance at my white button-front shirtdress belted over navy leggings reminds me why I never let him get me alone in my office.

"As you wish," he responds, hesitating in the doorway for a

moment as I approach. I slow and stop a respectable distance away. "You look lovely today."

"Thank you," I respond evenly, maintaining stern eye contact. "Shall we?"

He cocks a half-smile, one he's used to disarm me before, and stays put. But I'm practiced at ignoring his flirtations by now, so I simply stand my ground, waiting impassively for him to move.

For a moment we remain motionless, staring at each other, the tension in the room palpable. His smirk deepens, and he sighs lightly, stepping aside to end the standoff and let me pass. Most days I think he just enjoys the sport of it.

I breathe an inward sigh of relief, ignoring the tingling down my spine as he walks next to me, our hands swinging closely, threatening to brush against each other in the tight hallway. I hug my things to my chest, wrapping both of my hands around the warm laptop.

Before we can get very far, Jackson Williams, my assistant for the Buone Case project, spots us on his way to the conference room and joins us.

Relieved not to be alone with Mr. Giordano, I pull Jackson into a discussion that continues into our meeting.

But by the end of the hour we've made little progress, and both Jackson and I are struggling to find new ways to explain the contradictions at hand.

"Marco and I will review the legal descriptions this afternoon," Mr. Giordano finally promises as we wrap up the meeting. "But I'd still like to find a way to stick with our original scale."

I can see Jackson ready to beat his head against the desk.

"Again, the regulations simply don't support that," I insist. "You would need a significantly larger parcel."

"We're pushing our investors to their limit as it is," replies Maria Greco, Buone Case's finance lead. "We have no room there."

Mr. Giordano narrows his eyes at the report in front of him, as if challenging it to a staring contest will change what's on the page.

"Mr. Giordano, please," I say pleadingly, "review the data objectively. We'll get back together on Monday afternoon and try to find a path forward."

He leans back in his chair, his jaw twitching. He clearly has issues conceding defeat. I'd find it endearing if it wasn't so infuriating.

"It's time for lunch anyway," he finally says dismissively. "I'm sure we could all use a break."

There is a noticeable sigh of relief from everyone in the room, and I can't help but chuckle to myself. As everyone files out, Mr. Giordano stays fixed in his chair, running a finger slowly under his chin in thought.

"Ms. Evans, please stay," he asks quietly as I'm about to leave.

The last person files out in front of me and I glance back at him apprehensively. "All right," I concede slowly, leaving the door open and setting my things back on the table.

He rises, circling the table to close the door, then drops into the chair next to me. I attempt to control the pounding of my heart as he crosses his legs thoughtfully, leaning back in his chair.

"Serafina," he starts, and I'm jolted by his use of my first name. I've been very careful to keep things as formal as possible, so I'm wary of what he'll say next. "You are obviously an incredibly capable and knowledgeable businesswoman. Otherwise, I wouldn't be using your services. But surely you didn't get where you are by settling?"

I consider my response for a moment. I know he's trying, under the guise of flattery, to trap me into letting him persist with chasing his ideal.

"Mr. Giordano," I reply pointedly, and a smirk settles across his luscious pout, "I got where I am by working within the established system. What you're holding out for isn't going to work. I strongly urge you to review the data I've provided before we continue to discuss this further."

"Are you telling me what I want is impossible?" he asks shrewdly, with a look of such intensity on his face, I wonder for a moment if we're only talking about business.

"No," I admit, "but I am telling you what you want is going to cost you more than you have to spend."

He laughs suddenly, jarring me. "Despite what Maria says,

there is always a way to find more money," he replies dismissively.

I shake my head. "You misunderstand me, *signore*," I persist. "The biggest cost here is *time*. You've already spent more than two months pursuing your ideal, to no avail. It's April. If you want to build in the Seattle area, you're going to need to start. Soon."

His eyes darken a shade as he weighs my words, and he shakes his head lightly. He leans forward, placing his elbows on his knees.

"I appreciate your conservative approach," he allows, speaking into his lap at first. "It's a useful counterpoint to my methods, I see that. But what you must understand about me is, once I study a market, I have instincts about where and how to enter. I've found ignoring those instincts to be very dangerous." He looks up into my eyes for a long moment. "I'll review the data," he finally says. "But I'm not one to give up easily."

I regard him quietly. From everything I've heard of his success in San Francisco, one of the toughest markets on the planet, I can't argue that he must have good instincts. And his words make me realize my usual tenacity may have been replaced with reservations as a counterbalance to his dogged pursuit of what would amount to one of the best deals I've ever seen. But I'm hard-pressed to encourage him, as I know how often that kind of deal comes along and what the cost is of waiting for it.

"I'm sure you'll do what you feel is best," I reply

reservedly, switching the cross of my legs as I fidget under his heated stare.

"I know I'm a difficult bastard," he admits, smirking again. "I can't help that I'm used to getting what I want." He leans back in his chair, tilts his head, and cocks an eyebrow suggestively.

I bite back a snappy retort by reminding myself that it's his deal. His decision. And there's no way in hell I'm giving him the satisfaction of rising to his coy taunt.

As I remain silent, he purses his lips, and for a moment I think he looks disappointed.

"I'm sure we could do this all day," he says, abruptly changing the subject, "but you must be hungry. Can I take you to lunch?"

It's not his first invitation, and I'm sure it won't be his last. But my answer is always the same, and I'm sure he expects it.

"*Grazie*, but no," I reply lightly, rising from my chair. *Thanks, but no thanks. On all counts.* "I have work to do."

I can feel his eyes on me as I leave the room. Not for the first time I consider that his interest might purely be the simple intrigue of there being a female who spurns his advances. While he's not my usual type when I do bother dating, I'd have to be blind not to find him attractive. I'm just not sure why he's so interested in me. I'm pretty, in an average sense I suppose, with long, wavy brown hair, hazel eyes, and strong features, but I'm also thicker through my arms, chest, and thighs. Despite regular exercise and a decent diet, I'll never be the thin, gorgeous model type I imagine him with.

As I enter my office, I glance back to see him heading toward the elevator. His confidence radiates off him, his charm obvious even from the small greetings and interactions he has as he goes. If I know anything, it's that giving in to him would only bring trouble.

∾

That evening I drift toward sleep on the couch while watching an old movie. Between the tensions of the day, and my half-asleep mind, my thoughts drift back to Alessandro. I roll the name over my tongue and giggle.

Two months of working together, and he still continues testing my resolve on every front. The business side I can handle. The flirtation, though, unseats me more than I'd like to admit. He drops his hints shamelessly, though never publicly, and I wonder again if he's merely seeking the thrill of victory.

But in my drifting state I don't stop the thoughts like I usually would. Instead I dangerously start to wonder what might happen if I allowed it. The surprise on his face might just be worth it.

But then, things would get complicated. And I don't like complicated. Though it has been far too long since I've done, well, someone. I giggle again sleepily and push him and any thoughts of unleashing those desires back into their cage in my mind.

Monday afternoon we're at it again, late into the day. Jackson and I have spent the afternoon discussing the report with Buone Case's team. Marco Rossi and Giovanni Bianchi, Buone Case's architect and lead engineer, respectively, seem to understand the impediments. But ultimately it is Mr. Giordano's decision. And nothing we can say will convince him to back down.

The last hour has been spent formulating alternative possibilities to meet the project specs. Everything from looking outside the target area to contacting properties not for sale but ripe for an offer. All usual avenues, but none terribly likely to put us any closer to locking something down.

It's nearly seven when everyone else decides to go home. I'm so distracted by our conversation that before I realize it,

Mr. Giordano and I are alone in the conference room, and he has soundly rejected yet another of my proposed workarounds.

Completely exhausted and over the discussion, I seethe in silent fury and stand abruptly, stepping away from the table. "You can't dismiss me like that." His brown eyes flame with the same anger I feel.

"You work for me, yes?" he taunts.

It takes a lot to get under my skin, and he's done it. He's arrogant, demanding, and stubborn. He's been obstinate since day one, and I've hit my limit. And I'm done catering to him.

"No," I retort, "Evans Realty Services has contracted with your company on this project. We are not your servants, me least of all. And if you constantly refuse to see sense, I'm afraid we will be unable to meet your needs, *signore*."

He closes his mouth, runs a finger along his chin, and narrows his eyes. In one swift movement he stands and takes a step toward me. I step back, and my palms touch the wall behind me. He hovers over me and leans his head toward me with a wicked smile on his full lips. His dark eyes now dance with amusement, causing my stomach to tie into knots and my heartbeat to thunder in my ears.

"*Bravissima*. Finally. Not many people are willing to stand up to me," he says softly. He puts his lips at my ear and murmurs, "I like it."

I briefly register in surprise that he's been *waiting* for me to challenge him. But he's never been this close to me, and the sensation overwhelms me quickly. He smells of wine and spice, and it's making my head spin and my breathing accelerate. I shake my head, struggling to think clearly. He regards me for a moment and steps back.

"I apologize … I …" and for once this man seems at a loss for words. He clears his throat. "I have never … it won't happen again." He seems to realize he's crossed the line past his usual flirtation. But he looks disappointed.

"It's late. We're both tired. I think we should stop for the evening," I offer. But the tone in the room has changed. I am no longer angry, or exhausted. Against my better judgment, I'm intrigued.

He turns his palms out. "As you wish," he replies. But, perhaps sensing my weakness, he doesn't move. I examine the hard lines of his face, his thick, dark hair, his strong shoulders, and well-sculpted arms and chest in his designer button-up shirt. My eyes meet his, and I can tell he sees my thoughts. "If that's what you really want?"

I close my eyes briefly and take a deep breath, struggling to control the desire welling in me. But when I reopen my eyes he is standing over me. He raises his hand and runs a finger along my cheek as if asking for permission. My inner desires spring free of their cage, and my resolve melts. And I know what my answer is.

Dear God, yes. I tip my head back and part my lips. A small smile of triumph flits across his face and he grasps me firmly by the chin.

Softly, he touches his lips to mine, his mouth warm and

yielding, waiting for any sign of protest. It's been so long since I've so much as kissed anyone, and my whole body responds, shutting down any logic, any objections. A small sigh escapes me, and I kiss him back, gently moving my lips with his. My encouragement is enough. He wraps his arms around me and his kiss deepens, his tongue searching for mine.

My inhibitions melt away, and I run my hands through his hair, over his shoulders, down his arms as he presses me into the wall, his hands roving my body. His mouth moves along my jaw, neck, and shoulders, kissing and nipping a blazing trail before returning to mine.

With one hand he pulls my body to his, the other runs down my breast and circles my hardening nipple over my clothes. His warm, firm touch on my skin causes me to gasp with pleasure. He smiles and kisses my ear.

"You feel even more amazing than I'd imagined, *bella*," he murmurs into my ear, his voice like warm honey.

"Maybe if you'd spent a little less time thinking about that and focused on work," I tease him.

He puts both of his hands on my face and looks intently into my eyes, and my body tenses with anticipation.

"Yes," he admits, "but you've been a very pleasant distraction. And I'd very much like to do all manner of sinful things to you right here on this table." He kisses me softly.

"Mmmmmm," I moan. "This doesn't seem like the best place."

But even I know we are the only people in the office.

Though as I've found him as frustrating as he is fascinating for the months we've worked on this project together, I feel like I shouldn't let him persuade me so easily.

"It's just you and me," he assures me, and reading my hesitation, he trails warm kisses down my neck once more. I press my palms to his strong, broad chest and gently push him away. I look up into his deep, dark eyes. He sighs. "I see."

I shake my head. "Not here," I plead softly. He raises an eyebrow. "We meet here every day. It would be very difficult for me to pretend that it didn't happen when we're all in here tomorrow," I add. He laughs, and the full, deep noise echoes around the room.

"Yes," he concedes. "Though it won't matter where for me; I already have a hard time pretending around you." He folds his hand over mine and kisses each of my fingers in turn. "And it's getting harder by the minute."

Everything logical in me protests, distrusting his motives, his sincerity. But the part of me that's responded to him all that time has been let out of her cage, and she's taken over the driver's seat. His eyes sparkle as if he knows.

"Bring your things, we're going to my place," he commands.

And the proof that his kisses and caresses have clouded my judgment and obliterated my self-control comes in the form of a giggled response to his direction, "Yes, sir."

∽

A SHORT RIDE LATER, ALESSANDRO LEADS ME INTO HIS LARGE, high-ceilinged penthouse apartment. Placing his things on a small table, he pulls my bag out of my arms and lets it drop gently to the floor before restarting his sensual assault. He wraps his hands in my hair and pulls my face greedily to his. His kisses are hard and insistent, his tongue fighting with mine as he pulls me into his bedroom. I'm past resisting now, absorbed fully in the moment, as desperate for this to happen as he seems to be.

As he backs me to the bed, his hands fly down his shirt buttons. When he's done, I eagerly push the fabric away from his body. Running my hands down his sculpted chest and stomach, I marvel at their definition, the softness of his skin over his firm muscles.

"I've wanted you since the moment I saw you," he says huskily between feverish kisses.

My pulse races as I stare lustfully at him. "I find that hard to believe," I murmur.

He shakes his head and "tsks" at me. "Then perhaps I need to convince you," he grins lasciviously at me, grasps the hem of my dress, and pulls it abruptly over my head. His eyes rove hungrily over my soft curves and my white cotton bra.

I stare back, conscious of how my tall, fleshy body must compare to the tiny, athletic Italian women he must surely be used to bedding. Goodness knows I've seen that one who works for him — Francesca, his assistant — flirt with him shamelessly.

His thick fingers tug gently at my long, brown hair. They drop to caress the top of my breast, running down my stomach, lingering over the cloth below my navel. His touch is rough and warm, and each caress sends shivers of pleasure through my whole body. In a smooth, practiced motion he's worked my leggings and panties around my hips. They fall to the floor as he deftly unclasps my bra, freeing my breasts from the binding material. I gasp at the suddenness of my nudity and he chuckles pleasurably. I step out of the pile of cloth at my feet and kick it giddily away from me.

And suddenly I'm on my back, his tongue working its way into my mouth, his hands at my breast and between my thighs. His thumbs make mirror motions, both gently circling my sensitive flesh. I cry out in pleasure, overwhelmed by his touch. My cry clearly pleases him as he sighs into my mouth and presses the stiff outline under his trousers into my thigh.

"Hmmmm, I think you just enjoy torturing me," I breathe. I sit up and grab his belt, pulling him to stand in front of me. I maintain eye contact as I deftly unhook his buckle and lower his zipper.

His dark eyes lock on mine, and his breath quickens as my thumbs pull the rest of his clothing off, unfurling his erection. Breaking away from the heat of his gaze, I look on him. "Maybe it's time to return the favor," I say softly.

I lay my hands gently on his hips and bring my open mouth a hair's breadth from his waiting erection. His sharp intake of breath brings a mischievous smile to my face. Slowly, I ease the glistening tip between my lips, swirling my tongue from bottom to top and over again, slowly, relishing his obvious pleasure.

"Ohhhh, *mio Dio*," Alessandro moans and he reaches for me.

I weave my fingers with his to keep control. And for one breath more I maintain my slow rhythm before plunging him deep into my throat, sheathing him tightly with my lips, then sucking him as I pull him back out, and over again.

His breathing accelerates, his hands squeezing mine hard. "Serafina …" my name is a plea from his lips.

I relent and replace my mouth with my hand as I stand to meet his lips with mine. His kiss is fervent as I stroke him, and I can feel the hot moisture between my legs.

He guides me back onto the bed and kneels between my legs, quickly rolling on a condom. As I watch him, my whole body aches in anticipation, the wet heat between my legs practically unbearable. He presses his forehead to mine as he slips himself inside of me. The glorious, full sensation of him is like a wake-up call, and I bite back a cry of pleasure as his own rings through the room. He pauses, kissing me, running his teeth along my lip as he pulls back. My hips twitch under him, but he presses his hands against me, pinning me under him.

"Don't stop," I beg him.

He smiles sultrily, then draws himself back further only to quickly plunge deeply into me again, holding me in place to take his pleasure. His need is obvious in his rough, full thrusts, and my body responds. I wriggle free, wrapping my legs around him, using it to rise to meet his thrusts, my breath quick and gasping. I bite my lip hard, holding back a moan.

His chest lowers over me as he falls to his rest on his arms. "Let go," he says into my ear, his tone as rough as the sex. And it pushes me over the edge. I lock my mouth onto his, our tongues greedily consuming each other. He thrusts into me and I explode, grabbing the sheets under me, my back arching off the bed, a loud cry escaping me. He buries his smile of satisfaction in my hair, his lips pressed to my neck as he moves.

As my breathing recovers, I weave my fingers into his hair and whisper in his ear, "My turn." Resting on his arms once more to meet my gaze, he looks at me questioningly. "On top," I clarify.

He lets out a small, eager moan. "If you insist," he replies.

I wiggle out from under him and he rolls onto his back, propping himself up on his elbows and watching me curiously. Lying next to him, I meet his lips with mine, stroking him with my hand. As he wraps his arms around me, I slide my leg astride his hips, hovering over him. I push myself into a fully upright position, hands on his chest, allowing my thumbs to catch his nipples as I run my fingers down him.

Swinging my hips downward, I capture him between my legs and slide him inside me, eliciting a synchronized moan of pleasure from us both. My body quivers with the excitement of having missed this for so long.

I grasp his arms tightly, gently rocking back and forth. He goes still and moans in pleasure. I gingerly rise and fall, burying him deep in me before slowly easing him out again. His hands find my hips and follow my motions, his head flung back, groan after groan escaping his lips as I ride him, my own cries of pleasure mounting. I'm nearing orgasm again when his grip on my hips tightens, slowing my pace.

"Not yet," he growls, and he pushes me off him, climbing up onto his knees while flipping me on my stomach in front of him. He pulls my ass into the air. "Spread your legs," he commands.

I push myself up on my elbows and comply. A moment later I feel him slide into me, harder than ever. His hands grasp my hips and he lunges, burying himself so he's completely sheathed in me. I suppress a scream of pleasure. He leans forward, teasing my nipple with his hand.

"Don't hold back," he rasps, slowly easing in and out. "I want to hear you."

I groan in agreement, and he gradually picks up his rhythm and depth until he is slowly, steadily pumping deeply. I want to explode under the sweet torture, but it's just out of reach. I don't withhold my moans of pleasure and protest, and I'm aching for the frenzied pace that unlocked my body's long-dormant ability to send waves of pleasure crashing through me in climax. As he goes to ease into me once more, I buck my hips impatiently, driving him in deep and hard.

He gasps. "No, Sera," he cautions, taking himself out of me. I growl in frustration and I can almost hear the smile in his voice when he says, "What do you want?"

"Fuck me, Alessandro," I breathe. He moans.

"Ah, *dolcezza*, I love hearing you say that," he sighs.

And with that he's pounding into me, taking me so roughly that it's simultaneously painful and mind-blowingly delicious. Screams rip from my throat, and I've lost the ability to tense my own body when I come, so there's no escaping the pleasure when I shatter into a million pieces. I scream his name and tighten around him, making him cry out as his orgasm meets the last throes of my own.

We both fall, panting and sweaty, to the bed. I roll over and put my hand on his heart, and he lays a leg between mine. It is minutes before either of us can speak.

"Well, that was pretty okay," I deadpan.

He laughs, clearly exhausted. "If that was just okay, I can't wait to see what you think good sex is like."

After a few minutes of catching our breath, he props himself up on an elbow and peers down at me but says nothing.

"At a loss for words, Mr. Giordano? How uncharacteristic of you," I murmur jokingly.

He smirks at me and runs his hand down my chest. "Oh, I have words, Ms. Evans. Many words. Where do I start?" he muses. He drops a kiss on my neck. "Angel." Another on my clavicle. "Goddess." Another on my chin. "Siren." Another on my forehead. "Temptress." His mouth finds mine and when he pulls away I'm breathless. "At a loss for words, Ms. Evans?"

His chocolate eyes are twinkling, and a sideways smile hangs on his full lips. I can only manage a small smile in return before he pulls away and heads to the bathroom. And the sight of him walking away is a new joy, his backside as tight and well-muscled as his torso. His designer clothing did not do justice to the Adonis underneath.

He returns in a few minutes with a glass of water, offering it to me. I sit up slowly and take a sip. As he lays down, I slide next to him and we lay next to each other comfortably and quietly for a long while. I'm almost sure he's gone to sleep when he pulls away and sits up, leaning against the pillow to take another sip of water. Rolling onto my stomach to watch him, I can't help but stare.

"See something you like?" he teases.

I narrow my eyes and smirk at him before sliding up and reaching over him to sip from the glass he's put back on the nightstand, letting my breasts graze his arm and his chest, my hair tickling his shoulder.

His cock twitches. "Temptressss," he purrs and pulls me to him, cradling me in his lap and kissing me deeply.

Our play continues long into the night, until we are both sated and too exhausted to continue.

I WAKE SUDDENLY, MY HEART RACING, A GARBLED CRY DYING on my lips. I place my head in my palms and struggle to recall the feverish dream that disturbed my sleep, but it's fading away like a brief snow before the rain. Taking a deep breath, I steady myself and stretch my limbs.

Alessandro stirs next to me and the events of the previous evening rush back into my consciousness.

I've had sex with a man I'm in business with. Fuck. I ease gingerly out of bed and quietly walk to the wide windows across from the bed. The lights of Seattle twinkle around us, and the sky purples on the horizon. I look back at the clock on the bedside — five thirty-seven a.m. There's time enough for me to locate my clothing, sneak out, and get back to my condo to clean up before work.

How could I allow myself to capitulate to his advances? I look back at the bed, at Alessandro, and the answer is obvious — because I thought it merely a game to him. I never thought I'd actually end up in bed with the most stubborn, fiery, intelligent, and attractive man I'd ever met.

The exhaustion of our debates, the heat of the moment, it all made me throw my usually cautious nature to the wind. The very nature that's gotten me this far, that's made me so successful. How could I risk my company like this? My reputation? I close my eyes for a moment.

When I reopen them, my resolve is hardened. As stealthily as I can, I gather my things strewn around the floor. Thanking my lucky stars that the door is ajar, I slip into the living room and dress quickly. I don't worry whether the sound of the front door will wake him. Because once it does, it's too late anyway.

THREE

"Would you like me to call Mr. Giordano's cellphone again?" Maggie, my admin, inquires nervously.

My eyes find the clock again — nine nineteen a.m. "No, Maggie, thank you. Please have everyone meet in the conference room in five minutes. We'll proceed without him," I instruct her as confidently as I can.

But as soon as she leaves my office I chew my lip anxiously. *Did he wake up regretting this as much as I did? Have I jeopardized our contract?* The thought makes me feel as if my heart has been plunged into ice. Our firm has just started attracting clients like Buone Case. To derail that now would be catastrophic.

Get it together, Evans, I admonish myself. I chant a mantra silently to myself — *no amount of regretting can change the past, and no amount of worrying can change the future.* I let out a breath. Gathering my things, I head for the conference room.

✺

"So, you'll see on page fifteen that we've identified four new potential sites with the zoning, acreage, and most other parameters the project requires." Jackson is giving the part of our presentation we never made it to yesterday, but he may as well be talking to himself. The Buone Case team is in the room, but without Alessandro they are distracted and, frankly, useless. Jackson glances at me, and I nod encouragingly. My eyes flit yet again to the clock on the wall. It's nine forty-eight a.m., and still no Alessandro.

Mercifully, Jackson's presentation concludes a few minutes later. He thanks everyone for their attention. I control the impulse to roll my eyes. Closing my laptop, I clear my throat to gather everyone's attention.

"Thanks very much, Jackson." I pause. "Okay, ladies and gentlemen. Now that we've all got the latest, I think we should take some time to digest this and regroup. Obviously, Mr. Giordano will need to be informed upon his arrival and I'm sure his team will need some time ..." I trail off mid-sentence as Alessandro appears in the doorway, leaning casually against the frame.

He's dressed completely in black — fitted pants, button-up shirt, and well-cut jacket. He looks every inch the sexy devil, with his dark hair mussed just so as usual, his angular face in a relaxed, almost bored expression. Our eyes meet, and I can feel myself turning a myriad of shades of red. Everyone in the room turns their eyes to the door.

"Please, go on," Alessandro offers.

I clear my throat again. "Yes. Well. As I was saying, I think it best at this time that the Buone Case team meet to go over the latest and prepare for the upcoming site visits. Thank you everyone for your time. We'll leave the conference room to the Buone Case team," I say, trying to keep emotion out of my tone.

Alessandro steps into the room and places his bag on the table, letting my team pass.

Gathering my things, I steel myself, trying to shut down memories of the night before. I smooth a crease from my cream silk blouse with my free hand and step forward. "Mr. Giordano, *buongiorno*," I offer. "Extra copies of the latest site reports are here on the table. I'll be in my office. Please do let me know if you have any questions." And with that I brush past him before he can respond.

Keeping my pace even and casual, I smile shakily at Maggie on my way into my office. But as soon as I have collapsed in my chair, there is a small knock on the door.

"Yes?" I call, pulling myself up in my chair. I begin to reorder the things I've just dumped on my desk as Maggie's blond bob peeks around the door. I sigh in relief and smile brightly at her. "What is it, Maggie?"

"Ms. Evans, I wanted to remind you that you have a phone call at ten fifteen with Mr. Phillips about the meeting with the city for the Stone Way project."

I nod curtly. "Yes, thank you, Maggie. Is that all?"

"Yes, Ms. Evans." And with that she goes back to her desk.

I turn my chair to look out the window. Through the mist there looks to be a rainbow in the distance over the Smith Tower. I stand and approach the window when there is another small knock on the door.

"What is it, Maggie?" I ask impatiently, leaning toward the glass trying to see how far the rainbow stretches. When she doesn't answer, I turn, and Alessandro is standing behind me. Much too close. And a quick glance tells me that he's closed the door.

"*Buongiorno*, hmm?" he asks in a low voice. "*Sì, bella*, it is a good day." He reaches for me and before I can protest his hands are on my back, pulling me into a heated, fervent kiss.

And it's so good that I kiss him back, the dull ache between my legs flaring into a distracting yearning — until I remember myself. I pull away sharply, stepping behind my chair, putting it between us as I catch my breath.

"Mr. Giordano, please. I'm glad to see that you aren't upset by recent events, but I must insist that we try to keep this professional going forward." I'm putting on my best boss voice.

He looks confused. "Upset? Why would I be upset? Last night was incredible. Something I'd like to repeat with you here and now, in fact," he says, eyeing my fitted, navy pencil skirt.

"But if you would like to be professional while we are at work, I can respect that." He steps back to the front of my desk.

I give my head a small shake. "Thank you, but I think you mistake me, *signore*," I persist. "I would appreciate if we could return to keeping this *strictly* professional."

Alessandro's mouth opens in surprise as he takes in my meaning. Me, rejecting him after the insanely amazing sex we had. It's shocking to me too, but oh so necessary, and not just for my business.

"Surely you don't mean that? I can't say I've been with many American women, but your enthusiasm seemed to suggest you enjoyed the *unprofessional* nature of the evening," he counters, his tone amused.

"I'm sorry, but this is really not the place to have this kind of discussion," I say firmly.

His dark eyes fill with lust and fire, his full lips parting slightly. "Then over dinner tonight, perhaps?"

"It's not a discussion I wish to have anywhere," I insist.

He runs his finger under his chin in that way of his, and I know he's disturbed. "If that's what you want," he finally says.

"It is," I assert as steadily as I can.

"Then I must apologize for my lapse in professionalism," he says brusquely. "My team and I will see you at our meeting this afternoon." He turns to leave but pauses at the door. He opens his mouth but closes it again and looks at me searchingly for a moment before disappearing out the door.

As soon as I'm sure he must be back in the conference room, I call Maggie into my office.

"I need you to reschedule the call with Mr. Phillips. Tell him I'm free this afternoon. And please send Jackson Williams in to me."

She nods and quickly leaves the room.

Time to give Jackson a promotion to project management lead. It's long overdue, and I'm fairly confident he can handle it. And I can't handle being in the same room as Alessandro Giordano.

⌒

"I have full faith in you, Jackson," I reaffirm, shaking his hand warmly.

It's hard not to like Jackson, with his boyish looks — a young face, curly blond hair, and a tall, awkward frame. He radiates excitement and vulnerability, like now, as he's beaming from ear-to-ear, his pale blue eyes alight with enthusiasm.

"Thank you so much, Ms. Evans — I won't let you down. Will you be announcing it at the meeting this afternoon?"

"Yes, but I have other matters to attend to, so I will make the announcement first thing and then leave you to it," I respond. "But my door is always open if you need me."

Jackson nods eagerly. "Of course, thank you again so much."

∾

"And so, going forward, Mr. Williams will be your project lead. It's a formalization of the role he has been doing thus far, so I have no doubt you will be more than pleased with his efforts. I will, of course, stay abreast of things and be involved as necessary. And with that, I will leave you in his capable hands," I conclude. I've scarce dared to look at Alessandro, but I must now, and I extend my hand to him.

He shakes my hand with both of his, and he has something of the look of a wounded animal about him for a moment, but it's gone almost before I can register it.

"Thank you, Ms. Evans," he says simply.

I leave without looking back, my heart racing, and head to my private bathroom to compose myself.

∾

The week moves by in a blur of real and imagined tasks designed to keep me away from the Buone Case team. But Alessandro appears to have accepted my pushback in a way he never had before. Perhaps now that he's proven he can have me, he's no longer interested.

Though as much as I'm able to avoid more than glimpsing him during the day, the impact of what he's woken in me ripples through my conscious and unconscious mind, invading my dreams at night, beckoning me to him, touching me, wanting me. And every night I wake in a cold sweat with tears streaming down my face. By Friday I'm taciturn and withdrawn, and I'm not looking forward to the weekly tag-up meeting with Buone Case that I must attend.

∽

As our Friday meeting ends and everyone files out of the room to head home, I feel like I've been punched in the gut. Alessandro didn't so much as look at me the entire hour unless I was speaking. I'm unsettled as to why his finally respecting my boundaries bothers me, again ultimately chalking up his ability to cease his previously relentless campaign of flirting to having achieved his goal.

In any case at least the project is moving forward, finally. I sigh heavily and drag my laptop and folio back to my office. I pack my bag slowly and carefully, giving everyone plenty of time to leave. At nearly seven o'clock the office is quiet and dark, and I figure it's safe.

But on my way to the elevator I hear keys tapping. Following the noise, I find Jackson still at his desk.

"Jackson!" I say in surprise.

He jumps about a foot out of his chair in surprise.

"Oh my gosh, I'm so sorry, I didn't mean to scare you," I apologize.

He clutches his chest. "No worries, I startle easily. I thought everyone had gone home," he explains.

"I was just about to," I say, and then after a pause, "Hey, do you want to go to the pub next door for a drink? On me. As congratulations for the promotion, and the great work you've been doing."

He looks very surprised. Understandably, as I'm not exactly known for being social with my employees. Or at all.

"Oh! Uh, sure, yes, that would be great!" he exclaims. "Let me just close up here."

"Sure thing, I'll meet you at the elevator," I nod, and step away.

∼

THE PUB IS PACKED WITH END-OF-THE-WORK-WEEK EMPLOYEES downing two-dollar pints for happy hour. We manage to snag a table crammed into a corner.

"What'll it be?" I ask Jackson, dropping my blazer over the chair and putting my bag on the seat.

"I'll take a house pale ale," he responds.

Nodding, I head to the bar.

I return shortly with his beer, and a gin and tonic for me. This week has been rough, and hard alcohol is in order.

"So, Jackson, remind me how long you've been with the firm?" I ask.

Jackson replies almost instantly, "Three years, four months, and two weeks."

I laugh. "Wow, do you normally keep count?" I joke.

"Yes," he replies very seriously.

The smile drops off my face and I clear my throat. I start to realize this may not have been the wisest move when I see Maggie and Lucy enter the bar. I wave enthusiastically as Maggie stands on her tip-toes to make herself tall enough to scan the room for seats and, mercifully, she spots us and comes our way, with a very astonished look on her face.

"Maggie! Lucy! Please join us. We were just celebrating Jackson's promotion," I explain.

They both look at me skeptically but sit down. Jackson glances anxiously at Lucy and she tosses her long, dark hair over her shoulder nervously. Hmmm, an office crush maybe? Interesting.

"Actually, we were just discussing how long I've worked for ERS," Jackson says matter-of-factly.

Maggie and Lucy exchange a look.

"Oh? How long *have* you worked for Ms. Evans?" Maggie asks kindly, putting down the menu she'd started looking at.

"Three years. Four months. Two weeks," he replies stoically.

"Well, that's very nice," Maggie responds. "I've been with the company just over two years now, myself. Lucy?"

Lucy's eyes, which were scanning the room uninterestedly, snap back to Maggie. "A year next month," she replies dully, returning to looking around the room.

"Four years, five months, and … I don't know how many weeks," I insert jokingly.

Jackson blushes, and I feel stupid for mocking him. Maggie presses her lips together and looks in her lap, while Lucy finally looks amused.

"So, what's everyone up to this weekend?" I ask.

Thankfully, they rise to the bait and we all share our plans for the weekend. Lucy even manages to engage, especially once we order food and she's eaten. The change is startling, actually, as she goes from annoyed and aloof to engaged and animated. Maggie is, as always, her sweet and kind self. And Jackson is, also as always, adorably socially awkward, especially with his constant, furtive admiration of Lucy.

My own social anxieties usually get the best of me, but with the three of them chatting I manage to relax into the rhythm, answering the occasional question or offering a nod and encouragement at appropriate points in the conversation. Social situations have never been my forte — I'm good at numbers, deals, real estate. So, I'm surprised when I'm happily engrossed in their banter for more than two hours, until drinks and food have all been consumed and they start to make their goodbyes. I finish the last of my latest gin and tonic and set the glass down on the table. It goes in and out of focus for a moment and I groan, realizing I'm more than a little intoxicated.

What. The. Actual. Fuck. I haven't been drunk since college. How many did I have? I try to remember but can't. Yep, definitely drunk.

Maggie asks me if I'm okay to get home and I assure her I am, in as composed a manner as I can. Jackson and Lucy exchange a look, clearly surprised and amused to see their boss inebriated. As soon as I'm sure they're all gone, I pop outside to let the cool evening air sober me a little and hail a cab.

∾

Sitting in the back of the cab, I realize I am actually way more intoxicated than I thought. I should've eaten some of the food we'd ordered. I don't think I'm going to be sick, but I'm definitely woozy.

"Hey, you okay back there?" the driver checks.

I open my eyes to him eying me warily in the rearview mirror. *When did I close my eyes? Hmm.*

"Yessir," I slur, and I giggle at how drunk I sound.

Minutes later he stops the cab in front of a building that is not mine.

"Where are we?" I ask stupidly.

He gives me an address. "That's what you said right?" he asks suspiciously.

And it hits me. This is Alessandro's building. I gave him Alessandro's address. My subconscious smirks as I do my best deer-in-headlights impression and the alcohol inside me takes the driver's seat.

"Yes, yes, that's right," Alcohol says, shoving money in the cab driver's hand. So apparently Alcohol also controls my body now, I acknowledge as I slide out of the cab and strut into the building.

∽

A LESSANDRO OPENS THE DOOR, WEARING GREY SWEATS AND A dark T-shirt, looking confused. As his eyes light up with recognition, his mouth hardens into a thin line.

"What can I do for you, Ms. Evans?" he asks tightly.

"Uh oh, I'm in trouble, aren't I?" I giggle.

He steps toward me and Alcohol throws my arms around his neck. He stiffens, sniffing me, then pushes me away to arm's length, examining my face.

"You're drunk," he chastises me, then pulls me into his apartment. "Get in here before you throw up all over the hallway."

I shake my head and wobble to the couch. "Not gonna throw up. And not drunk. Just tipsy," Alcohol says sinking into the warm leather. He must have been sitting here because it smells like him too.

He sits further down the couch and shakes his head at me.

"You're more than tipsy," he accuses me. "Did you drive here?"

"Pfffff, 'course not!" I say, waving my hand dismissively.

"Well, that's a start," he says, grimacing. "Why are you here?"

I frown and Alcohol slides toward him and runs my hand up his leg. "Isn't it obvious?" Alcohol tells me to climb into his lap. "Aren't you happy to see me?" Alcohol tells me to kiss him. *Mmm.* His mouth is warm, and he tastes like wine.

He disentangles my arms from around his neck and pulls his face away, holding me in front of him. "I wish I could say that I was, but after what happened earlier this week ..."

Alcohol pouts and runs my hands down his chest, to his pants. "Let's just pretend that didn't happen for tonight," Alcohol leans into his ear and whispers, slipping my tongue along his lobe. I feel him hardening under his trousers.

"*Porca miseria*! Serafina, that's not fair," he grumbles. He stands suddenly, and I tumble back onto the couch. "And I'm not going to take advantage of you in this state." He goes into the kitchen and comes back with a plate of bread and oil with herbs, and a glass of water. "Eat. Drink."

Alcohol likes when Alessandro is commanding, and it makes me eat the bread as kinkily as I can. He stares at me impassively.

After a few minutes the food and drink do their work, and I'm able to push Alcohol back into the passenger seat, though my head is still foggy and my reflexes slow. Tears of rejection well in my eyes.

"Okay, then. Well, thanks for the food. I guess I'll go now," I say in a soft voice. I stand and put the dishes in the kitchen, gripping the edge of the counter and breathing deeply. I can feel him watching me.

"You'll do no such thing," he snaps. "There is a guest room just there." He gestures to a door. "I don't trust you to get yourself home, and I'm too tired to take you. It's been a trying week, and I'm going to bed." He fumes all the way out of the room down the hall to his bedroom.

I hear his door click shut. I sit back on the couch to steady myself and contemplate leaving anyway. But he's probably right. The tears sting at my eyes again as the effects of the alcohol wear off and the humiliation sets in. What am I doing? Why the hell *did* I come here?

Because he makes you feel, my subconscious whispers. I shake my head. No. He can't make me feel anything I don't want to feel. I head angrily to the guest room, determined to escape after I've slept off the booze.

⁓

MY EYES FLY OPEN IN THE DARK, MY BODY SHAKING. TEARS are streaming down my face. Warm arms pull me up.

"Shhh, *bella*, I'm here," Alessandro's husky voice whispers to me in the dark as he wraps his arms around me. "It's okay. You're okay." He kisses my hair.

I choke back a sob and bury my face in his naked chest, trying to will my body to stop convulsing. After a moment I'm able to stop the tears but not quite the shaking. I pull away, wiping my face with my hand.

"What are you doing in here?" I ask him weakly.

He brushes my hair out of my face. "You were screaming," he says, holding my chin and tilting my face up so I must look in his eyes. They are full of worry. "Is it just the alcohol?"

I laugh drily. "No," I reply shortly. "It's not the alcohol."

"I see," he says. "This happens often?"

I shake my head. "Not usually, no. Just lately." *Since the night I gave in to you.*

He raises an eyebrow, but mercifully doesn't inquire further. His eyes examine my face, my shaking shoulders. He places his warm palms on them and the shaking stops. I look up into his eyes again and his expression is soft and full of concern. I curse under my breath and pull away from him. "I'm fine," I scoff. "You can go back to bed." I fully intend to dress and leave as soon as he's gone, silently angry at myself for putting myself in this position.

He shakes his head, his mouth a thin line again. "Just when I think I'm starting to understand you," he murmurs angrily and starts to slide off the bed.

Without thinking, I circle my hand around his wrist, stopping him. "Alessandro, please," and my voice is thick with the tears that start flowing pitilessly down my cheeks.

He yanks his arm out of my grasp. "Please what? Make up your mind — do you want me to stay or do you want me to go?" he demands.

I shrink back from his understandable anger and confusion. I'm thinking one thing and feeling another, and it's making me behave in a manner even I find appalling.

"Please just don't be angry with me. I'm not doing it on purpose," I explain.

He sinks onto the bed and strokes his chin with his finger. "I know," he finally says, his frustration obvious in his tone. "But that doesn't make it any less infuriating to be toyed with."

I narrow my eyes. "I'm *toying* with you? How did you get there? As you may recall, *you* were the one who pursued *me*, who seduced *me*," I fume. "I wasn't confused about anything until you started this."

Anger flashes in his eyes and he rests his hands on the bed in front of me, leaning forward so his face is inches from mine. "Maybe you could do with a little confusion, Serafina," he breathes. "Maybe it's exactly what you need." And he lunges forward, his lips grabbing mine, his weight toppling me onto the pillows behind me. He pins me to the bed with his mouth and his naked torso, his hands holding my hips.

I can only resist angrily for a moment before my resolve crumbles and I'm kissing him back passionately, my hands pulling him completely onto me.

He pushes up abruptly, yanking his sweatpants to his knees and roughly sheathing himself with a condom from his pocket. He shoves my underwear aside with one hand and puts himself in me with the other. His weight falls on me again, pinning me under him as he thrusts angrily into me. I scream gutturally in pleasure, wrap my legs around him, and pull his mouth to mine. Our mouths battle, hard and hot, while we meet each other hard on each push.

His mouth drops to my ear, his hand gripping the hair on the back of my head hard, and he roughly speaks into my ear between carnal grunts of pleasure, "Damnit, you drive me crazy." His pace quickens, he bites my shoulder and licks up my neck only to reclaim my mouth with his. As his thumb starts working one of my nipples, I pull back and bite my lip hard.

"Let go," he commands.

I stop holding back and let him hear me cry out. He greedily kisses me as I climax, my screams dissolving in his mouth.

He pulls out of me, still hard, and yanks my panties off. He kicks off his sweats and sits back on his haunches, stroking himself with one hand. "I want you on top of me," he demands.

I nod, flushed with pleasure, and take him in my hand as he lays down. Quickly climbing on him, I guide him into me.

I lean over him, my breasts grazing his chest as I rise and fall hungrily, slamming into him. He bucks his pelvis each time I fall, driving deep and hard into me. Our pace is frenzied, and it's not long before I climax again, squeezing him tightly and tipping him into orgasm with me. We both let out our last cries. I sink onto the bed next to him and I know no more.

FOUR

I'm woken by Alessandro squeezing my nipple, rolling it between his moistened thumb and finger. Seeing my eyes open, he plants a kiss on it, flicking it with his tongue. It grows hard and long, and he sinks his mouth onto it, pulling it with his teeth. A moan escapes me.

"You are an amazing alarm clock," I manage.

He laughs and strokes my face. "Imagine, if you'd just make up your mind, all the many wonderful ways I could wake you each morning," he says, smiling.

My face falls and his smile falters.

I sit up and gather my knees to my chest. "Pretty sure it was you who seduced me again," I point out. "You can't begrudge a girl a little confusion when an impossible and gorgeous man tries to lure her into a questionably ethical arrangement."

"I'm impossible?" he pouts.

I chuckle. "Come off it, we both know you're insuffer-able," I say, pinching his jutting bottom lip. His full, beautiful lip. I shake my head. I'm well rested, and I'm not drunk or terrorized now, so it's time to take back control of this situation. "You can't take 'no' for an answer."

"'No' is a word I don't recall actually passing your lips," he counters. "And your actions this week have unmistakably said, 'yes.'"

I sit, weighing his words, dumbfounded. And I realize he's right. He corners me in a conference room, and I end up spending the night with him. And then I stumble drunkenly into his apartment, enabling another steamy encounter.

Alessandro nods knowingly and stretches on the bed next to me. The sheets shift revealing his erection, and I'm distracted out of my forming protests.

∽

BASKING IN THE POSTCOITAL GLOW, I EXPLORE ALESSANDRO'S chest and arms with my fingers while he strokes my arm tenderly.

"A man could get used to this," he sighs.

I start to tell him not to, but he puts a finger over my lips.

"Breakfast?" he asks.

I look at the clock over his shoulder. It's almost eleven a.m. We've spent all morning in bed together.

"It's nearly lunchtime," I reply, "and I need to go." I sit up and start to dress.

He strokes my back and I swat playfully at his hand.

"Stay," he pleads. "*Per favore, bella.*"

I sigh and turn to him. "Alessandro, I have things to do," I reply. I hesitate a moment and turn to hold his hands in mine. "I've enjoyed this. It's more than I thought to look for right now. But I have responsibilities. My company, my employees." *My heart.* "I don't have room for breakfast. Or lunch." I see the familiar persistent gleam in his eye. "*Or* dinner, Alessandro." He chuckles, and I sigh. "You know what I mean."

He shakes his head. "No, I don't," he states.

"The sex is amazing. But that's all this can be. We have a professional contract. If emotions were to get involved, that could put our working relationship in jeopardy, which in turn could put my company in jeopardy. I can't allow that," I clarify.

"So just sex."

I let his words sink in. Just sex. Yes, I think I can do Just Sex. I've done Just Sex before. Sometimes ending amicably, sometimes not, but always manageably. Then again, it's never been with a client.

"Can you do that?" I ask him. And I realize I hope his answer is yes.

His thoughtful stare goes on and I start to get nervous. Somewhere in the apartment a phone rings.

"*Cazzo!*" he swears, rising from the bed. "Don't go," he

commands, pulling his sweatpants on and scrambling to the phone.

I finish getting myself together, use the bathroom, and head into the living room where I hear him speaking rapidly in Italian.

He finishes his call abruptly and turns to me. "I'm sorry, I forgot I had a phone appointment. I will have to call them back shortly," he says apologetically.

"It's okay, as I said, I need to go anyway," I say, leaning my head toward the door. "Goodbye, Alessandro."

He sweeps me into his arms and kisses me deeply. "*Ciao, bella*," he murmurs, picking up his handset. As I reach the door he calls me, "Serafina?" I pause by the door. He looks appraisingly at my rumpled clothes, his dark eyes once more filled with lust and fire. He raises an eyebrow suggestively as his eyes meet mine. "Yes. Just sex." He winks and starts to dial.

Smiling, I let myself out.

∽

Despite my best efforts to keep busy on Sunday, by early afternoon I find myself back in his bed, recovering from our latest antics.

"So, what are the rules?" he asks me, trailing his fingers over my naked breasts.

I purse my lips in thought. "Hmmm. Well, I'd say, for

starters, we only have sex here or at my place," I begin. "Never in the office. And we don't tell anyone."

"I can live with that," he responds, running his tongue along my nipple.

I push him away playfully. "I can't think while you're doing that," I admonish him.

He wiggles his eyebrows and I laugh. "What about other men?" he asks.

I stare at him in mock shock. "I don't know what you're into, but threesomes aren't really my style," I say, doing my best to sound horrified. His eyes widen, and he freezes. I shove him gently. "I'm *joking*."

He lets his breath out in relief. "I don't mind a little kink, but no, no threesomes," he agrees. "I meant do you still plan to see other men?"

I snort. "I don't see *any* men," I reply honestly. "I go on the occasional first date here and there, but nothing ever goes very far. So, there are no 'other men' to worry about."

"Wow," he replies.

Unsure of the nature of his astonishment, I shrug self-consciously. "It's just not on my radar," I say simply, hoping to bypass the discussion. "What about you? Surely there are other women?" I look at him expectantly, having seen his flirting both directed at myself and nearly every other woman in the office at one point or another. And I employ a lot of women.

"From time to time, but nobody serious for a very long while," he says. I look at him skeptically. "Really. In any event, there will be nobody else while I am with you. And I'd appreciate the same in return."

I weigh the possibility that he's just a huge flirt but am still dubious. "That's fair," I concede. "But if you decide you want to be with someone else, physically or otherwise, please just tell me. And I'll do the same." And I'll just have to hope he actually does.

"Fair enough. Is that all?"

I think for a moment. "I think so. You?"

"Do I get to take you on dates?" he asks.

I sit up abruptly. "No, no dates. I don't want anyone we work with seeing us together. And we only spend time alone together if it's between sexcapades. We are together for sex only, as our schedules allow. I'm okay with sleepovers if it's the most obviously convenient option."

"Sexcapades?" he laughs. I smile. "You drive a hard bargain, but I'll take what I can get."

His words worry me. "Alessandro, if you're hoping for more, this won't work." He regards me thoughtfully.

"*Bella*, I'm always hoping for more from life," he explains. "But if you're worried about me falling in love with you, don't." He kisses my fingertips. "Now, I think we've done enough talking."

RETURNING TO WORK ON MONDAY MORNING CARRIES NONE OF the stress of the previous week. And with the project management handed over to Jackson, I don't have to worry about being caught staring lustfully at Alessandro or having an argument with him that boils over into a passionate liaison behind closed doors. Now that I've unleashed that long-suppressed part of me, I just don't trust myself around him anymore.

As the elevator climbs to my floor, I do my best to suppress the memories of the weekend enough to wipe the humongous grin from my face. But I'm still positively chipper when I greet Maggie on my way into the office. She looks at me questioningly as I float past her into my office. I laugh as I get settled in for my first call of the morning.

∾

AFTER LUNCH I SETTLE BACK AT MY DESK TO REVIEW A NEW purchase and sale agreement for one of our client's acquisitions when I'm interrupted by Nick Conrad, my finance lead, poking his head around my door.

"Got a minute, Ms. Evans?" he inquires.

"For you Nick? I have five."

He takes a seat in front of my desk. "Did you by any chance take any petty cash out on Friday afternoon?" he asks.

I frown. "No. How much is missing?"

Nick sighs. "Four hundred."

My eyebrows shoot up. "Well, *that's* a little obvious," I remark.

He nods in agreement. "Yes, usually thefts are smaller amounts over longer periods of time."

"So, you think it *is* theft, then?" I prompt.

"I've checked with the last few people on the ledger and the bookkeeper, and nothing. So yes, unfortunately, likely it's theft," he says.

"Email me the ledger, and please let me know what additional security measures you'd like to take while this is being investigated. Once I have that, I'll contact an independent investigator and get back to you as soon as we find something," I promise. "Thanks for bringing this to my attention."

Nick leaves and I push back from my desk, turning to the view of the city behind me. I take measures to make sure we attract the best employees and treat them well, so I'm especially disturbed by the theft. The amount is a pittance, it's more the principle of the matter.

My email pings, grabbing my attention — it's the ledger from Nick. I forward it and pick up the phone to talk to my PI.

⌇

It's Wednesday and I haven't heard from Alessandro, besides catching a glimpse of him here and there coming and going from meetings, so I decide to text him.

Busy tonight?

I chew my lip and wait impatiently. Thankfully, his reply comes quickly. *I am now. 20:00, my place. No underwear.*

So bossy. I grin widely.

∽

His door opens, and I toy with the straps trailing from the belt of my long, red trench coat. Alessandro's eyebrows jump when he sees me.

"Are you going to make me stand here all night, or can I come in?" I tease.

He steps aside. "*Per favore*, come in," he offers. "Is it raining?" he inquires, trying to sound casual, but I can hear a note of excitement in his voice.

I laugh shortly. "No." As I turn I open my coat and let it fall to the floor, revealing that I'm wearing nothing but heels. His jaw drops, and he is speechless. Exactly the effect I was looking for. "You said no underwear," I say, fixing a confused look on my face. "Should I put it back on?" I reach for the trench and he pounces, pushing me onto the couch.

"Not unless you want me to rip it back off you," he growls.

∽

Late that evening we lie in his bed as he absentmindedly strokes my hair.

"I can't believe how much sex we've managed in one evening," I say, giggling like a teenager.

He smiles down at me. "That's what happens when I'm made to wait three days for you," he admonishes me, kissing my neck gently, running his fingers lightly over my body.

"You could've asked anytime," I remind him, lazily running my fingers through his thick hair.

"I wanted to see how long it would take you to ask me," he replies.

I catch his eye. "Seriously? Why?"

He muses for a moment. "Just curious," he says finally.

I frown, unsatisfied by his answer, but unwilling to push the issue. "Well, you're going to have to wait again, because my mother is coming into town tomorrow and I don't think I'll be able to get away until she leaves on Sunday," I inform him.

He grimaces. "I take it then that I won't be meeting her?"

"We're not telling anyone else, remember? And it might be a tad hard to explain why I'm running off to meet a client at all hours of the night," I chide.

Alessandro shrugs. "So, don't explain. Wait until she's asleep, come have fun with me, and then return to your own bed," he suggests.

"She's a light sleeper. She'd hear me leave," I protest. "It's only four days, Alessandro."

He rolls toward me and hitches my leg over him. He kisses my neck and lightly skims my sex with his palm. *"Bella,"* he pleads, "that's an eternity. It's like asking me to go four days without air. Or light. I'll go mad."

"Don't be so dramatic," I say, pushing away from him playfully.

"I'll just have to break down your door at night then. Take what is mine," he emphasizes the last word in a way that effectively ends the discussion.

◈

LATER, AS I'M DRIFTING TOWARD SLEEP IN HIS DARK BEDROOM, Alessandro tugs my chin gently and I look up into his eyes.

"Are you ashamed of being with me?" he asks, his voice vulnerable.

I snap awake. "No," I protest. "Why would you ask that?"

"Surely your mother would understand if you see me while she is here. But if the thought of even suggesting I exist is so awful for you, I thought," he pauses, "that you might be worried about more than our colleagues finding out. That you might be embarrassed by me, by our arrangement."

"No," I insist again. "I don't tell my mother anything. It's like handing her weapons," I explain.

He looks at me, bemused. "Your mother hurts you with what you tell her?" he asks. Afraid to speak, I swallow hard and hesitate a moment before nodding, afraid of this getting too real. "Why doesn't your father step in?"

And the fear crashes in. *Oh, Alessandro.* I shake my head

vehemently. *No, no, no. I cannot have this conversation.* I go to leave the bed and he wraps his arms around my waist, pulling me back in.

"Serafina, no, don't run from me," he insists, pulling me in to his lap facing him in the dark. "You can tell me. I'm not here to judge you, I just want to understand." His soft words and warm flesh against mine work their magic.

I melt into him, burying my face in his neck so he can't read my face. "My father left my mother and I when I was twelve. I was her only outlet for all of her fear, anger, and hatred for seven years," I say thickly as a few tears escape. I brush them away immediately. "I left as soon as I could, and I try not to tell her anything about my life that you couldn't learn about me on the internet."

He smooths my hair and strokes my back. "Then why do you see her?" he asks.

I snort. Good question. "She's my mother." It's the best response I have. "Even if she's awful, she's all I've got. It's why she doesn't visit often, or for very long." *And I couldn't stand to have her rip this to shreds, to destroy the small comfort I find here in your bed.*

I slide back to the other side of the bed, and he watches me silently as I compose myself.

"*Mi dispiace*," he murmurs. "I didn't mean to upset you."

I smile wanly. "It's okay," I say. "But really, I should go home tonight. I just realized I have some things I need there." Lies and more lies.

FIVE

" **S**erafina, darling, I don't know why you refuse to cut your hair. It's far too long and unruly," my mother says, pulling at a stray, wavy lock.

I blanche at the contact and focus on driving. We haven't even made it back to my condo and she's already lobbing insults at me.

"It's good to see you too, Mom," I reply.

She huffs a little and smooths her own shoulder-length perfectly coifed brown hair. "Do you have to work tomorrow, or do I actually get to spend time with my daughter?"

"I have to go in for a few hours in the morning, but after that I'm all yours." A few hours of peace. And getting to see Alessandro, if only briefly, and not exactly in the way I'd prefer.

"Why don't I go with you? I've never been to my big-shot

daughter's company. I would just love to see you in your element," she simpers sweetly.

I cock an eyebrow at her. "Mom, you've never been interested in my work. What gives?"

"Well, you work all the time and you never mention anything about getting out socially. So, you must have friends at work. Maybe even a boyfriend?" she suggests.

I can't help it; my mouth drops open in shock. I close it quickly, hoping she didn't notice. It's like she has a sixth sense about how to go for my vulnerable spots.

"They're my employees, and I certainly have never dated anyone that works for me." Well, that much is true.

"All the same, I'd love to see it," she insists.

I sigh internally and resign myself to adjusting my morning. "Fine, Mom. I need to make a brief appearance for a meeting, but I can give you the tour," I concede. *And I'll watch you like a hawk, so you don't have a chance to humiliate me any more than absolutely necessary.*

"Oh goody," she enthuses, clapping her hands together.

AFTER MY MOTHER HAS GOTTEN SETTLED IN THE GUEST ROOM, I call Maggie to let her know to cancel my morning calls and let Jackson know I'll be in for the last fifteen minutes of the tag-up meeting with Buone Case. I don't tell her my mother will be with me. I know what a gossip Maggie can be, and I don't want to spark anyone's interest ahead of time. Especially not Alessandro's.

∽

THE ELEVATOR DOORS SLIDE OPEN, AND I EXIT INTO OUR reception area with my mother in tow. I can practically feel her vibrating into another plane of existence with excitement. I'd like to think maybe she's just proud of me, but years of experience have me wondering what she's really hoping to get out of this.

"Good morning, Ms. Evans," Lucy greets us as we pass.

"Good morning, Lucy," I reply, smiling warmly at her.

"Oooh, is that your secretary?" my mother asks loudly as we pass.

I face-palm internally. "That's our receptionist," I reply tensely. I lead her through the outer office, pointing out the various departments as we go. "All our support functions are on the south side of the office," I gesture, "human resources, finance, IT, marketing, and sales. All of our direct functions are on the north side of the office," I gesture again, "project managers, land use and zoning specialists, property managers, leasing agents, and so on," I explain.

Her eyes are wide as she takes it all in. "Where are the other real estate agents? Are you the only one then?" she asks.

"Mom, legally many of our functions can only be

performed by a real estate agent so more than half of our direct staff are real estate agents," I explain.

"Wow, Sera, everyone here must be so smart," she says in awe. I feel like I'm in the Twilight Zone. Is my mother impressed? She catches me staring funnily at her. "What? I'm just glad you're not trying to do this all on your own. At least you have smart people doing all the work."

And she's back.

"My office is over here. I need to pick up a few things and check in with my assistant before catching the end of a meeting," I say, moving on.

Maggie looks puzzled as I approach her desk.

"Good morning, Maggie, this is Christine Evans." I pause. "My mother."

My mother's eyes take in Maggie's plain face and short, chubby frame with disdain.

"It's a pleasure to meet you, Mrs. Evans," Maggie exclaims, extending her hand eagerly.

My mother deigns to shake it briefly. "Thank you, but it's *Ms.* Evans," she says coolly. "I'm not married. Sera's father left years ago."

The smile slips off Maggie's face.

"Well, Maggie, if you have the papers I requested, I'll be heading to the Buone Case meeting," I interject swiftly.

Maggie stares at my mother in bewilderment for a moment longer before tearing her eyes away. "Yes, of course, here they are," she replies, handing me a stack from her desk.

I work them into my bag and thank her, then lead my mother by the elbow down the hall to the conference room.

Before we go in, I pause. "Mother, please remember these are my employees. I typically don't share details of my personal life with them and I'd appreciate if you didn't either," I implore her.

She looks totally taken aback by my words. "Oh, Sera, I would never! That thing about your father was about me, not you," she rationalizes. "She called me 'Mrs.'!"

I rub my temples in frustration. "Okay, whatever, fine. You can either wait in the reception area or come in with me, as long as you sit by the door and don't say a word," I warn.

"Oh, of course I'd love to come in and see you in action!" she exclaims.

I put my hand on the doorknob and pause a moment wondering why I'm doing this. I must be a glutton for punishment.

As I go to turn the knob, the door swings open and I jump back as people start filing out. I glance in panic at my watch, wondering if I'm late, but it's only ten forty-seven. Apparently, the meeting is over early for once. When the exodus stops I look in the conference room and see Jackson and Alessandro still in discussion, standing in front of the projection screen. My mother follows me in as Jackson is animatedly talking to Alessandro about going forward on the site he's selected.

"Looks like I missed the party," I joke, interrupting their tête-à-tête. Both of their heads turn to me, and then to my mother. I look at her and she is staring at Alessandro. Hard. "Gentlemen, this is Ms. Christine Evans." I try to keep the sarcasm out of my voice at the "Ms."

Jackson hurries excitedly over to us, pumping my mother's hand. "A pleasure to meet you," he gushes to her. "I had no idea our Ms. Evans had a sister!" From his tone it's obvious he knows she is not my sister. Alessandro and I share a smirk.

My mother titters, flattered, though she hasn't more than glanced at Jackson. "How *sweet* of you! But heavens, no, I'm her *mother*," she coos, her eyes on Alessandro. "Though I was *very* young when I had her." And she *bats her eyelashes* at Alessandro.

He looks at me in astonishment and I laugh soundlessly, mouthing *I'm sorry!*

"Yes, well," I say, composing myself and moving on swiftly. "This is Jackson Williams, one of my top project managers." She finally looks at him and smiles. "And this is Mr. Giordano. We've contracted with his company to assist in expanding their development into the Puget Sound Area."

Alessandro extends his hand, which my mother grasps tightly with both of hers.

"Mr. Giordano," she says breathily, "it's so nice to meet you. I hope my daughter is taking good care of you."

I cover my mouth with my hand and cough, suppressing another laugh. *Oh, Mother, if you only knew.*

"*Piacere*," Alessandro replies, his lips twitching. "And *per favore*, call me Alessandro. Your daughter is a fine business-woman, we are very pleased with our progress."

I'm reminded what a good first impression he makes with his ability to turn on the charm, his melodic Italian accent, and his intense good looks.

"Oh! Of course, *Alessandro.* And where are you expanding from?" my mother inquires, all but turning into a puddle of goo on the floor.

He senses the effect and lays it on thick. "Our original development was in the Campania region of Italia," he replies in a tone far more accented than usual. "We have been developing in the United States for more than five years now, mostly in California until our recent business here."

"Well, I do hope you'll decide to stay in the area," my mother replies breathily.

"I'm definitely warming to it," he says, looking at me suggestively over her shoulder.

I notice Jackson shifting uncomfortably at the charged atmosphere, and I flush with embarrassment.

"Now that we've all been introduced, Jackson, Mr. Giordano, it sounds like things are going well. I take it there was nothing you needed me for if you've already adjourned?"

Jackson straightens to attention. "No, ma'am, I think we're set. Everything is moving along nicely. We've all agreed on a site and the buyer's agent has all but said his client will take the offer. Hopefully, we'll have acceptance by early next week," he assures me.

"Excellent, Jackson, that's really excellent," I reply. *Finally.* "Thank you."

Jackson nods to Alessandro and offers a small wave to my mother, "It was nice meeting you."

"Yes, you as well, dear," she replies, barely glancing away from Alessandro long enough to acknowledge him, and Jackson disappears.

"Mr. Giordano, we don't need to take up any more of your time," I reassure him.

"Yes, I'm sure you have so many *important* things to do, Alessandro," my mother says, putting her hand on his arm. "We wouldn't want to keep you."

"Not at all, ladies, I'll just be counting the minutes until the end of my day from here," he laments.

My mother's eyes light up. "Well, we can't leave you to such misery! Come, Sera has taken the rest of the day off. We were going to have lunch and go shopping. You should join us for lunch," she proposes. I freeze and my heart drops into my shoes.

"I couldn't impose, really, and I'm sure Ms. Evans wouldn't want to be unprofessional," he says, hiding his grin.

"Yes, Mother, please, I'm not sure it's appropriate for us to intrude upon Mr. Giordano's time," I quickly agree.

But my mother isn't having it. "Don't be silly, he's just being polite. Of course, you'll come, won't you? You can tell us all about Italy, and I can tell you all about Western Washington. I've lived here all of my life, and there is so much you should see."

I look at him pleadingly, but I already know what he's going to say.

"An offer I cannot refuse," he replies, gathering his things.

"Wonderful," my mother chirps gleefully. "I just need to use the powder room. Sera?"

"First door on your left," I instruct her, pointing down the hall. And as soon as she's gone I close the door and turn to face Alessandro, shaking with anger.

"Now, before you explode," he cautions, "look how happy it's made your mother. And you'll have some help managing her for a bit of her visit."

I clench my fists and breathe deeply through my nose. "How is it going to look if we're seen leaving together for lunch with my mother?" I spit at him.

He fingers his chin. "We'll leave separately then. I'll say I forgot something and I'll meet you there. And we'll go some-place on the Eastside," he suggests.

I mash my lips together to keep from saying what's on my mind. *She'll tell you things I don't want you to know.* He steps forward and draws me into his arms, holding my chin and looking deeply into my eyes.

"What was I to do?" he asks in his softest, most winning voice. "If I had said no, do you think that would have improved your afternoon with her?" He has a point.

"You're right," I say resignedly. "Please, just try to keep her on neutral topics."

"I have a feeling there's no keeping that woman from wherever her mouth wants to wander," he laughs. "Or her eyes." His mouth droops into a frown and now I laugh.

"She's totally into you," I tease him. "Maybe it's *her* that will be sneaking out to meet you after *I'm* asleep."

He makes a disgusted face and I laugh again. I stop as I hear footsteps approach, and we spring apart. Moments later the door opens, and my mother enters.

"Let's go!" she says jubilantly.

༄

MY MOTHER DOES NOT SHUT UP ABOUT ALESSANDRO THE whole way to the restaurant. She asks questions about him, but immediately launches into her own speculations without waiting for a response.

Once we're finally all seated together I immediately order a glass of wine. Alessandro raises an eyebrow at me, but I ignore him, sipping it gratefully.

Thankfully, my mother starts to bombard Alessandro with all the questions she couldn't wait for me to answer, though frankly I didn't know the answer to most of them anyway. Through three glasses of wine and an amazing ribeye, he tells her that he is thirty-seven, has four siblings — an older brother and two younger sisters, is from Bologna, and that he wanted to

be a vintner when he was a child. The last fact cracks me up —
only an Italian child would want to grow up to make wine.

He's painted a vivid picture of his home country and shared
several of his California exploits, and my mother has lapped up
every minute of it. But after my mother orders dessert, her
expression turns serious.

"Tell me, Alessandro, are you seeing anyone?" she asks
baldly.

He is, understandably, surprised at the abrupt change in
conversation, his eyebrows shooting up. Classic Christine
Evans. Lull them into a false sense of security, then go for the
jugular.

He sets down his fork and considers his response carefully.
"Not as such," he hedges.

"A handsome man like you? I'm sure you are dating several
women but are too chivalrous to say," she purrs. "I'll take that
to mean there's no one woman in particular." She winks at him.

"I'm afraid I don't understand the purpose of your question," Alessandro says tentatively.

"Oh, dear boy," she laughs, "I don't mean to frighten you.
I'm not after you. Unless you like cougars." She winks at him
again and he *blushes*. And now I'm kind of enjoying the specta-
cle, my urge to rescue him waylaid by the shock on his face.

"I ... that is to say, I'm sure you're very ... but I'm not ..."
he stutters uncomfortably.

"I was *joking*," she assures him. *Sure, you were, Mom,* I
think to myself, *unless he'd said yes.*

"No, no. Don't mistake me. I just wondered, since single men tend to pay more attention to single women. Now, I know my daughter keeps herself very busy at that company. But you seem to spend a lot of time with her." I don't like where this is going. "Have you seen her with anyone special?"

Oh, dear lord. "Mother, if I was seeing someone do you think I'd wave it under a client's nose?" I ask with exasperation.

"Well, you never know, and it doesn't hurt to ask. I just wish someone would catch your eye," she says pointedly, glancing at Alessandro.

Alessandro gives me a look that plainly says, *See? Even your mother wants you to date me.*

"This is not exactly a conversation I want to have with someone I'm doing business with. In public no less," I say tightly.

"You worry too much," she says dismissively. "We're all friends here! Besides," she says to Alessandro, "a mother worries. I knew that good-for-nothing ex-fiancé of hers was just going to break her heart. I mean, she was only nineteen and he was twelve years older than her! It was bound to end badly, but I didn't know it would set her off men for a full ten years."

"*Mom!*" I am livid. "I can't *believe* you!" I'm torn between anger and horror, the mixture causing my stomach to begin roiling uncomfortably.

"Oh, Serafina, calm down," my mother says sharply. "Everybody has a past. I have a past too — your father left me, just like Tom left you. And I had an almost teenaged daughter to take care of! I'm sure it's nothing as salacious as all that to your friend here."

"That's not the point! You can't go around telling my personal business to people I work with." I can't even with her right now. "Alessandro, I am *so* sorry, this is not anything you needed to hear, and I'm sure you do not want to be dragged into our family drama. Thank you very much for a mostly enjoyable lunch. I think it's best if we leave now."

I leave the table as quickly as I can without running, avoiding his reaction and hoping I can keep my lunch down long enough to escape.

"I'm sorry my daughter is so dramatic. Thank you very much for lunch," I hear my mother say behind me.

I don't speak to her on the ride home, or once we're in my condo. My stomach has settled, but my head aches and I need to be alone. Without a word, I go to my room, shut the door, and let the angry tears flow into my pillow. I cry for what feels like hours before I'm able to regain control. Two of my most painful, private histories laid out at the feet of a man who makes me feel something. It's a fool's hope that he won't use the knowledge against me.

But even my mother doesn't know everything about my relationship with Tom. How he charmed me into my first sexual experiences, which due to my naivety naturally resulted in my falling completely and hopelessly in love with him. And how he then became controlling and abusive every way but physically. Until one day when I dared to suggest we might get married someday, only to have him laugh at me, insult me, and then leave me.

And even my mother doesn't know that, to my utmost shame to this day, I begged him to take me back. For months I pursued him, until I was practically stalking him. Only to have him cruelly tell me he'd found someone else. That he was marrying someone else. So quickly. And it wasn't until years later that I realized he'd probably been cheating on me all along. Or that maybe *I* was the side piece. In any case, I also never, *never* told my mother that Tom's parting words were so close to my dad's: "Who could ever love *you*?"

SIX

Darkness had fallen when I finally emerged into the living room. My mother was sitting on the couch reading a book, which she quietly set aside.

"I made you some dinner," she says softly. "Mac and cheese casserole — your favorite. It's in the fridge."

"Thanks," I mumble, and I realize I'm ravenous. I retrieve a dish from the refrigerator and numbly watch it turn in the microwave.

After I've eaten what little I can manage, I put the rest away. I turn, and my mother is seated at the kitchen bar.

"Sera, if I'd know you were in love with him, I never would have said anything," she says.

I laugh mirthlessly. "I'm not in love with Alessandro, Mother," I retort. "I'm just fucking him."

Her eyebrows shoot up. "I see," she says rigidly. "Well, still, I had no idea, and I *am* sorry."

"It's a recent development," I allow. "You couldn't have known."

"Well, I would have if you talked to me more," she says, hurt in her voice.

"I would talk to you more if you didn't violate my trust constantly," I retort, leaving the kitchen. "I can't have this conversation with you again, Mom, we just go in circles. And the damage is done. I'm sure Alessandro will stay far away from me from now on."

"No, Sera," she pleads, following me into the living room. "You should go to him and give him a chance to prove you wrong."

I whirl in place to face her. "Why? You're my mother, and every time I give you a chance to prove me wrong you just hurt me! Why do you think I don't date? How can I trust anyone if I can't trust my own mother? Or my father, who obviously wanted away from our drama too? Not that I blame him," I add. "I can't do this, Mom. Please just leave me alone."

"You're overreacting," she says angrily. It's the mention of my father, I'm sure. It sets her off every time. Maybe I wanted to set her off. Push *her* buttons for once. "When you're done acting like a child, let me know." And with that she closes herself in the guest room.

And for reasons unbeknownst to me I start laughing manically. Sinking to my knees, I wrap my arms around my torso as I laugh, tears streaming down my face. *Boy, I'm really losing it.*

I focus on taking a few slow, deep breaths to steady myself and rise sluggishly. I need to go somewhere I can get a break. Take back control. I grab my keys and my bag and head to my office.

✑

AT NEARLY MIDNIGHT I TURN AWAY FROM MY DESK AND SINK into my chair, putting my feet on the credenza by the window. The lights of Seattle twinkle in the mist, and the sky is as dark as my mood. I don't know how long I've been sitting there when I hear footsteps. I tense up and look wildly around the room for something to use as a weapon.

"Serafina?" Alessandro's voice calls from the hall. I breathe a sigh of relief knowing there is no danger. Well, not the physical kind at least. My door swings open and he's there. "Thank God you're here, we were so worried."

"Alessandro, what are you doing here? Who is we?"

As if in answer, he pushes a button on his cellphone and stares at me until the other person answers. "Christine? I've found her, she's at work." He pauses. "Yes, thank you. Have a good trip, *arrivaderci.*" He ends the call, tucking his phone in his pocket and striding toward me.

He drops to his knees in front of my chair. He looks a mess, his dark hair disheveled, his top two shirt buttons opened, and his clothes crumpled. He wraps his hands around mine and kisses them, looking up at me with wild eyes and a worried expression.

"I've been trying to reach you all day," he says. His voice is strained and tired. "I figured you didn't want to talk to me until your mother called me this evening to say you'd vanished."

I shake my head. "She said I *vanished*? That's a little melo-dramatic," I reply, rolling my eyes. "We had a fight, she went to her room. I left. And how the hell did she get your phone number?"

"I'm in the phone book," he says, waving his hand dismis-sively. "Why didn't you tell her you were leaving? She was in a panic. You haven't been answering your phone, and the office line goes straight to the answering service."

"You're in the phone book?" I laugh. "How terribly old fashioned of you."

"Well, it worked out pretty well in this case," he retorts, glowering at me.

"I didn't know you were such a worrywart," I fume. "I haven't been gone that long, Alessandro. I turned off my phone because I didn't want to talk. To either of you. You both knew I was upset. Can't I just be alone for a while?" I pull my hands out of his and he stands.

"I was just concerned for your well-being. I didn't know if you'd go out and get drunk again or do something else equally stupid."

"I'm a grown woman, I don't need a babysitter."

He narrows his eyes. "Yes, you've made it perfectly clear that you don't need anyone," he says flatly. "I'm sorry I came." He throws his hands in the air, but rather than leave, he sinks into one of the chairs opposite my desk.

We sit in tense silence for a few minutes.

"I'm not going to stay away from you," he says softly, breaking the stalemate. Clearly, my mother is incapable of keeping any sort of confidence. No big surprise there. "Your mother shouldn't have told me those things, of course, but it explains a great deal. I'm not going to leave you."

A great lump forms in my throat and my eyes sting. "Spare me your pity, please," I manage to choke out. "I don't want you to stick to our arrangement merely because you feel sorry for the hurt little girl who always gets left."

He steeples his fingers under his chin and shakes his head gently. "I would have said the same before I knew those things, had you cared to ask. I will not be the one to end this," he promises.

I want to believe him, but it doesn't make any sense. "I don't understand."

"I started this, as you said," he begins. "I pursued you. You told me your terms, and I accepted them. And only on your terms will this be over."

"You say that," I whisper, "But you didn't like my terms. I can tell you wanted more. You'll get frustrated and find someone who is willing to give you that." I shudder at the thought. I may be confining our tryst to a small sliver of what he wants, but it's all I can give. Even so, now that I have it, the thought of losing it is intolerable. Nothing has cleared my mind of doubt and worry like the moments of pure bliss spent with him.

"I accepted your terms, and I'm a man of my word," he assures me. He rises from the chair and walks around my desk. He offers his hand and I take it without hesitation, as if my body has a mind of its own. He pulls me up to him and grasps my chin, forcing me to look up into his eyes. "In any relationship, even one such as this, there needs to be trust. I need you to trust me." His dark eyes burn fiercely into mine, his breath hot on my face. "Do you trust me, Serafina?"

Conflicting emotions rage inside me. But trust is not something I know how to give easily. "I want to," I admit breathlessly.

He regards me for a moment. "That will have to do for now, then." And slowly he lowers his mouth to mine, circling my cheek with his thumb. His tongue invades my mouth, melting my thoughts and emotions until they drain away completely.

I return his kiss fervently, running my hands up his strong arms. This is what I need — to touch him, be touched by him, and let everything else fade into the background.

He pulls back and grabs my hand, leading me out of the room and down the hallway.

"Where are we going?" I inquire.

He turns back to me with a mischievous grin but doesn't

answer. A moment later he opens the door to the conference room and pulls me in.

His hands pull at my blouse, working it out of my skirt and over my head. "I told you I wanted to have you on this table," he explains.

He unhooks my skirt and tugs it with my panties over my hips and to the floor while backing me to the table. In one swift motion he places his hands under my behind and lifts me onto the smooth surface. As he removes his clothing I unhook my bra and we're both completely naked. In the conference room. The inviolable nature of it is thrilling.

He climbs up with me and places a condom beside us. He trails kisses up my legs and then stomach, stopping to lick and tease each nipple. I moan and arch my back into the pleasurable sensation. His hand disappears between my legs, testing my readiness. He flicks me down there with a finger and I moan again. Laughing and smiling he brings his mouth to mine briefly, then drops his head between my legs, plunging his tongue into me while continue to work the area with his hand.

I'm dizzy with desire as he pleasures me, but it's just making me want him more. I call out his name in a desperate plea. It has the desired effect, and he brings his mouth back to mine. I reach between his legs to stroke him until he's moaning in my mouth.

"Condom," I whisper yearningly into his ear.

He rears back, slipping it on, and eases into me torturously slow. My back arches off the table, and I grit my teeth.

"Let go, Serafina," he urges me.

Oh yes, he likes it when I don't hold back the screams. I let my breath out in a groan and he rewards me with a hard thrust. I cry out and grip his back.

"You like it rough, don't you?" he asks.

"Oh God, yes," I moan, "please!" My plea spurs him on and he's pounding into me, his strong body heavily pinning me into the table causing me to feel the full effect of each thrust, my cries echoing through the room.

He rears back and hitches one of my legs over his shoulder, dragging me into his lap. Bracing himself with one arm, he uses his kneeling position to circle his hips, dipping in and out of me slowly and deeply, suspending my ascent to climax. I'd be frustrated at the delay, but it feels. So. Good. Finally, I've had all I can take.

I pull away from him and climb to my knees. "Lie down," I command him.

He grabs me and plunges his tongue into my mouth, his desire evident in every move, every noise he makes. I push his chest until he's lying under me, then squatting over him I sink him deep into me. We both groan in satisfaction. He offers his hands and I hold them, using them to balance as I work my hips over him. As I feel myself getting closer to climaxing, I drop my legs under me. Our flesh meets fully, and the new angle takes me closer to release. His hands are now free to rove my breasts and stomach. He licks his thumb and uses the moisture to work one nipple hard. The combination of sensations upends me into orgasm, and my muscles tighten over him. He cries out at last as we both finish.

He sits up, holding me in his lap, still inside me. We kiss softly, breathing heavily from our antics.

"I hope that lived up to your expectations, Mr. Giordano," I tease.

His teeth graze my ear and he runs his hands over my shoulders, down my arms, then brings my fingers to his lips.

"You always exceed my expectations, Ms. Evans," he agrees, brushing my hair behind my shoulders and kissing my neck.

As I'm studying his face I suddenly remember something. "Alessandro, why did you tell my mother to have a nice trip?"

He laughs loudly. "Took you long enough!" he chuckles. "She went home. She seemed to think you were in the wrong for not taking her apology gracefully, but she said she figured it was best if she removed herself from the situation nonetheless." He pauses thoughtfully. "You really weren't kidding about her."

I smile blandly. "Nope. I wish I were."

SEVEN

The weekend passes quickly in a blur of flesh, gratification, and relaxed pillow talk in between our exploits. It's an unexpected and most welcome departure from my usual workout, errand, and reality television–packed weekends. But Monday morning is the inevitability that puts a pause on our stolen moments.

Now, it's back to business. And the first thing I do is get my private investigator on the phone.

"Peter, I need an update on the petty cash theft," I dive right in, skipping the pleasantries.

"Yes, Ms. Evans, of course. I was going to call you soon," he responds. Peter Jeffries and I get along well because he's as direct as I am. "We couldn't find any deposits, but one of your employees, a Megan Stanwood, has been struggling financially recently. Lots of payday loans, that sort of thing. Her rent check payments have been most irregular so, with the open background check consent form your employees are required to sign, I was able to get her landlord's cooperation in confirming that she made a cash payment of four hundred dollars the day after the money went missing."

Bingo. "Good work, Pete. Can you please send what you've got over now? We'll need a full official report for our records, but I want to get moving on this ASAP," I request.

"Sure thing, Ms. Evans. I'll do that now and have the report to you within the week."

"Thanks."

Megan Stanwood. I purse my lips, trying to remember her. With almost fifty employees, though, I'm hard-pressed to keep track of them all. In any event, it's time to talk to HR.

I knock on Alison Kramer's door.

"Come in," a muffled voice calls.

I swing the door open to see a strawberry blond head buried in a filing cabinet drawer. With a mighty pull she emerges triumphantly holding a torn and bent folder.

"Sera, dear!" she shouts, tossing the folder on her desk. She rushes over and hugs me tightly. "If it isn't my favorite boss!"

I laugh. "I'm your *only* boss, Allie," I remind her.

"And one I haven't seen for a while! You haven't been hiding from me, have you?" She winks at me slyly and I blush.

Her green eyes miss nothing and narrow curiously at my reaction. I have, in fact, been avoiding her.

I've been friends with Allie since college, where I got to see her brilliance with both reading people and business. It's the reason I recruited her when I started my own company, and she's been my most trusted confidant and ally.

As a friend, I've been dying to tell her about Alessandro. As the head of my human resources department, not so much.

"Just busy, as usual," I reply innocently. "How are you and David? Is the honeymoon over yet?"

"We're super," she replies dreamily. "And funny that you mention it, but we were just talking about taking another honeymoon to celebrate our first anniversary."

I roll my eyes jokingly. "Why am I not surprised?" I tease her.

She scrunches her nose up and sticks her tongue out at me. "Anyway, *boss*, what can I do for you today?"

I stick my tongue out at her too and chuckle. "Did Nick talk to you about the petty cash theft?"

"He mentioned it." She nods, gesturing to the chair in front of her desk and taking a seat herself. "Was Peter able to find anything out?"

"Yes," I say and fill her in on what he told me. "I'm sorry to say the name Megan Stanwood doesn't ring any bells with me."

"Don't be, she's a relatively recent hire and she only works part time," Allie says kindly. "She shares reception duties with Lucy Drummond. She mostly answers phones."

I look at her blankly, unwilling to admit I didn't remember that we'd hired another receptionist until she just reminded me, much less know her name or what she looks like.

"Mousy brown hair, brown eyes, average height, and generally unremarkable," she summarizes. "Easy to miss."

"Ah. How recently was she hired?" I ask.

Allie wakes up her laptop and taps a few keys. "Four months ago," she confirms.

"Why is she only part time?"

Allie skims her file. "She's twenty-six, but she's still a student. It looks like she changed schedules and reduced her hours about a month ago to accommodate her new classes."

"Well, that would certainly explain why she was suddenly short on cash," I reply drily.

"I don't know her well, but I've spoken to her several times outside of her hire process. She's quiet, reserved. She doesn't seem to be socializing with any of the other employees out of work hours that I can tell."

"How on earth do you keep track of what everyone is doing outside of work hours?" I ask her, aghast.

She cackles cheekily. "It's my *job* to know what people are up to around here. And I rather enjoy it," she explains with a twinkle in her eye.

I shake my head in amazement at Allie's commitment. "So, what's the procedure now?" I probe.

"Now, I bring her in and talk to her. Present her with the evidence, and see what she says," Allie says simply.

"Should I be in that meeting?" I ask.

"I think it would be better if you weren't," Allie says pointedly. "You can be a little intimidating. And she's likely to talk more freely when her boss isn't glowering at her." She smiles sweetly at me.

"Fine, but I'd like this dealt with swiftly, please. Call her in immediately. Then have Lucy keep an eye on her and come talk to me. I want this handled by the end of the day," I insist.

"Sure thing, boss." I stand up to leave. "Was there anything else you needed to tell me?" She gives me a probing look.

"Nope, not a thing." I avoid her stare.

"Mhm. Well, I'm here if you want to talk," she says meaningfully.

"Thanks, Allie," I say, turning before she can see how red my face is. "Talk soon."

∽

MY ONLY MEETING THAT MORNING IS WITH SHAWN PHILLIPS, for whom we are working with the city on rezoning a portion of his property. It's been a slow and tough process, and going over the latest round of proposed easements and legal descriptions with him, while necessary, is boring me to tears.

As the assigned project manager, Ben Fuller, talks Mr. Phillips through the easement diagrams, my mind wanders to Alessandro. His perfectly muscled body still amazes me no matter how many times I see it, touch it, and revel in it. His commanding tone when he demands a kiss, a position, or to hear me scream his name echoes in my thoughts, and I wonder how I'll react when he inevitably uses that same insistent cadence in the office again. I shudder lightly and struggle to bring my attention back to the meeting.

Thankfully, Alessandro won't be back in our office until Friday. He's sent most of his team back to their offices in San Francisco until further notice, and he and his assistant are working out of their temporary offices south of the city on some peripheral development tasks in preparation for closing on their new property. So, there's nothing but my own imagination to distract me from the doldrums of rezoning, property management, and the other myriad day-to-day needs of the business.

Ben asks me a question, snapping me out of my reverie, and I dig deep to find the will to re-engage in the meeting.

∽

As soon as I'm back at my desk I text Alessandro. *Buongiorno. I can't concentrate this morning thanks to you. Hope your morning is good. x*

And almost instantly he responds: *Ciao bella. Prego. Busy day, talk soon.*

I frown. Too busy for banter. Time to be a little less clingy and put my head back into work.

∽

As I'm reviewing a rather promising bid request for sourcing a large parcel to create a combo commercial retail and residential development, Allie pops her head around my half-open door.

"Good time?" she asks.

I gesture to a chair. "Please," I offer.

She sits, adjusting her skirt nervously.

"I take it your talk with Ms. Stanwood didn't go well?"

Allie grimaces. "Unfortunately, no. She was extremely guarded from the start but went completely silent after I presented the evidence."

"Did you accuse her directly?" I ask, itching for details.

Allie sighs, knowing I won't be satisfied with anything less than a blow-by-blow. "I told her we'd noticed money missing from petty cash. I didn't tell her how much. I asked her if she'd ever taken anything out of petty cash. She said no. I told her that we investigated further and had strong evidence to suggest she'd come into possession of the exact amount missing immediately after it went missing. She didn't respond. So, I asked her where she got the money from," Allie describes.

"And?" I prompt, literally on the edge of my seat.

"She said she got it from a friend." Allie rolls her eyes. "So, I called her bluff with one of my own. I told her if that's true then she'll be cleared when we recover those bills from her landlord and the serial numbers don't match those of the missing petty cash."

"Holy shit. Did she take the bait?"

"She turned as white as a sheet! Then she told me I can't make her admit to anything and to tell you to go fuck yourself."

"Seriously? That's a bizarre response," I muse. And a disturbing one. "What did I ever do to her? I don't think I've ever even met her."

"I don't know, Sera," Allie sighs. "But she wouldn't say any more."

"Can we fire her based on circumstantial evidence?"

"Sera, we can fire her for any reason we want. Washington is an at-will employment state. I fired her on the spot and had security escort her out," she says blandly. "I didn't want to give her the chance to steal anything else or spread her vitriol amongst the troops before getting your approval."

I nod my head. "You absolutely made the right call. And you don't need my approval — you're the head of HR."

"I figured you'd say as much. Still, I was sorry to have to do it. And I wish I knew what her story was. She definitely made me nervous," Allie admits.

"Yes, I'm pretty alarmed by the whole situation," I agree. "Let's call together a meeting with Nick and Will tomorrow. I'd like to brief them on the situation and revise some procedures."

∽

By the end of the day I'm utterly spent, and all I want to do is go home, drink wine, and let my cares melt into a hot bath. I'd rather they melted under Alessandro's skilled caresses, but wine and bubbles will have to do as I haven't heard a peep from him since his brusque text this morning.

When I get home, the first thing I do is dig through the cupboards only to find I'm out of wine. I lean my head against the cold steel refrigerator door and groan. Just a bath then, I guess.

Stripping quickly in the bathroom, I'm pleased to find that there is still bubble bath. I run the bath and drop a generous amount in. As I tie my long brown locks up into a bun, I hear my cellphone ring in the kitchen. I contemplate letting it go to voicemail, but knowing it'll just bother me if I don't answer, I turn off the tap, wrap a towel around myself, and retrieve my phone begrudgingly.

"Hello," I say moodily.

"You don't sound happy to hear from me," Alessandro's warm voice says.

"I didn't have time to look at the caller ID," I reply, suddenly grinning like an idiot. "You know I'm always happy to hear from you. Not that I expected to since you were so *busy* today."

"Awww, don't be mad at me," he pouts. "I think I know what will make you feel better."

"Unless it's you, naked and holding a bottle of wine, I'm not particularly interested," I reply dismissively.

There's a knock on the door. "Not bad — two out of three," Alessandro says. "And if you open the door I can make that three out of three."

I drop my phone on the counter and open the door a crack to see Alessandro, wine bottle in hand as promised, smiling broadly on my doorstep. He is dressed casually in a grey cable-knit sweater and dark wash jeans, and has a very rugged five o'clock shadow on his jaw. It may be the first time I've ever seen him out while anything but perfectly coifed in a designer suit.

"Aren't you full of surprises?" I say, hiding behind the door as I open it wider in invitation.

He slips in and, grabbing me, pushes me against the back of the door. As it slides closed he runs his nose up my neck to my ear.

"*Ciao*," he murmurs, nibbling my earlobe and running his hand up my naked thigh. "Do you greet all of your guests dressed in a tiny towel that barely covers you?"

"Mmmm," I moan. "Only the good-looking ones that bring me wine." I slide under his arm and flit into the kitchen, grabbing two wine glasses from the cupboard and a corkscrew from a drawer. "Follow me."

"I'm intrigued," he answers, trailing closely behind me.

I lead him into the steamy bathroom and set the glasses and corkscrew on the wide counter before I restart the flow of hot water. "Now, are we going for three out of three or not?" I demand.

He laughs heartily and sets the wine bottle next to the glasses. Staring licentiously at me, he slowly pulls his sweater off, dropping it to the floor. He makes quite a show of removing his shoes, and then his pants, turning away and bending pointedly to move his things into a pile. Now gloriously naked, he picks up the wine and raises an eyebrow. "Is this better?" he asks.

I pretend to consider for a moment and he gives me an exasperated look. "Yes," I grant him. "Perfect."

"Now that we have that settled," he replies, uncorking the wine and pouring a generous amount in both glasses. "A toast."

He hands me a glass and touches his glass gently to mine. "To beautiful women, who can make you forget even the most frustrating of days with one tiny towel."

"To accommodating gentlemen with magnificent bottoms who rescue you from a dearth of wine and a lonely bath," I reply.

His eyes shine playfully as we both take a sip. I place my glass on the wide ledge around the sunken tub and step in, beckoning him with a finger to join me.

As I settle into his arms, I use my foot to turn off the tap and breathe a sigh of relief.

"Why was your day so frustrating?" I ask, skimming my hands over his thighs.

He sighs heavily. "I've spent all day chasing contractors and materials and all manner of details that should be in place by now. But I'm finding it ridiculously difficult to rely on anyone," he fumes.

He continues in detail about all the supplies that have been sub-par or missing, contractors who don't seem to understand what permits are required, and the like for quite a while. I find it strangely relaxing to listen to him rant at length about his troubles, as he occasionally slips out of English and into Italian when he is particularly frustrated.

Thankfully, I've worked with him long enough to understand most of it, and my ability to care about the rest has mostly been wiped away by the wine, the bath, and the gorgeous man with his legs wrapped around me.

Finally, he halts his diatribe and looks down at me apologetically. "*Mi dispiace, dolcezza*," he murmurs, kissing my forehead. "How was your day?"

"We had to fire someone today," I grimace. "Not something I enjoy doing, but I'm particularly unsettled about this one. Something is just not right." I proceed to explain everything, and Alessandro listens intently.

When I'm finished Alessandro runs a finger along his chin. A gesture that is starting to seriously turn me on.

"I can see why you're so upset." He pauses. "Have you reported it to the police?"

"Not yet," I reply. "I was waiting until we'd confronted her, but we'll probably discuss all that tomorrow."

He frowns. "Are you at least going to have someone keep an eye on her?"

I look at him in surprise. "I hadn't even thought of that. Obviously, she has it in for me or my company, I don't know, but what can she do now?"

He shrugs. "As they say, keep your friends close and your enemies closer. Or keep a closer eye on your enemies? I don't know. I think it would be a good idea in any case," he suggests.

I take a sip of wine and weigh his words. He's probably right. I'll add that to my list for tomorrow as well. I finish my wine and place the glass on the ledge. Turning slowly so as not to slosh water on the floor, I climb into Alessandro's lap.

"You know, you are incredibly smart," I whisper into his ear. "Which is incredibly sexy." I run my tongue down his ear, along his neck.

He pulls my face to his and kisses me softly. "Says the naked, wet goddess straddling me," he purrs, and starts to work his magic on my body.

I realize quickly that I no longer care about the water cascading over the edge onto the floor as our bodies entwine, our need for each other sudden and pressing.

∽

While I dry off, Alessandro puts his clothes back on. I look at him inquisitively in the mirror.

"You're not staying?"

"Not tonight," he states, "I didn't realize how late it is, and I have matters to attend to before the day is done."

"Okay," I say begrudgingly. "I'll see you later then."

"Yes, you will," he reassures me. He kisses me sweetly. "*Buona notte, mio tesoro.*"

And he's gone.

I walk, naked, to my bed and slip between the sheets. Eventually I fall into a fitful sleep and, for the first night in more than a week, the nightmares return.

EIGHT

"**O**kay, recap, team," I say. "Go." I point at Nick first.

"I will personally keep petty cash under lock and key in the safe," Nick states. "Any withdrawals will require company ID and a signature with weekly audits. And I'll do a check of our books and, with Will's help, our client accounts to make sure there was no skimming anywhere else."

I point at Will Baxter, my IT guy. "I'll do a check of all of our systems and software to support Nick's needs and to make sure she didn't tinker with anything else she wasn't supposed to."

"Why would you do that?" Allie asks, confused.

"She was a computer science major," Will replies. "She asked me for help with her homework from time to time. She was bright too. Better safe than sorry." He shrugs.

"Agreed," I say.

"And while our background checks are sound, I'll add a few psychological profiling questions to our hiring process to attempt to identify any undesirable tendencies in the future," Allie says. "I'll need you to run them by our attorney, Sera."

I nod. "Good thinking. And I'll talk to Mr. Jeffries about reporting this to the police and instituting ongoing surveillance of Ms. Stanwood until we're satisfied she will not continue to be a threat," I conclude. "Let's reconvene Thursday morning. Thank you for your time."

Nick and Will leave the conference room already in deep discussion about financial reports. Allie closes the door behind them then retakes her seat opposite me.

"You okay, Sera? This is heavy stuff," she asks tentatively.

I rub the back of my neck and nod. "It does take more out of me than I thought it would, but I'm fine," I assure her. "What about you?"

"Oh, you know me. Five by five," she says, grinning. "So, are you going to tell me why we haven't done lunch and shopping in weeks? I didn't think you could stay away from retail therapy for that long," she jokes.

"Hardy har," I reply wryly. "I've just been busy. We've got a couple major accounts and a new one possibly coming down the pipeline. It's a crucial time for the business. We're just starting to get good word-of-mouth business, and I don't want to slack off and waste that momentum."

"You know what the funny thing about that answer is? It

sounds good — but it's complete bullshit. Cut the crap, Sera. I've known you for ten years. Who is he?" she asks shrewdly.

And I can't stop the dumb ear-to-ear grin from breaking across my face in time.

"I knew it!" she exclaims, slamming her hand on the table. "Details!"

"It's not what you think," I hedge. "We're just sleeping together. You know, fuck buddies."

"There's your fear of commitment again," she admonishes me. "Why can't you ever admit you're dating someone? Then you might actually have a relationship that lasts more than a month."

"Because maybe I don't want a relationship? It's working for me," I reply, a little testily.

"You only *think* it's working for you, Sera," she says, shaking her head.

"Allie, please, don't," I plead. "I'm happier this way. We've built this amazing business, I'm having incredible sex, and my mother only managed to last a little more than twenty-four hours on this last visit." I grimace slightly at the memory. "Life is pretty good."

"A day? That's all? What happened?" she presses, and I'm immediately sorry I mentioned it.

"We had a fight. Or three," I reply cautiously. "Her usual crap. I'm surprised you didn't hear about some of it. She told Maggie my father left us. Oh, *and* she told Alessandro about Tom!" I blurt the last part out before I can stop myself.

Allie's eyes widen, and she covers her mouth. "I shouldn't be surprised," she says. Then a funny look crosses her face. "Alessandro? You mean Alessandro Giordano of Buone Case?"

Shit.

"Yes," I reply, trying to breathe normally — and not turn red. And failing miserably.

"I've never heard you call him anything but Mr. Giordano," she says slowly. "When did you guys get so … oh oh oh!" She starts flapping her hands frantically.

"Allie, shhhh!" I chastise her.

"You're *sleeping* with a client?" she hisses. "That is *so* not like you!"

"Allie, I never said I was sleeping with him," I joke clumsily. She shakes a finger at me.

"Oh no you don't, Serafina Evans," she says gleefully. "Holy shit!"

I cover my eyes like a child, hoping it will make her disappear. "Allie, you're killing me," I mutter. The lack of response is worrying, and I realize she's gone silent. I drop my hands to find her frowning. "What, Allie, what is it? Am I violating some sort of contract clause? Oh, god."

"No, no," she says hastily. "It's not that."

"Then what?"

"Well, you know I keep my ears open for juicy gossip, especially when we start with a new client?" she starts.

"Go on," I say tightly. I don't know if I want to hear this.

"He's kind of a womanizer, Sera," she cringes.

I shrug. This isn't news to me. "I don't really care. Fuck buddies, remember?"

She clears her throat. Oh god, there's more. "You know Francesca, his assistant?

"Of course," I reply. "Short, ridiculously gorgeous with long, dark hair and big lips?"

"That's her. Big lips *and* a big mouth. She told me a couple months ago that they had something going. You know, 'something' with heavy undertones of 'I'm doing my boss.'"

My fears during our first sexual encounter of him bedding perfect-bodied tiny Italian women come rushing back. Ugh. "Well, that was a couple of months ago," I say, trying to sound blasé.

"Maybe," she says thoughtfully. "I hope so. But still, even through other channels he's got quite a reputation. Just be careful."

"You know me," I counter.

"Yes, you're usually the epitome of prudence," she allows. "But if he hurts you I *will* have David break both of his legs."

"As any true friend would," I joke. "I appreciate the concern. Can I go back to work now?"

"You're the boss," she replies.

THE DAY WHIPS BY IN A HAZE OF ODDS AND ENDS, DISTRACTING me from reviewing the contracts for our, hopefully, new client.

It's a big deal not just because of the size of the project, but because of the company we'd be contracting with, Sutton Developments. They have a very large chunk of the commercial real estate market right now, and I somewhat suspect they're testing my services for a buyout. But I'm happy to play that game as, in the meantime, it will bring us quite a lot of business and, potentially, prestige.

Having promised them preliminary contracts for review by midweek, though, I really need to crack down and review the documents Keith, our contracts point man, has provided ahead of our internal review tomorrow.

I pick up my phone to check the time and notice two missed texts and a missed call with voicemail. The first text, from Alessandro, was from late this morning — *Busy tonight?* The second, also from Alessandro, was from late afternoon — *Everything okay?* The missed call and voicemail are from my mother. Knowing I won't call her back anyway, I listen to the voicemail first.

"Serafina, it's your mother. Just calling to see how you are. Hope everything is okay. I love you." That's all. She's probably just testing the waters after our fight to see if I'm still mad. No need to call her back right away, or possibly at all.

I quickly type a message to Alessandro. *Sorry, busy day. Hope yours was better than yesterday. Unfortunately, I have a hot date with some paperwork. Tomorrow night?*

I check the time once more and pay attention this time — it's almost six. I should probably eat something before attempting to read legalese. Standing up and stretching, I make for the break room to scrounge in the fridge for something to eat.

∾

At eleven I close my laptop and rest my head on its warm surface. Good enough for now. Time to go home and sleep. I look at my phone for the hundredth time, and still nothing back from Alessandro. I try not to think too much about it and head home.

∾

On the drive my phone pings announcing the arrival of a text message, but I'm thankfully able to resist the urge to look until a few blocks later when I'm home. It's from Alessandro, of course. *Can't. Leaving for San Francisco tomorrow. Back Friday. Don't miss me too much while I'm gone.*

I scrunch my face into a frown. San Francisco. With Francesca, no doubt. Allie's warnings echo in my brain. Can I trust him to be sexually exclusive? I don't really know him that well. I'm sure *she* knows him much better. She's certainly known him a lot longer.

Gah, get ahold of yourself, Evans. You don't *want* to know him that well, right? Friends with benefits. Exclusive friends with benefits. That's not like dating, right? We don't ever go anywhere. Just sex.

Except he did want to take you on dates. And with so much sex, the pillow talk has been frequent and, occasionally, surprisingly deep. And he has met your mother.

No. No, no, no, no, no. We are not dating. And even if he is sleeping with Francesca, what do I really care? We're not in love. We use protection. It's not like we signed a contract with the terms we agreed on. *Move, Evans, and leave your thoughts behind.*

∽

THURSDAY MORNING FINDS ME NERVOUS AND OUT OF SORTS. We've provided contracts to Sutton Developments, and while I'm certain we won't hear back until early the following week, I have a very good feeling about it.

Refocusing, I go over my calendar for the day. My follow-on meeting with Nick, Will, and Allie is in twenty minutes, so I give Peter Jeffries a call to check in.

"Ms. Evans, good morning. I presume you'd like a status report?"

"You presume correctly, Mr. Jeffries."

"Our research deeper into Ms. Stanwood's history hasn't provided any additional connection or incidents that would raise any flags. We've also established the subject's schedule and haven't noticed any abnormal behavior during our surveillance. Everything's pretty quiet here," he summarizes.

"*Beware of the danger signals that flag problems: silence, secretiveness, or sudden outbursts,*" I murmur. "I'm afraid we now have all three, Mr. Jeffries."

"Yes, ma'am," he replies, his tone bemused.

"Thanks, Pete, I'll check in again soon."

∿

AS SOON AS I ENTER THE CONFERENCE ROOM I CAN FEEL THE panic rolling off Will and Nick. Allie sits silently, a deeply concerned expression on her face.

"They wouldn't tell me, they wanted to wait until you got here," Allie greets me.

I've never been one for beating around the bush, and I'm especially impatient given the situation. "Out with it then," I direct.

Nick speaks first. "So, first, our books are fine. Nothing additional skimmed out of our various accounts and direct dealings," he assures me.

"Am I to take it, then, that's she's stolen from our clients?" I reply, trying to stay calm.

"Not exactly," Will chimes in hesitantly.

"Mr. Baxter, please be as direct as possible before I have a heart attack at twenty-nine years old," I insist.

"Okay. Someone has rigged our property management software to ignore maintenance requests. Some have been extremely serious, but most were nuisances. Unfortunately, it has steeply increased turnover in some properties, included our largest account — Evergreen Homes," he explains. "There were two particular cases that caused large dollar figure damage, both in that company's properties."

Questions swirl in my brain.

"For how long? Is anything else in the system affected? How did this go unnoticed with both us and Evergreen?" I demand.

"Three months. The tampering also changed the daily, weekly, and monthly reports printed for both maintenance data and turnover data. Those were the only functions and parameters affected. I think if it was more widespread we would have noticed, so it was a smart attack," he explains. "I talked to our point property manager, Rachel Harris. She was made aware of both costly maintenance incidents by phone calls directly from the tenants when they didn't get a response through our automated system. Unfortunately, in both cases the tenants had to be let out of their leases due to the extent of the damage once professionals arrived on the scene. Both Rachel and Evergreen Homes agreed at the time it was the tenant's faults for either not using the maintenance reporting system correctly or not calling the emergency numbers soon enough. While not untrue, this new information definitely brings that back into question."

"What about all the other stacked maintenance requests? How many resulted in turnover?" I ask, rubbing my temples.

"Almost ten percent so far, ma'am."

I look at Will in shock. In this business, ten percent is an astronomical figure in such a short time. Evergreen Homes is going to be furious, and rightly so.

"Has the software been fixed?" I ask.

"Not yet, ma'am, I'm working on it," Will replies shakily.

"What do you need to get it done quickly?"

"It's not a matter of staffing, ma'am. It needs one set of eyes comparing previous coding to current coding and looking for hidden traps. Whoever did this was quite sophisticated," he laments.

"Can't we just reset it to the last clean data point?" Allie asks.

We all shake our heads. "That would mean losing months of cost and revenue data," I grimly respond. "I need to speak with our attorneys before I inform Evergreen Homes and anyone else affected about the issue." I pause. "You said 'whoever did this' — you don't think it was Ms. Stanwood?"

"Not alone, no," Will responds.

"She has an accomplice," Allie infers, and Will nods. "Anything from Pete yet?"

"No, but I'll let him know what's happened," I respond. "Will, keep working and let me know if you need anything. If you can, find a way to funnel out the maintenance requests so we can see them and get someone manually calculating the turnover data and editing the reports accordingly before they're filed. If you'll all excuse me, I have a good number of phone calls to make."

∾

BY THE END OF THE DAY MY ATTORNEY HAS WORKED WITH ME on an opening statement and what I should and should not say to the affected clients. Will's team has provided me with a numerical accounting of the extent of the errors and the estimated monetary damages associated with them, both in repairs and turnover.

Three smaller companies have a minor enough hit to where we can pay the sum outright. Evergreen Homes, however, has, conservatively, overall long-term damages in the hundreds of thousands due to the high number of units we manage for them. Paying such a high amount at once would be a huge hit to the company, or to our ability to keep affordable — or any — insurance.

But most damaging will be the hit to our reputation and continued success. We will weather the current predicament financially, certainly, but that gives me little comfort knowing what this will do to our prospects.

I trudge home reluctantly, knowing I probably won't sleep anyway.

∾

Friday morning finds me bleary-eyed and in desperate need of caffeine. After a healthy dose of coffee, I call all four companies affected. Predictably, the smaller three, while unhappy, were placated with the promise of recompense and correction of the issue going forward, but the relationship will be tenuous at best for a long time, I know. Evergreen Homes, on the other hand, fired us on the spot.

I've called an afternoon meeting with the property management team to deliver the news, and another meeting right after for Nick and me to talk with our insurance agent. It's going to be a long and discouraging afternoon.

At six o'clock I decide to throw in the towel for the day, as my mind is just not up to slogging through the forms that need to be filled out for our insurance claims. As I'm heading for the elevator, Allie appears.

"Maggie told me you'd headed out for the day," she explains. "Dinner and drinks. Now. On me."

"No argument here," I promise.

"Pub next door?" she asks.

"No, let's go someplace closer to my place so I can drop off my car," I request.

Allie raises an eyebrow. "Planning on getting stinking drunk, are we?"

"Just being smart." *And yes.*

"Okay. Not that I would blame you in any case after the day we've had," she says.

Twenty minutes later we're happily settled in a booth and I'm nursing a gin and tonic. Allie is working on the plate of fries in the middle of the table. While I know it's probably a good idea to eat something, food is the last thing on my mind.

"How did the meeting go this afternoon?" Allie inquires.

I groan. "Do we really have to talk more about work? I'm so spent," I complain.

She looks at me apologetically but doesn't retract her question.

"Fine. People were pretty upset. I'm sure they're afraid for their jobs. I tried to reassure them we aren't planning to get rid of anyone, we still manage hundreds of units, and that we'll turn that frown upside down, there are sunshine and rainbows just beyond the yellow brick road, blah, blah, blah," I grouse.

"Well, I'm sure you were very convincing," Allie says sardonically.

And we both burst out laughing.

"I believe it, I do, it just feels like we've worked so hard to get where we are … were," I correct myself with a grimace. "You know me. I'll do it again no matter how hard it is. But that doesn't mean the thought isn't utterly exhausting."

"Sounds like you need a nice, relaxing weekend," she offers suggestively.

"Ugh, don't get me started on that either. I think he's

supposed to be back today. But honestly, I'm not really in the mood to see him right now," I admit.

"Trouble in paradise?" she feigns surprise. "Almost right on time."

"What the hell does that mean?"

"It means you've been ... seeing him? Is that the right word? Doing him? I don't know, whatever you guys call it, for what, almost three weeks now? I've never seen anyone last more than a month," she reminds me.

I scowl. "Not really the pep talk I need right now," I snap.

She shrugs. "Sorry." And after a pause, "Is it what I told you about him? I didn't mean to cause trouble."

I take a long sip of my drink. "I think it might be," I confess. "I know I brushed it off at first. But the more I think about it, the more it bothers me. I mean, I know this isn't a real relationship, but I'm not ok with him sleeping with other women."

"Does he know that?"

"Yes. Decidedly," I pause. "Though, admittedly, while I did ask him to tell me if he wants to be with another woman while we are together, I didn't exactly specify that he should do it *before* he sleeps with someone else."

"You're worried he's been sexing it up in San Francisco," she deduces.

I nod weakly.

"Only one way to find out," says Allie. "That is, of course, assuming you trust him to tell you the truth?"

I ruminate on that for a moment. "I do, actually," I decide. "But I don't know if I'm up for hearing that kind of truth right now."

"You'd rather be in the dark?" she asks, confused.

"Lord, no. I just don't have the energy to deal with it at the moment," I reply. "It's been one of the worst weeks on record. And that's including my Third Deal Disaster."

"You mean the 'remodeled' place you bought where the previous owner had hidden more than a hundred thousand in damages, so he could unload it?" she asks. "That was a legal battle for the books, for sure. You pretty much ruined that dude's retirement with that judgment."

I shake my head. "First of all, he ruined his own damn retirement. But that was my Second Deal Calamity. My Third Deal Disaster was the chick who trashed my car and tried to set fire to the apartment building I was evicting her from because I also inadvertently outed to her deployed boyfriend that she was living with someone else." I pause. "Why the hell did I keep going? Much less start my own real estate company?"

"Uhhh, because you've made a shit-ton of money doing it?" Allie reminds me. "And, let's be honest, you love it. Catastrophes and all."

"Not today, Allie," I sigh.

Allie considers me with a knit brow. "I don't understand how you can persevere through so much professionally, but you're not willing to take the same chances for a much greater reward."

"You mean *love*?" I tease her.

"Yes, Sera, *love*. Not all guys are like Tom," says Allie. "When you find a good one, it's all worth it."

"I really don't think that's Alessandro," I laugh. Good sex? Absolutely. Soul mate? I shake my head at the thought.

"How do you know for sure if you don't give him a real shot?"

"Allie, you are Captain Mixed Message Pants," I tell her. "Didn't you recently warn me off him?"

Allie grabs my drink and sets in on the far side of the table, shoving the plate of fries under my nose. "Okay, first, no more booze for you. 'Captain Mixed Message Pants'? Honestly, Sera," she laughs. "Secondly, I don't dislike him, per se. I will always want you to be careful. I just want you to give someone a shot. Because even if it doesn't work out, I can almost guarantee you it will never be as bad as that first time."

"I definitely need to slow down on the alcohol because that almost made sense," I grouse.

"Good. Fries!" she commands. Grumpily, I comply.

"Thanks, Allie, tonight was really what I needed. But you didn't have to walk me back to my building. I'm fine now," I say.

Allie hugs me tightly. "That's what friends are for," she replies. "There's David!"

A dark blue sedan pulls up and the passenger window rolls down to reveal David leaning over the passenger seat.

"Well, hello there, lovely ladies," he waggles his eyebrows. "Can I convince one of you beautiful gals to come home with me tonight?"

I point with both hands at Allie and she giggles, climbing into the car.

"Nice to see you, David," I call.

"You too, Sera, have a good night," he replies.

"Goodnight, Sera. Call me if you need to talk," Allie offers.

"Thanks, babe, see you Monday." I quickly turn so I don't have to witness their reunion and head up to my condo.

❧

ONCE INSIDE, I NOTICE I'VE MISSED A TEXT FROM ALESSANDRO. *Tonight?*

It's after ten and I just want to cocoon myself in bed and sleep off my buzz. *Can't. Hope you had a good trip.*

His response is immediate. *No kisses?*

He's in a playful mood. Great. *Rough week. Not in the mood. Ttyl.*

I turn my phone off before he can respond and head to bed.

NINE

On Saturday I do everything I can think of to keep myself busy and my mind off work — and Alessandro. By early afternoon I've run on the treadmill, showered, had breakfast, cleaned the condo, caught up on bills and emails, had lunch, and gone grocery shopping. I'm just about to start purging my closet when the phone rings.

I glance at the screen. It's Alessandro. Knowing it will only delay the inevitable not to answer, I answer.

"*Ciao*," I greet him.

"*Ciao*," he replies. "Apparently you haven't missed me as much as I missed you."

"I did miss you," I reply honestly. "It really has just been a bad week."

"How about I come over and you can tell me about it. I'll bring wine," he promises.

I hesitate. It would be nice to work through my thoughts on everything with him. He understands the issues at stake, he's smart, and logical. But I'm vulnerable right now, and not just about the issues at work.

I suddenly feel like I'm standing on a precipice. I can either pull myself back from the edge or I can fall into a dark, unknown space.

I remember Allie's advice. "Okay," I agree.

WHEN HE KNOCKS ON THE DOOR I GRAB THE HANDLE, TAKE A long breath, and open the door. Dressed in dark slacks, a white button up shirt, and sporting a new, close-cropped beard, he looks even more handsome than I remember. He smiles brightly as he holds both hands behind his back.

"*Ciao*," I greet him. "Whatcha hiding back there?"

"*Ciao*," he replies. "I said I would come bearing wine, didn't I?" And with a flourish he extends his right arm, holding not one but two bottles of wine.

I laugh appreciatively. "You sure know how to brighten up a girl's day," I joke, gesturing for him to come in.

"Ah ah ah," he protests, and with another display of fanfare, he rolls out his other hand, which is holding a dozen long-stemmed red roses swaddled in baby's breath. His expression is guarded as he measures my reaction.

I grab the front of his shirt and pull him inside, pressing my lips firmly to his. "Thank you," I say as sincerely as I can, taking the bouquet. "They are gorgeous."

"As are you," he replies, obviously pleased with my response. He follows me to the kitchen and uncorks one of the bottles while I put the flowers in a vase.

Accepting a glass gratefully, I settle onto the couch.

"How was San Francisco?" I ask warily.

He raises an eyebrow. "Unremarkable. Why don't you tell me what's going on?"

I take a long sip of wine and pull my knees to my chest.

He shakes his head lightly, slides next to me, and pulls my legs over his lap. "Much better," he murmurs. "Now, come, talk to me, Serafina. You're worrying me."

The concern that fills his soft, insistent tone unravels my nerves, and I begin to tell him everything that's happened at work.

I go slowly, making sure I'm remembering everything, describing my concerns, my devastation, my uncertainty for the future. He listens quietly and intently without interrupting, for which I'm grateful as it lets me release everything and meander freely through what has mostly been inner dialogue until now.

By the time I'm done, a few tears have found their way languidly down my face and his expression is dark. When I have no more to say, I drain my wine glass and set it on the coffee table, waiting expectantly for his response. Alessandro is silent for several more minutes.

Finally, he asks, "Your private investigator — do you trust him?"

I look at him, bemused at his choice of question. "Yes, I've worked with him for years. He came extremely highly recommended and has never given me reason to doubt him."

"That's a start," he says thoughtfully. "But this sabotage, this *betrayal,* is unacceptable." He frowns deeply. "And you've really decided not to report this woman to the authorities? Even with your most recent findings?"

"No," I reply firmly. "I agree with Peter. Everything we have is circumstantial. She didn't admit to anything, and we don't have anything to concretely tie the theft or sabotage to her."

"So, nobody is going after this woman and her consorts?" He curls his fingers into fists menacingly and a few of his knuckles crack.

"Alessandro, please, I agree it's troubling, but don't do anything foolish," I caution him.

He laughs deprecatingly. "The joy of having ridiculous amounts of money is I don't ever personally need to do anything foolish. I have people that keep me safe. That can keep you safe."

"You're not suggesting," I can barely say it, "that you have mob ties that can take care of this?"

Alessandro laughs so hard he has to put his wine glass down. "No, *bella,*" he gasps when he's able to catch his breath long enough to speak. "I'm talking about private security guards." He finally calms and wipes away the tears of laughter that had leaked from his eyes. "Truly, that was the funniest thing I've heard in a long time."

My cheeks redden, and I pull my legs back to my chest. "Sorry," I mutter, ashamed at my assumption. "Okay, so private security guards. Do you really think this is as serious as all that?"

His smile slips, and he takes my hands in his. "Serafina, when it comes to you, it's as serious as all that if there's even a chance that this person wants to harm you," he insists.

I stare into his dark, troubled eyes, alarmed at the force of his conviction.

"Alessandro, I need to ask you something."

He kisses my fingers each in turn. "Anything," he responds.

"Francesca Del Vecchio. Are you sleeping with her?"

His head snaps up in surprise. He stares at me, open mouthed for a solid minute.

"My assistant?" he hisses finally. "No. I'm not sleeping with, fucking, or doing anything else with her." His eyes are like ice and he picks up our empty wine glasses, taking them into the kitchen.

"Then why has she told people at work that you two have something going?" I press, seating myself at the counter.

He closes his eyes and shakes his head. "I don't know."

"Why would she make that up?"

His eyes fly open, and they are angry and cold, and I can tell he's on the verge of losing his temper. "Who knows? I am not interested in Francesca. She has expressed interest in me in the past, which was never returned. I. Am. Not. Fucking. Her. Nor will I *ever* fuck her," he says, quiet rage echoing in each word. He pins me with a steely stare. "I've given you my word and kept it. I am yours. I have not strayed, and I will not leave until you tell me to. I think the better question is, will you ever trust me, or are we doomed to repeat these conversations ad nauseam?"

"Okay, so you haven't fucked her," I concede, ignoring his question. "But apparently she's not the only one painting the picture of you as a Lothario."

His knuckles turn white as he grips the counter. "I really don't give a fuck what people think of me," he snaps. "They should mind their own damn business."

"So, it's true?"

"Have I asked you how many men you've been with? No. Because it doesn't matter. This," he gestures between us, "is what matters. Do you really want a number? Will it make you feel better?"

He is angrier than I've ever seen him, and its sent my pulse racing. Tears sting my eyes.

"You're right, it's none of my business." My voice is barely above a whisper, the stress of the conversation, the week, crushing my ability to speak up.

"I didn't say that," he sighs, frustrated. "My sexual past is your business. But you don't *need* to know more than that I'm healthy. And in any case, we're careful. What I'm trying to say is that the rest was before. But if you really *want* to know more, if you want to know me, I'm an open book to you. Just be careful that you want me to answer the questions."

I stare morosely at the refrigerator as I process his words. "Part of me wants to know," I admit. "But not today. I can't handle any more today." My eyes fill with tears of exhaustion. I rise slowly and walk to the bathroom, where I close the door behind me and melt to the floor, silent sobs racking my body.

A few moments later the door opens softly, and Alessandro gets to his knees in front of me, pulling me into his arms. "Serafina, I'm sorry, darling, please don't cry," he begs. "I forget. You act so strong, I forget."

"Forget what?" I ask between sobs.

He raises my chin so I'm looking into his eyes.

"That you have such a tough outer shell, but you're made of glass inside," he breathes.

I sniff deeply and brusquely wipe the tears away. "I'm not so breakable as all that," I insist, slightly insulted.

"I didn't mean to offend you," he hedges. "You have a heart. A big, beautiful heart. And you carry so much on your shoulders. That's all." He cradles my face in his hands and looks deeply into my eyes.

I don't see a trace of judgment or pity. It's like he just sees right into me. And I should be scared, but somehow, here in this moment, I'm not.

I wrap my arms around his neck and allow him to sink back

onto the floor, pulling me into his lap. I rest my head on his chest and I feel him wrap his arms around me.

An indeterminate amount of time later, it could be minutes, or even hours, I hear a great rumble tear through his midsection and I laugh, breaking the spell of our embrace. I stand up gently, pulling his hands until he rises too.

"Come on," I prompt. "I'm going to make you dinner."

$\sim$

AFTER WE HAVE CLEANED THE LAST BITES FROM OUR PLATES, Alessandro leans back, rubbing his stomach appreciatively.

"You're a damn fine cook, woman," he grunts.

I smirk at him. "High praise coming from you," I reply archly.

He grins widely and ferries the dishes into the kitchen. "How about we watch a movie?" he suggests. I gape at him for a moment and he laughs. "What? I need to digest," he explains.

I shrug. "Suits me."

He settles onto the end of the couch and I climb between his legs, resting my head on his chest.

I hand him the remote and bring up my digital movie library. "Pick whatever you'd like."

He starts scrolling through the list, and I wrap my arms around his torso, snuggling into him.

$\sim$

Warm breath and soft tones flutter across my eyelids. A low, melodic hummed tune reaches my ears as I'm rocked gently. The rocking stops and something cool touches my skin briefly before the warmth and familiar scent of wine and spice wrap around me, lulling me back into nothingness.

∾

I'm woken gently by the soft light of early morning. I've been stripped to my underwear and I'm in my bed. I roll onto my side to see Alessandro sleeping soundly next to me, naked from the looks of it. I watch him sleep for a few minutes, noting fine wrinkles from the laugh lines he gets at the corners of his eyes and mouth, and a faint line on his forehead. Without the myriad of unpredictable expressions that constantly flit across his face, he looks stern and distinguished, his thick eyebrows set in a hard line over his dark lashes, and his full mouth in a slight natural downturn. Unconsciously, I run a finger over the corner of his mouth and across his firm, square chin in the same way he habitually strokes it himself.

His fingers wrap around mine, bringing my hand to his lips for a kiss as he opens his eyes. "*Buongiorno dolcezza,*" he murmurs sleepily, wrapping his arms around me and pulling me closer. "I like sleeping with you. Why don't we sleep here more often? Your bed is better than mine, I think."

I nuzzle into his chest and consider whether to tell him it was my way of keeping him in a box. Last night ended so comfortably, and he looks so happy that I decide against it. "I hadn't thought much about it," I lie.

"Well, I like it," he declares. "And not just because we actually just slept together."

"What does that mean?" I ask, amused.

He grins down at me. "It means you're starting to trust me," he replies.

I consider for a moment and decide there's probably some truth to that. And strangely I'm still not freaking out.

"Maybe," I reply slyly. "Or maybe I'm just lulling you into a false sense of security, so I can take advantage of you." I roll him abruptly onto his back and straddle him, running my hands up his chest and leaning in to kiss him deeply.

He wraps his arms around me and sighs contentedly. "I can live with that," he says, tracing my lips with his fingers, then running his hands down my back. I can feel him hardening beneath me, and he tugs at the hem of my panties. "Off," he demands. "Condoms?"

I climb over him, off the bed and point to the nightstand on my side of the bed. As he retrieves his quarry, I remove my panties and slide into bed behind him, capturing him with my hand as he turns to me. Stroking him evenly, I trace the lines of his torso with my tongue, dropping the occasional kiss as I work my way downward. Replacing my hand with my mouth, I take him in all at once, eliciting a deep groan of pleasure.

With him fully in my mouth, I work my tongue on the underside of him, lengthening and hardening him. I watch as each pull makes his breath come harder, his moans louder. When I sense he is close, I retreat, sitting back and taking him in for a moment. His breathing slows, and he gazes at me imploringly.

He goes to reach for me, and I lazily roll my hand up the length of him and back down. He falls back onto his elbows, throwing his head back in pleasure. I stroke him harder until he's panting again. And then I stop.

He goes to move for me again, and I descend upon him using both mouth and hands in a frenzy of motion, torturing him to the edge before stopping once more. He groans in frustration.

"What do you want?" I prompt him.

He stares at me hungrily, recognition in his eyes. "Fuck me, Serafina," he begs.

"Oh, I love hearing you say that," I grin, quickly retrieving the condom and slipping it onto him. Swinging my leg over him, I descend roughly and begin to ride him. I draw his hands to my breasts and he strokes my nipples, causing my cries to meld with his.

I grind on top of him, thrusting him deeply until I'm on the brink. As I topple over the edge, I lean forward, screaming his name loudly as waves of orgasm crash through my body. Utterly spent by the rapid ascent into passion, I slide onto the bed beside him.

He doesn't move, either, and I breathlessly manage, "Did you ...?"

He nods. "Screaming too loud to notice?" he smiles.

Now I nod, and he laughs his deep, throaty laugh.

When we've caught our breath and cleaned up, I pull on a T-shirt and panties and head into the kitchen to make breakfast.

As I'm grilling French toast, Alessandro emerges in his undershirt and boxer briefs, looking just-sexed rumpled and ridiculously hot. He grabs me from behind and runs his hands over my breasts. "You're all kinds of distracting," he murmurs into my ear, pressing his hips into my backside. "I have half a mind to take you on the counter."

I turn and hand him a plate of French toast. "Then you better eat something to keep your strength up," I tease him. Glaring facetiously, he takes the plate and sits at the bar. I join him shortly, and we both tuck into our food like we haven't eaten in weeks.

I look over at him with a full mouth to see his cheeks bulging and we both laugh, bits of French toast and syrup spraying over the bar, which only makes us laugh harder. I manage to swallow my mouthful, and I use my napkin to wipe bits off his chin and shirt. He playfully kisses my neck with his mouth still half full.

I beam serenely and go about finishing my breakfast.

While Alessandro cleans up from breakfast, I pop into the shower. As I'm rinsing the soap from my body, he enters the bathroom and strips.

"Mind if I join you?" he inquires.

I gaze keenly at his gorgeous body. "Not at all," I respond.

He jumps in beside me, and I run my wet hands over his chest, leaving a lingering kiss on his lips. "I was just finishing up."

"Good, now I can get you all dirty again," he replies, running his fingers between my breasts, over my stomach, and along my sex before sliding them into me.

I'm extra sensitive from our exploits first thing this morning, and I groan pleasurably and wrap my arm around his neck, sinking into him for support. My other hand finds his stiff cock under the hot water, and I work him to the same rhythm he's working me.

He pushes me against the wall of the shower, leaning his head on the cool tile behind me and groaning into my ear. The sounds of his enjoyment spur me on, and I stroke him harder and faster. He responds in kind, and we continue to urge each other on with our hands and voices until I'm screaming in ecstasy, barely managing to stay upright as he also finishes in my hand.

His mouth finds mine under the steaming stream of water and I'm lost to the feel of his hard, wet body against mine.

Unsurprisingly, the day finds us abed for the most part.

"I think it's time to decide which nickname I'm going to call you," Alessandro declares as he runs his fingers up and down my arm.

I scrunch my brow, confused. "You already call me Sera sometimes," I respond. "That is my nickname."

He laughs. "True," he allows. "But I was thinking more of a nickname only I call you."

"You mean a *pet name?*" I ask, aghast.

"I don't know why the suggestion offends you so. I've already given you several, if you hadn't noticed," he replies. "You can pick which you like best."

"I think you called me 'darling' once or twice," I reply, "but I don't remember any others."

He smiles. "In English, yes. Perhaps you don't speak as much Italian as I thought," he muses. "There's also been *bella, dolcezza,* and *mio tesoro.*" He ticks each off on his fingers. I stare at him blankly. "Beautiful, sweetheart, and my darling."

He regards me carefully. "I was only testing them out to see how they sounded. If you don't like any of those, you can pick a different one," he offers.

"No," I say, blushing. "I had no idea. I like those. You pick."

"Hmmm," he muses. "*Bella* is good, but so common. Everyone Italian and American with the '*Ciao, bella!*' all day long."

"So, no," I laugh, resisting the urge to point out that he, too, frequently uses the expression.

"No," he replies. "*Dolcezza* is a nice word, but a little too sappy for general use, I think. But *mio tesoro* I like."

"Why?"

"Because I get to say you're mine," he says softly, his eyes warm and inviting.

I find myself both touched and, finally, scared by his sentiment. Attempting to lighten the mood, I offer, "I can live with that, but I get to give you a nickname too. How about I call you 'buttercup'?"

He laughs heartily. "No. Decidedly not," he responds.

I turn my head to look up at him ponderously, searching for something a little less intimate. "How about Alex? Isn't 'Alessandro' the Italian version of 'Alexander'? Seems like that would work."

His brow furrows. "Yes," he replies shortly. "But it's not a pet name." A dark look passes over his face. He disentangles himself and rises from the bed.

"Have I offended you?" I ask, bemused.

"No," he sighs, pulling on his pants. "It's just not a name I want to be called from your lips."

"Sorry," I mutter self-consciously, pulling on my own clothing. "Let's just drop it." I push past him to leave, but he grabs my arm.

"No, I'm sorry," he apologizes, wrapping me in his arms. He sighs resignedly. "I told you once I was an open book to you. And I meant that. When I was younger, I did go by 'Alex.' But at some point, I decided there were too many bad memories associated with it. So, I started going by my full name."

"Ah," I say. "I see."

"Call me anything else you like. I just don't want to be 'Alex' again," he says pleadingly.

I stand on my toes and kiss him lightly. "Okay, buttercup," I whisper.

⁓

ALESSANDRO RETURNS HOME FOR THE EVENING AND I'M LEFT to crawl into bed alone. But the memory of his warmth, of our deepening connection, and the amazing moments in his arms help me drift peacefully to sleep, ready to face whatever comes next.

TEN

Mid-Monday morning I'm at my desk poring over monthly reports when Maggie buzzes me.

"Ms. Evans? I have Charles Sutton on the line for you."

My heart races in anticipation. "Thanks Maggie, I'll take his call now."

I slowly draw in a couple of long, deep breaths to steady myself before picking up the phone.

"Mr. Sutton, I'm so glad to hear from you," I greet him.

"Ms. Evans," he replies brusquely. "Perhaps you should wait to hear what I have to say before you get too excited."

My heart beats harder and faster, and my breath catches in my throat. "Of course, sir, what can I do for you?" I reply as steadily as I can.

"We heard a rumor last week that you had some sort of software issue that created some costly issues for your clients," he puts forth baldly. "Now, we were ready to sign on the dotted line, but naturally this has given us pause for concern."

Fuck. How on God's green earth did he hear that so quickly?

"Completely understandable," I reply smoothly. "And I hope I can allay any hesitations on your part."

"I certainly hope so too," he responds. "Are you able to tell me what happened?"

"Yes, sir. It was, unfortunately, due to tampering by an employee who has been discovered and let go. We've done a full security scan and isolated the issue to two property management report parameters which did, unfortunately, create performance and cost issues for several clients, all of which we took full and immediate responsibility for, both professionally and financially," I assure him. "It's given us the opportunity to review our position and procedures, and strengthen our systems and processes going forward. I can give you my full assurances that this was an entirely isolated incident that I have never experienced in nearly five successful years of running this business, and that I am taking every measure possible to ensure nothing like this ever happens again."

My words are met with silence and I count ten of my own frantic heartbeats before he responds.

"I'm glad to hear you've taken responsibility and are taking the appropriate measures," and I can hear the "but" coming, "but with such a large financial hit, will your company have the resources it needs to fulfill the terms of this contract?"

"Without a doubt," I say without hesitation. "I am a woman of my word, Mr. Sutton, as evidenced by our instantly bringing this to our client's attentions, owning the issue, and seeing that action was taken as soon as possible to make our clients whole again. I've been in this business long enough to have dealt with my fair share of trials, and I've got a track record that proves my ability to take them in stride and come out on top. The real estate business isn't for people who can't handle problems like this and turn it for their betterment."

"I like your attitude," he says. "Nonetheless, I propose we add a quick exit clause in case the remaining fallout renders you unable to perform any of the duties under the contract. One that doesn't require litigation to terminate the contract."

"As in, you can walk away anytime with no repercussions, no strings attached?" I ask.

"More or less, yes."

I ponder that for a moment. I'm not sure I have much of a choice, and I think he knows that.

"I can agree to the spirit of that, but I need the clause to stipulate that all expenses for work completed to date will be paid in full," I counter.

It's a minute before he responds. "I'll want detailed invoices twice a week."

Twice a week? Bit of a control freak, are we? Then again, if

I were in his shoes, I'd probably ask for the same thing. Maybe more, even.

"That sounds perfectly reasonable, sir," I respond.

"Then we have a deal, Ms. Evans. I'll have my attorneys revise the paperwork for signatures this afternoon. Can you be at our offices at two?" he inquires.

"Absolutely, Mr. Sutton," I say, relieved. "I'll see you this afternoon."

After we've hung up, I consider my predicament. Alessandro's concerns rattle around my brain. I decide that there's more than a chance of harm coming from this situation, and not just for me personally, but for the dozens of employees relying on me. I call Maggie in.

"Yes, Ms. Evans?"

"Maggie, I want you to find a highly recommended corporate security firm. I want to schedule an in-house consultation and full review of our current situation, with an eye to implement new procedures across the board as necessary to secure our office, systems, records, and anything else they see fit to recommend," I direct her.

"Yes, Ms. Evans," Maggie says, quickly making notes.

"I'll be meeting with Mr. Sutton this afternoon at two p.m., otherwise you have my current schedule. I'd like a meeting as soon as possible." She nods. "Oh, and Maggie?" She pauses at the door and looks back inquiringly. "If they also cover personal security, so much the better."

"I'll see what I can find, ma'am."

∽

CHARLES SUTTON IS A FORMIDABLE MAN IN HIS LATE FIFTIES. His short, dark hair is peppered with silver, and he wears a no-nonsense dark grey suit that looks like it easily costs as much as my first car did. He also wears a no-nonsense demeanor.

But it's not for nothing I've successfully grown my company in a field filled with men like him. A mix of frankness, a thick skin, and being difficult to intimidate have gotten me far in this business.

As the notary hands each of us our copies of the documents that have now been signed, he rises from his seat at the head of the table and shakes my hand firmly. I return in kind, keeping eye contact while smiling agreeably.

"I look forward to working with you, Mr. Sutton."

He inclines his head to me. "And I look forward to seeing if you live up to the hype," he replies shrewdly. "Recent unpleasant events aside, of course."

I laugh genuinely. "You're not a bullshitter, sir," I say. "I think this will work out well for everyone."

He chuckles and releases my hand, gesturing for me to precede him out of the conference room.

∽

BACK IN MY OFFICE, I ALLOW MYSELF A SMALL HAPPY DANCE around my chair. I'm so gleefully enjoying my return to success after recent events that I don't hear Maggie come in. As I round my chair, I notice her watching me, a very surprised expression on her face.

"Maggie!" I exclaim, blushing a little. "Just celebrating our new contract. What can I do for you?"

She laughs nervously. "Congratulations, Ms. Evans," she says. "I just wanted to catch you before your project management tag-up. I've scheduled you with Hoyt Corporate Services for one p.m. tomorrow afternoon. They were highly recommended by multiple sources for corporate security."

"Wonderful! Is that all?" She seems very unnerved by my uncharacteristically chipper demeanor.

"That's all," she replies, backing uncertainly out of the room.

"Okay, off to my meeting then," I grab my laptop and breeze past her, chuckling to myself at her bemused expression.

IN THE MEETING WITH MY PROPERTY MANAGEMENT TEAM, I instruct the lead project manager, Ana Englund, to oversee redistribution of the approximately two hundred remaining units among the other nine team members and to focus on researching area properties ripe for a property management switch. The team continues to seem understandably uncertain about the drastic reduction in workload, and I do my best to reassure them of my commitment to their positions and our recovery as a company. Leaving the conference room, I wonder to myself if it will be enough.

∾

THE NEXT MORNING, I HAVE MY ANSWER IN THE FORM OF THE first property manager resignation — Sam Nichols, who has served one of our smaller clients exclusively for almost three years. He is apologetic but is concerned for his growing family and admitted to having been looking for a larger, more stable company for some time. I'm not surprised, though I am still disappointed. As I watch him leave for Allie's office, I wonder how many more there will be before all is said and done.

∾

THAT AFTERNOON, SHORTLY BEFORE ONE P.M., MAGGIE BUZZES me to let me know that Bryce Hoyt of Hoyt Corporate Services has arrived.

"See him to the conference room and let him know that I'll be there shortly," I instruct her. I finish the email I was writing and gather my things.

On the short walk to the conference room I observe the usual hustle and bustle of the office on a weekday afternoon. Everything seems so normal, despite the fallout from the recent sabotage. But I sigh inwardly, knowing it all hangs on a thread.

As I enter the conference room, Mr. Hoyt stands to greet

me. I'm taken aback instantly by his rugged good looks. He's probably in his early thirties, easily six-foot-four, with a broad, strong frame, chestnut brown hair, and bright blue eyes. He wears a well-tailored navy suit and smiles warmly as he extends his hand, which I take.

"Ms. Evans," he says in a deep baritone. "So nice to meet you." His handshake is firm and warm, and he exudes a calm strength.

"Mr. Hoyt," I reply, "I appreciate your taking a meeting with me so quickly." I release his hand and gesture for him to have a seat.

Once he returns to his chair, I seat myself across the table from him and set my things beside me.

"Call me Bryce, please. It worked out well, as we had a cancellation this afternoon," he explains.

"Their loss, my gain, then, Bryce," I reply. "And please, call me Sera. I've done some preliminary research on your company and was most impressed. Your company has a long history of happy and, most importantly, secure customers."

"When my grandfather started the company over forty years ago after leaving the FBI, he felt very strongly about avoiding red tape, jargon, and any other barriers to the everyday Joe or Josephine," he smiles, "being able to protect the businesses they'd built."

"I'm glad to hear it. Unfortunately, I'm in need of a little more protection than I'd like to be. I'm afraid I didn't think to engage your services soon enough," I say.

"That's not a problem, I'm here to help," he says, leaning toward me. "Why don't we start, then, with you telling me what's going on."

"The short version?" I sigh.

He smiles indulgently. "Whichever version you'd prefer."

I huff a small laugh and gather my thoughts. "A little more than two weeks ago we discovered a theft from our petty cash of four hundred dollars. I engaged a private investigator and through him was able to discover that one of our employees had made a cash rent payment in that exact amount the day after the money went missing. We confronted the employee. While she wouldn't admit to it, her reaction was troubling." I grimace. "She was immediately terminated."

"What troubled you about her reaction?" he presses curiously.

"She told my HR director that we couldn't make her admit to anything," I pause. "And to tell me to go fuck myself."

He laughs. "That seems like a pretty normal reaction, if you ask me," he replies.

"Except I've never met the woman that I can recall," I explain. "She was a part-time receptionist for whom we made allowances in changing her schedule to accommodate her education. Even for part-time employees we cover a portion of health insurance and offer a myriad of other benefits. We go out of our way to source good employees and treat them well."

"I see. Well, that does make her reaction somewhat odd," he allows. "Go on."

"After her dismissal we discovered that someone had tampered with our property management software," I say. "There were business and financial damages to four of our clients, one of whom represented more than half of the units we managed."

"Managed? Past tense?"

I nod. "They terminated our services as soon as they were told. Some of the issues required us to go through our insurance to ensure each client received full restitution for their damages. It also put a pending deal in jeopardy, though I was fortunately able to save that."

He gives me an assessing glance, clearly impressed, and I can't help but blush a little. "Your assistant mentioned on the phone that you are also interested in personal security. Do you have reason to believe this woman is dangerous?" he asks.

"I don't know," I admit. "The people closest to me are concerned. Will, our IT person, says he was aware of her programming skills and doesn't think she would have been able to accomplish the software damage on her own. I guess I'm concerned, too."

"I'd say you have reason to be," he agrees. "Have you filed a police report?"

"No. My PI suggested there isn't much that would accomplish," I explain. "That all of the evidence is circumstantial."

"At this point there isn't much they would do, that's true," he allows. "However, if there are issues in the future it would help establish a pattern of behavior."

I blink hard. "I hadn't thought of that."

"That's why I'm here, Sera," he replies kindly. "I suggest we meet with the rest of your team as soon as possible and start going over the various parts of your business to refine your security measures."

"Absolutely," I respond.

"Okay, you may want to write this part down, so you can bring what's needed to discuss the various aspects of protecting your business," he pauses so I can bring up the notepad on my laptop. "Human resources will want to bring their hiring documents and procedures, copies of all background checks and re-checks for employees and clients."

"We haven't done any background checks on clients," I interrupt.

"Then we'll want to do those right away," he replies, making a note. "We'll also want to review badging systems and employee training procedures. That should get us started from the people side of things."

I finish my notes and nod for him to continue. "I'll need to know from your IT person the firewall details, what kind of encryptions are used on your hard disks, if any, and the names of all software you use."

"What about in-house solutions?" I ask.

"You've created your own software?" he replies, obviously stunned.

"Mainly to connect outputs of various systems for our own reporting needs," I explain.

"Then I'll need the details on all that code and, eventually, access," he replies. "But in all honesty, in almost all cases having ad-hoc software solutions is extremely unsafe."

Will is not going to like this guy.

"Are your phones landline or VoIP?"

"Landlines," I respond. "Less secure?"

"No, actually, you're better off keeping your landlines," he replies. "I also didn't see any security cameras?"

"Correct," I confirm.

"That's an easy change. I'll bring some information on systems sized for the office, so I'll need a tour when we're done here. They range in price and obviousness, which I'll be prepared to go over with you," he explains. "And just to make sure we're on the same page, you do understand that this will be an ongoing process and partnership? We will, of course, let you know what our recommendations are and the cost for those services after our initial consultation, but maintenance of your security plan as your business grows is just as crucial."

"Absolutely," I agree emphatically. "I'm honestly a little embarrassed I hadn't thought about it sooner."

He shrugs. "I think most people want to trust their employees and their clients," he replies. "It's understandable."

I can't help but laugh and he cocks an eyebrow, clearly confused.

"The irony there being I'm not a particularly trusting person," I explain.

He considers me for a moment. "Do you have issues delegating?" he asks.

I laugh again. "You could say that," I reply. "I have to out of necessity, I suppose, but it's very difficult for me."

He examines my face carefully for a moment. "That's a lot for one person, Sera," he said softly. "Let's talk about a full delegation plan, too." He makes another note.

"Is that a security issue?" I tease.

He smiles indulgently. "It may not seem like one, but concentration of power is actually a problem," he explains. "When a lot of people rely on you, being the only one who knows how to run everything, who makes all the decisions — that can cause some serious business-flow problems. You need to be able to take a sick day, take a vacation, or otherwise just step away and have the business continue to run in your absence."

"That's a good point," I admit. "I can't remember the last time I was sick and didn't just work through it." He makes another note. "Uh, you didn't need to write that part down." I blush, and he laughs.

"So, the last thing to discuss today — personal security. I'd like to do a home review as soon as possible and discuss your usual routine."

"That sounds reasonable," I respond. "I'm usually in the office until around six or seven each evening. I'm free any night this week."

"How about tomorrow then? Say eight p.m.?"

I make a note. "Sounds good. If that's all, I can give you the office tour now."

"That's all," he agrees, rising. "After you, Sera."

⁓

As I conduct his tour, nearly every woman in the place follows Bryce's progress over the floor, and some of the men too, for that matter. He makes a sketch and covers it with notes as we loop around the office. As we approach reception, Lucy eyes him appraisingly, tossing her long, black hair over her shoulder coyly.

He shakes my hand firmly, holding eye contact. "It's been great meeting you, Sera," he says genuinely. "I sincerely believe we'll be able to help you safeguard your business." He pulls my hand gently so that we both are leaning in slightly, "And, more importantly, you."

For a heartbeat the chemistry is palpable in the air. He gives me a dazzling smile and lets my hand go.

I smile back giddily. "I look forward to it," I reply. I watch him climb into the elevator, and he gives me a little wave as the doors close. I do my best to ignore Lucy's knowing smirk as I pass by.

As I enter my office, I'm surprised to find Alessandro sitting in one of the chairs opposite my desk.

"Alessandro!" I exclaim. "You startled me. What can I do for you?"

He rises and closes the office door. "Who's your new boyfriend?" His tone is dangerous.

And I'm zero to mad in three seconds flat. "You can't seriously think that was anything but business," I retort.

"You looked pretty friendly," he says in a flat voice.

"Yes, we were," I say firmly, "because he's from the corporate security company. He was here to discuss our *security* needs."

He has the good grace to look surprised and ashamed. "I didn't know."

"Well you could've asked before accusing me of openly cheating in front of you and everyone else in the office," I respond, pouting.

"That would require everyone else in the office to know you have someone to cheat *on*," he points out.

I throw my hands up. "You want me to go around and tell everyone I'm fucking you? Fine." I make for the door and he grabs my arm.

"Don't be a child," he snaps. "And I'd say we graduated past 'fucking' this weekend, wouldn't you?"

"Not really, no," I reply obstinately.

His mouth tightens into a hard line. "Have it your way, then," he replies, and leaves.

I don't hear from him the rest of the day. As I'm drifting to sleep, his angry words echo in my head and weave into my nightmares.

ELEVEN

The next evening, I meet Bryce in the lobby of my building to start the home security assessment. He arrives right on time, this time in a pair of faded jeans and fitted white T-shirt. In his casual clothes his large muscles are unmistakably on full display. I smooth my hands nervously over my black, knee-length shirtdress that is hopelessly wrinkled from the day.

"Hey, Sera," he greets me, grasping my hand firmly.

"Hey, Bryce," I return.

He smiles brightly and I'm a bit giddy again — his pleasant nature is ridiculously infectious. "I'm going to start with your concierge, if that's okay? I just want to ask him a few questions about the building's security features," he explains.

My phone pings. "Sounds good, I'll just see what this is while you do that."

He heads off, and I watch him hand his business card to the older gentleman at the desk before I look down at my phone.

It's a text from Alessandro. *I think we should talk.* I'm angered that he thinks that's a good way to start a conversation after he stormed out and didn't talk to me for more than a day.

Can't, busy. Having a security assessment of my place. I hit "send" a little more furiously than I intend to and take a deep breath to calm myself.

His response comes quickly. *By the giant?*

I roll my eyes. *His name is Bryce Hoyt.* Looking up, I see Bryce heading back toward me, so I put my phone to silent and drop it back in my pocket.

"Okay, got what I needed," he says. "Shall we go up?"

I'M STANDING IN THE KITCHEN MAKING TEA AND ANSWERING Bryce's questions about my routine as he examines the doors, windows, and fire escape when someone knocks on the door.

Bryce stops what he's doing and gives me a look. "Expecting someone?" he asks.

"No, but it's okay, keep going," I gesture to him as I go to answer the door.

He shrugs and heads to climb out the window onto the fire escape. I swing the door open to reveal a clearly piqued Alessandro.

"Darling," he says exuberantly, "I missed you." He strides in and makes a show of kissing me passionately.

I push him away firmly, frowning. "Are you out of your mind?" I demand in a hushed tone.

His eyes narrow and his voice drops to a whisper. "Yes," he hisses. "I tend to get that way when the woman I'm with doesn't tell me a handsome, young stranger will be in her apartment at night."

"So, you came to mark your territory?" I retort quietly. "Would you like to piss all over the apartment, or perhaps you could just challenge him to a duel?"

He glowers at me as Bryce climbs back in the window, looking at me questioningly.

I clear my throat and try to wipe the angry expression from my face.

"Bryce, this is …"

Alessandro throws his arm around me and extends his hand. "I'm Alessandro Giordano, Sera's boyfriend," he offers.

My head whips toward Alessandro, my nostrils flaring, mashing my lips into a hard line to contain my outraged response.

"I'm Bryce Hoyt, doing a personal security evaluation for Ms. Evans," Bryce replies formally, giving me a concerned side glance. "It's nice to meet you, Mr. Giordano."

"I'm glad you're here Bryce, I want my girl well take care of," Alessandro says, squeezing my shoulder.

I shrug his arm off me and return to the kitchen in disgust, trying to suppress the shaking rage that's rippling through me.

"Understandably," Bryce replies. "Though I wouldn't discount how well she's done for herself up until now. She seems like a very smart woman." He smiles at me reassuringly and it melts my anger for a moment. I give him a grateful smile in return.

Alessandro stares at him icily.

"Who wants tea?" I interrupt, hoping to dissipate the tension in the room.

"I'm actually done here, I think," Bryce replies, giving Alessandro a nervous glance. "I'll be in touch soon."

"Thanks, Bryce, I really appreciate it," I reply, showing him out the door.

"Talk to you soon, Sera," he says, giving me one last small smile before he goes.

I close the door behind him and count to three. I turn slowly and stare at Alessandro, who has settled himself on the couch.

"Ready to talk?" he asks pointedly.

"No," I reply angrily, marching into the kitchen.

He approaches the bar. "Don't be like that," he urges.

I slam the teapot back onto the stove and turn the burner off. "No, *you* don't be like that," I retort. "How dare you come over here unannounced to claim me like I'm your property? And to refer to yourself as my boyfriend — without even talking to me about how I'd feel about that — un-fucking-believable. That's what you are." I can practically feel the steam coming out of my ears, and my hands are shaking.

He rounds the counter, putting only the kitchen island between us. "What was I supposed to do? Don't you see the way he looks at you?" he demands. "You invited someone who is practically a stranger into your home. One who was willing to undress you with his eyes in front of everyone. God only knows what he'd do in private." He seems perfectly composed except for his tone, which radiates fury and wrath.

Privately, I'm pleased that he's upset, given how much he's upset me. Outwardly, I scoff. "Don't be ridiculous. I thoroughly investigated his company. I would never have agreed to him being here if I thought he or his company was in any way questionable. Don't treat me like I'm stupid."

"Do you want to fuck him? Is that it?"

Every word he utters stokes the fire of my fury. I despise being treated like a child. Like my word means nothing. And his petty accusation is both untrue and unfair. He can flirt with every woman in sight, but I so much as speak to another man and this is what I get? I have to suppress the urge to throw things, to scream at him. Instead, I close my eyes, hoping when I open them I will stop seeing red.

"No, Alessandro. I didn't want to fuck him," I say carefully, as calmly as I can manage. I open my eyes and stare at him, still fuming. "The only person I want to fuck is you."

In a flash, he rounds the island and pulls me to him, claiming my lips with his, my body with his hands. The turmoil inside me responds to his hot, rough touch, and my body screams to release its anger and tension in carnal conquest. I kiss him back ferociously, my hands tearing his shirt buttons open, then quickly opening his belt and zipper.

He lifts me onto the counter, sliding my shirtdress up over my hips, and rips my panties off viciously, sheathing himself quickly with a condom. Then, throwing my legs over each of his shoulders, he pulls me to him and violently takes me. He's leaned over me, gripping my thighs tightly, eye shut firmly as we set a frantic rhythm. Every powerful lunge mixes my anger with my desire until I'm screaming in furious pleasure, egging on the enraged pounding of flesh on flesh. I climax quickly, my body arching off the counter. My muscles clench around him, and he growls gutturally in orgasm.

After a moment, he pulls away and falls back against the refrigerator, panting heavily. As he discards the used condom in the kitchen bin, I climb down from the countertop and retrieve my panties while he rights his clothing. He watches me silently, his eyes narrow and dark.

"Now get the fuck out," I demand. I go to my bedroom and slam the door behind me.

A moment later I hear the front door close sharply.

⌒

ALLIE COMES OVER IN RECORD TIME, RESPONDING TO THE anguish in my voice, even though it's late on a work night. We sit under a blanket on the couch, passing a pint of chocolate caramel chunk ice cream back and forth.

"So, he just left?" she asks in awe.

I nod glumly. "And I know I told him to, but …"

"You wanted him to stay?"

"No. I just wish I hadn't been so *angry* at him," I admit.

Allie hands me the last of the pint and doesn't say a word.

"What?" I prompt her.

"You're not gonna like it," she promises.

I shrug. "I pretty much feel like shit right now anyway, Allie, just spit it out."

"You have feelings for him," she says.

I savor the last spoonful of caramelly, chocolatey comfort as I weigh her words.

"Anger is a feeling, yes," I hedge, and she rolls her eyes.

"You know what I mean, Sera," she insists.

I sigh and put the empty carton and spoon on the coffee table. "I don't know what I feel. I've spent so long trying to avoid doing exactly that." I pause. "I thought I could contain my relationship with him to only the things I wanted to feel."

She shakes her head vehemently. "You know that's not how it works."

"I know," I say, and I feel small and overwhelmed. And foolish.

"Tell me what he's made you feel. Besides angry," she says wryly.

"The good stuff or the bad stuff?"

She hesitates. "Start with the bad stuff."

"Besides angry? Scared, confused, and jealous, just off the top of my head," I list.

"And the good?" she prompts.

I think about this one for a moment. "Sexy. Desired. But he also listens to me. More than that, he understands me," I admit. "And I've felt more alive since this started. Before him I was so engrossed in my routine. I didn't realize how lifeless I was." I pause. "He has pet names for me," I admit sheepishly.

"And how does that make you feel?" she asks.

"Well, doctor," I joke, leaning back on the couch pillows.

"Seriously, Sera," she insists.

"At first it made me feel …" I grasp for the right word. "Cherished? Then it just scared the shit out of me."

"It sounds like he wants to be with you, Sera. Like really be with you. And it sounds like you want that too, until your fear kicks in."

"Obviously, if he's going around telling perfect strangers that he's my boyfriend," I gripe.

"He was *jealous*," she says, exasperated. "I'm not excusing his behavior, but that's a pretty normal reaction. What did he say when you got jealous of Francesca?"

"He was angry at first. But when he calmed down he told me he wanted me to know that I can come to him with anything, ask him anything." As complicated as Alessandro is at times, she's right — he obviously wants to try.

Allie presses her fingers to her temples. "I'm going to cut to the chase here, because it's late and we have work tomorrow. Think about how he makes you feel, good and bad. Picture his face," she directs me. "Do you want to end it with him? Or is there enough good for you to fight your fears and frustrations and give this guy a real shot?"

I sigh heavily and rise to clean up.

Standing in the kitchen, I place my hands on the kitchen island, remembering our exploits from earlier in the evening.

"I want to give it a real shot," I admit. "I just don't know how. And after tonight, he may not want to anymore anyway."

Allie approaches the kitchen bar. "Tell him, Sera," she pushes. "Give him the chance to tell you what *he* wants."

I glance at the clock. It's almost eleven. "Not tonight," I reply. I approach Allie and embrace her tightly. "Thanks for talking me off the ledge, Allie."

"Anytime," she offers, squeezing me back. "Good night, babe, love you."

I let her go and walk her to the door. "Love you too."

When she's gone, I fall fully clothed onto my bed. I let the small well of exhausted tears fall and close my eyes, surrendering to my fatigue.

I throw myself into the Sutton Developments project the next day, pounding through piles of preliminary research to build a base for one of our project managers to start from. It feels good to turn myself over to the Serafina that used to shut off the world and lose herself in the details of a project, emerging only for caffeine and bathroom breaks.

My staff seems to sense my reclusiveness, as the few times I emerge throughout the day their conversations cease and they scatter back to their desks, pretending to be working diligently. It would make me laugh if I wasn't still so out of sorts.

Just as I'm about to head home at six, an email hits my inbox from Hoyt Corporate Services with their proposal. I open it eagerly and skim the contents. It's lengthy, but the bottom line seems more than reasonable. I save a copy to my desktop for perusal after dinner and pack up to head home.

∽

SITTING AT THE KITCHEN BAR, I'VE FINISHED MY LONELY dinner and am sipping a glass of wine while reading the rest of the contract when my eyes wander to the kitchen island. I stare at it for a moment and a wave of shame washes over me at the way I treated Alessandro. I eye my computer for a moment, then snap it closed, decided that I'll finish my review in the morning. I grab my keys and purse and head out the door.

∽

I KNOCK SOFTLY, MY STOMACH IN KNOTS. PART OF ME IS hopeful and excited. But when the door opens that evaporates when I see Francesca standing in the doorway. All long, dark hair and big, red lips. She is clothed, thankfully, but barefoot. I'm too shocked to speak.

"Alessandro, *qualcuno a vederti*," she purrs toward the living room.

Alessandro appears behind her, sexily clad in black sweatpants and a black T-shirt, and he's also barefoot. When he sees me he stops cold and glances guiltily at Francesca. His shamefaced expression rips my heart out of my chest and I back away from the door.

I try to form an excuse, but the words won't come, and I turn to flee.

"Serafina, stop!" he calls commandingly. He catches up to me easily before I can get anywhere near the elevator.

I try frantically to hold back the tears a moment longer, but it's a dicey proposition. "I shouldn't have shown up unannounced," I say thickly. He shakes his head and his expression is heartbreakingly sad, but he doesn't reach for me.

"I didn't expect you," he says awkwardly.

I laugh drily. "That much is obvious."

"It's not what you think," he says, predictably.

"I very highly doubt you know what I'm thinking right now," I say sharply.

"Fine, it's not what it looks like," he clarifies. "I wanted to give you some space. We're just working." He finally touches me, tentatively sliding his hand in mine. When he realizes I won't pull away, he guides me back to the apartment, and I follow reluctantly.

He releases me and pushes the door open to reveal Francesca deep in conversation with Marco, who is similarly casually dressed in jeans and a sweater. Chinese food takeout containers litter the coffee table, and there are stacks of documents and blueprints everywhere.

"Oh," I say meekly, ashamed.

"We're almost finished," he promises. "You can stay, if you want. Or I can come over when we're done."

"I'm already here," I say timidly. "I'll just stay out of the way until everyone's gone."

"Come," he prompts, leading me down the hallway. He opens the door to a room I've never been in before. Overflowing bookshelves line the walls, and a large desk occupies the far corner of the room. "You can wait here," he points to an overstuffed chair. "Be back soon."

I set my bag on the chair and peruse the shelves. Many of the books are in Italian, so I can only make out a few titles here and there. The books in English cover a wide variety of subjects, from car maintenance to classic literature.

As I flip through a beautifully illustrated book on Da Vinci, Alessandro reappears. He leans against the doorframe and regards me sternly. I slip the book back into its place on the shelf and face him.

He continues to watch me silently for a few moments, then turns and walks out of the room. Assuming he wants me to, I follow him into the living room. I look around, noting that everyone has gone. He gestures for me to take a seat on the couch. I sit and wait nervously for him to break the silence.

He runs a finger along his chin and my heart jumps. I want to reach out and touch him, to fix what is broken, but I remain still.

Finally, he speaks. "Before I say anything else," he begins, "I owe you an apology for my behavior last night. You were right, I had no business showing up unannounced and declaring us as something we'd explicitly agreed not to be."

"Apology accepted," I say quietly. He offers a grim smile that doesn't reach his eyes. "But?" I prompt.

"But," he agrees, "whether you're willing to admit it or not, we've progressed past a casual relationship. Neither of us is treating this like just sex. And you were right — I want you to be mine, to be with me completely. But not if you're going to treat me the way you did last night."

"Alessandro, I'm sorry for the way I treated you last night too," I allow. "But you started it. And I don't want to be treated the way you treated me last night, either." I breathe slowly, trying to move past the anger.

"Fair point," he concedes. "And while I am not one to make excuses, I would like to offer you an explanation. I've never had to pursue a woman for this long before, never had a woman push me away and pull me in within the course of the same conversation for weeks on end. It's driven me a bit out of my usual sensibilities. I'd like it to stop."

My face falls. "Are you breaking up with me?" I ask fearfully.

"*Porca miseria*, woman, I just told you I want to be with you," he replies testily. "And as much as I'm used to being in the driver's seat, it would seem it's up to you. However, the one thing I can do is ask you to choose. To either be with me completely, or not at all."

"Hmmm," I feign ponderously. "Those are my only options?"

He gives me a bewildered look. "Yes," he replies slowly.

I slide toward him on the couch and look up into his eyes. I tilt my head and drop my hand on his leg. "Then I guess completely it is."

He stares coolly into my eyes for a moment longer, and I wonder if he's heard me. A smile creeps slowly onto his face. "Good," he says. "Now get the fuck out."

I slap his arm and he bursts out laughing.

"Joking! Of course, I'm joking, *bella*," he yelps as I repeatedly smack him.

I cease my attack and cross my arms over my chest, with an affected pout. He pulls me onto his lap and strokes my hair, my cheek, my chin. He drops light kisses on my nose, cheeks, and, lastly, lips. His kiss deepens, and I sink into his arms, breathing in his special wine-and-spice aroma.

He slides his arms under me and carries me to his bedroom, setting me down gently on my feet next to the bed. Pulling his T-shirt over his head, he lets it fall to the floor. I lay my palms lightly on his chest, his heart beating strongly under my hand. He hooks his thumbs into his sweats and eases them around his hips, and they drop to the floor with his shirt. He steps out of the mound of clothing, now completely naked. I shudder in anticipation, eliciting a smile from him.

I drop my hands to the large belt cinching my shirtdress at my waist and unhook it, adding it to the pile at our feet.

"I love that you wear these dresses," he murmurs, running his hand up my thigh, then along my backside. "So easy to remove."

His other hand joins in and he slowly slides my dress up. I raise my arms compliantly to let him strip the fabric off my body, then swiftly unhook my bra and shimmy so it falls away from my body.

He lets out an appreciative sigh, dropping to a knee to allow his tongue to explore my nipples. I run my hands through his thick hair and gasp in pleasure as he teases me. His mouth continues to trace kisses downward, to my hip. He slides my underwear off to make room for his roving tongue.

His mouth returns to mine and he lifts me onto the bed, lying next to me, running his hands over me. I wrap my leg around him and shift my body against his, enjoying the feeling of his skin on mine.

"You're on birth control?" he asks. I nod. "Good. Do you trust me, Serafina?"

He rubs against me and I choke back a tortured moan. And I know I've already surrendered.

"I trust you," I breathe, and my heart expands at the truth behind the words.

He cups my cheek with one hand and covers my mouth with his, sliding his tongue along my lip. Dizzy and breathless, I feel him shift himself on top of me, into me, and the feeling of just him inside me is unbelievably incredible and overwhelming.

"Go slow," I plead.

He nods softly. I pull my legs back to receive him fully and settle my heels on his behind as he carefully tests the effects of the new sensation. He holds me gently in his arms, keeping his mouth on mine, and tilts himself slowly out, leaving me void. Just as slowly, he reenters me, and I gasp loudly into his mouth.

He shifts his head to bury his face in my hair, his mouth at my ear, "*Mio tesoro*, you feel amazing."

Even just his words are enough to pleasure me, and I moan in response. "Don't stop," I plead.

He draws up, resting himself on his forearms over me and stares into my eyes as he begins to move. He keeps a slow rhythm, but the lack of barrier makes me feel everything intensely, and I know when I climax it's going to be something to behold. For now, I focus on the building sensation and his eyes on mine.

His pace increases, and I grab him in encouragement, moving to meet him. He sits up further, now resting on his palms, and the change in position brings new waves of pleasure. I grasp the sheets beneath me and work my hips with his, moaning in abandon as he stimulates me in ways he never could before. Suddenly, I want to know what it feels like to be on top of him this way, and I tell him so.

His eyes go wide, and he leans into me, wraps his arms around my back, and flips our positions in one swift movement. A giggle bursts from my lips and he smiles up at me beatifically.

Adjusting to being on top, I bring myself up to a sitting position and the fullness of feeling deep within me causes me to cry out in pleasure. He shows his approval and enjoyment at the change and moans with me. Going slowly, I work myself over him. Once I master the sensation, I move faster, my orgasm building inside of me. He plays with my nipples, his thumbs circling and pressing my sensitive flesh, while he watches me closely, grunting appreciatively every time I slide him deep into me. As I feel myself starting to climax, I lean back, and my world explodes. It's so powerful that I can only moan lowly, even moving is difficult and my body slows.

Alessandro grabs my hips and braces me as he works himself beneath me, prolonging the pleasure. I cry out unreservedly as the orgasm continues to rip through me, and I can feel the subtle shift when he hardens further, causing a blackout level surge of pleasure. But I hang on, wanting to watch him come beneath me, his cries signaling the depth of his gratification.

My whole body tingles distractingly, and I fall on his chest, his mouth finding mine. Finally, we part breathlessly, and lie facing each other with our legs still partially entwined.

He grasps my hand and brings it to his lips, kissing each of my fingers. I gaze at him adoringly and he grins transcendently.

"Now you're really and truly mine," he declares. He props himself up on his elbow and kisses me. "Are you happy?"

"Blissfully," I reply with a sigh.

TWELVE

On Friday morning it takes me a while to get my head out of the clouds and refocus on work, but I finally manage to finish reading Bryce's proposal. It looks phenomenal, and I'm eager to start making the changes, but realize I should probably check with Nick first so he can prioritize it in our upcoming expenses. I mark the forwarded email urgent and send.

Standing a stretching widely, I go looking for Nick to ensure he reviews it as soon as possible.

⁓

Entering his office, I find Nick seated on the floor surrounded by paper.

I laugh. "Wasn't the digital age supposed to put an end to this kind of thing?" I tease.

Nick looks up in surprise.

"You'd think," he chuckles, "but they didn't account for fuddy-duddies like me who need to see everything on paper, sometimes all at once, to start putting things together. Technology may advance, but it's hard to unlearn your own processes."

"Speaking of processes, I've forwarded you the Hoyt Corporate Services security proposal. I'd like to accept today and get on their schedule ASAP," I say pointedly.

"I hear you, boss," he agrees, shuffling a couple pages. "I'll wrap up here and get back to you early this afternoon."

"Thanks, Nick," I reply. I frown thoughtfully. "Is Helen enough help, or could you use another bookkeeper?"

"What?" he asks looking up, confused and distracted.

I gesture around his office. Aside from the floor around him, the whole desk and both of his extra chairs are covered in papers, and the wall behind his desk in sticky notes and ledgers.

"Oh, that." He sighs heavily. "Maybe temporarily? I've been paranoid since our discovery, so I've been redoing all of our reports by hand based on hard copy receipts, bills, and so on, and comparing them to the software reports."

"Is that really necessary?" I ask skeptically. "I thought Will didn't find any other issues besides the property management software?"

"He didn't," Nick admits. "I just can't shake the feeling."

I shiver. "I understand, Nick," I assure him. "Believe me. Of all people, I get it. But maybe you can focus your concern into reviewing the security proposal? They're going to re-review all of our systems, and hopefully be able to reassure us on that front."

"Really?" he asks hopefully.

"Yep, that's kind of the idea," I point out.

"Okay," he concedes. "I'll give it a rest for today. Thanks, Sera."

"No problem. Talk to you this afternoon," I reply.

He turns back to the stacks on the floor and I watch him for a moment longer to see if he'll keep going or not. Thankfully, he starts to pile the papers together, adding the small stacks to the teetering piles on his cabinets. I smile tolerantly and meander back to my office.

"Ms. Evans," Maggie says as I approach. "Mr. Giordano came by. He wanted to speak with you before the weekly tag-up."

"Oh?" I ask in surprise. "Where is he now?"

"I think he went to the break room for coffee," she replies. "In any case, he said he'd stop by again shortly."

"I see. Well, I'll just be doing some research, so please send him in when he returns," I instruct her.

When I get in my office I duck into my private bathroom to check myself in the mirror. I'm pleased to find my long, brown hair is still soft and wavy after the lengths I went to this morning to tame it. I also note there are flecks of green in my usually brown eyes. I smile shyly at myself, knowing that only happens when I'm really excited about something.

I return to my desk and do my best to focus on research. I haven't been working long when Maggie pokes her head in to announce Alessandro's arrival. He thanks her, and she closes the door behind him.

We stare at each other across the room for a moment.

"Are you here for business or pleasure?" I ask teasingly, rising to meet him in front of my desk.

He wraps me in his arms and kisses me gently. "I thought you had a 'no sex in the office' rule?" he jokes back.

I run my hands over his back, grabbing his behind. "Old rule," I say silkily, pulling his face to mine.

He kisses me briefly and pulls away laughing. "My, you are feisty today," he comments. "We should've ditched the condoms sooner. But I don't think I can properly pleasure you in six minutes."

I jut my lip out in a pout. "Wanna bet?" I challenge him.

He hesitates for just a moment before smirking suggestively and pushing me into the bathroom, closing the door behind us.

He presses me against the back of the door, his breath hot against my ear. "No screaming now, *mio tesoro*," he says huskily. He kisses me passionately, sliding his hand under my skirt.

I bite my lip as his thumb finds its target, revolving tantalizingly. He pulls my blouse away from my neckline, caressing my neck and shoulder with his lips, then returning his mouth to mine to work his tongue with mine. As his fingers brush along my sex, I release his mouth, gasping softly. I press my face into his chest to stifle a moan.

"Tsk, tsk, tsk," he whispers, "how are you every going to come quietly if you can't even take a little teasing?"

"Why don't you stop teasing me and find out?" I urge him.

He smiles wickedly and plunges his fingers into me suddenly, taking me as roughly as he would if he were inside me. I grip his shoulders and choke back a scream. I can feel him hardening against my leg as he watches me respond to his rapid assault.

As my breathing becomes frantic and my grip tight, he loosens his last onslaught and circles hard with his thumb and forefinger inside and out while pumping hard with the other fingers. It pushes me over the edge and I come, squeezing my eyes shut and letting out a low moan into his shoulder.

"Shhhhh, *bella*," he murmurs, pulling my face up. He covers my mouth with his and lets the last of my moans dissolve in his kiss. He gently removes his hand from between my legs and checks the watch on his other wrist. "Two minutes to spare."

I laugh softly, resting my head against his neck. "See? We may even have enough time to get to the meeting without looking like you just fingerfucked me in a bathroom."

We both dissolve into quiet, conspiratorial laughter. He gives me one last brief kiss and we prepare ourselves to head to the meeting.

Putting his hand on my office door handle, he winks at me roguishly. "I'll go first."

I blow him a kiss and he leaves me to gather my things for the meeting. As I exit my office and head to the conference room, I realize another perk of him leaving first. I get to watch him walking in front of me, his fitted trousers accentuating his gorgeous backside. I suppress a giggle, realizing he's right — I am feisty today.

As I take a seat across from him at the table, I feel my insides ache tantalizingly from our brief encounter, and I gingerly adjust myself, enjoying the sensation. He raises an eyebrow distractedly at me as Jackson calls the meeting to order.

"Great! Now that everyone is here," Jackson begins. "There's not a lot to cover, as the deal closes in two weeks. I'll give the floor to Marco and Giovanni to discuss build readiness and any remaining issues at hand."

Alessandro's architect and engineer take the floor, running through the build process open items. I start to notice midway through the meeting that every time Alessandro goes to engage, he glances sidelong at me first. It starts to make me blush, and I hope nobody else in the room notices our reactions to each other.

As the meeting wraps up, Jackson approaches me for a word. Alessandro lingers momentarily, but I shake my head faintly in a sign for him not to wait. He takes the hint and leaves reluctantly, and I'm left to wonder for a moment if he intended to make me return the favor in the conference room once everyone had left.

Shaking myself out of my hedonistic musings, I turn my attention to Jackson. "What's up?"

"I was wondering," he begins, "if you've decided who will be lead on the Sutton Developments project."

"I'd given it some thought, yes," I admit. "And while I know the Buone Case project is wrapping up and heading into a development phase that we won't be terribly involved in, the Sutton Developments project is an entirely different beast."

"I know," he agrees enthusiastically. "That's exactly why I wanted to express my interest. I know I don't have as much commercial leasing real estate experience as Ellie, but I think that with my extensive commercial residential experience and my outstanding research skills I'd be more than capable."

"Jackson, I appreciate that, but this is a very important project for us," I say gently. "And Ellie has more experience than both of us combined, on both sides. I need her pinch-hitting for us here. We have to nail this to regain our momentum."

Jackson nods despondently, and I consider the situation silently for a moment. "But," I hedge. "Since it *will* be such a large project, and you have obviously shown talent and initiative, it might be a good experience for you to assist Ellie."

His eyes brighten. "That would be awesome! Thank you so much, Ms. Evans," he gushes happily.

I smile warmly at him. "No, thank you, for carrying so

much of the Buone Case project lately, Jackson," I reply. "It's been a challenging time for me, and I couldn't have managed without you."

I excuse myself for lunch, and Jackson practically skips out of the room behind me. Chuckling quietly, I return to my desk to find Nick prowling around Maggie's empty desk.

"Sera! There you are!" He sounds excited.

"Hi Nick," I reply, looking at him warily. "Had a few cups of coffee since I saw you last?"

"No!" he exclaims, waving his hands comically, and I suppress a dubious chuckle. "I read the security proposal and I wanted to tell you as soon as possible that we can absolutely make that happen from a financial end."

"That's great, Nick, but weren't we supposed to meet after lunch?"

"I couldn't wait," he admits. "I had no idea how many ways there were to deal with this. Better software, better data protection, better training — I feel like a huge weight has been lifted off my shoulders."

His clear relief radiates in his tone and mannerisms and something clicks in my brain. "Oh Nick, you didn't think any of this was *your* fault, did you?"

He stops pacing frantically and a gloomy shadow passes over his face. "I know it's silly," he admits. "But I feel like I should've known better. Done better. But this," — he waves a printout of what I can only assume is the security proposal — "I would've never thought of half of this."

I lay a hand on his shoulder reassuringly. "Nick, it wasn't your job to think of all that. This is all on me. I should've thought to seek this kind of help before it became necessary," I say. "I'm sorry." My heart breaks for the hours he must have lost worried about this.

"Thanks," he says slowly. "I know this is your company, Sera, but I've been with you almost the whole time. I see how hard you work. I just felt like I let you down. Like I let everyone down making it so easy for someone to steal from us."

"I get it, but shit happens," I say blandly. "You know how good a judge of character Allie is, how thorough she is with the hiring process, and even she was duped."

"I hadn't thought of that," he acknowledges.

"We all could have done better," I allow. "But all that matters now is what we do next."

Nick smiles and holds up the security proposal.

I nod and laugh. "I'll call Bryce Hoyt."

"Sera, I'm so pleased you've decided to work with us," Bryce's warm, deep voice says through the speaker phone.

"Me too," I respond. "We'll see you first thing Monday morning then?"

"Bright and early," he confirms. "We're going to hit the ground running on this one, Sera. I'll have someone start on your client background checks and I need you to tell me when you have a block of time next week to file a police report on your saboteur."

"I'll have my assistant send my schedule over," I assure him. "Have a great weekend, Bryce."

"You too, Sera," he says huskily.

After I've hung up, I can't figure out what about the exchange has left me unsettled until I remember Alessandro's accusations regarding Bryce's intentions toward me. I make a mental note to observe his interactions to see if he's the same with everyone, or if I really am getting special treatment before turning back to organizing the preliminary Sutton Developments research.

$\sim$

JUST BEFORE SIX, AS I'M WRAPPING UP TRANSFERRING MY organized research to a shared directory, Alessandro appears in my open doorway.

"*Ciao*," he greets me, grinning like a schoolboy. "Almost finished?"

I give him a fake stink eye. "Yes, but if you keep coming in here everyone's going to know what's going on," I grouse.

He saunters in, plopping happily in a chair. "I thought the rules had changed?" he asks, a twinkle in his eye.

I raise an eyebrow at him delicately, pursing my lips. "Yes, I suppose they have, Mr. Giordano," I concede.

He rises from the chair and stands next to me, leaning against the desk.

"But that doesn't mean we need to broadcast it," I warn.

He leans his face close to mine. "Maybe I want to broadcast it," he replies seductively, then takes my lips with his, pulls me to a standing position and wraps himself around me.

I break my lips away from his, gasping for air. "Alessandro, please."

His hand holds my chin, thrusting it upward so he can kiss my neck. I let out an involuntary sigh of pleasure. His lips move to my ear, his tongue wreaking havoc with my brain.

"Don't worry, *mio tesoro*, almost everyone is gone anyway," he murmurs, returning his mouth to mine.

I give in and wrap my arms around his neck, returning his heated kisses.

Suddenly I hear a small "Oh!" of surprise, and I jump out of Alessandro's embrace to see Maggie standing in the doorway.

"Everyone except Maggie," he says innocently, flashing a devilish smile.

"I'm so sorry, Ms. Evans," Maggie says, scurrying away and turning bright red.

"Wait here," I instruct Alessandro tersely.

He suppresses a smile and slides into my chair, putting his feet up on my desk. I shake my head, half annoyed, half amused, and leave the room to catch Maggie hurriedly packing her things.

"Maggie," I say, and she looks up, abashed. "I'm terribly

sorry to have put you in that position. Mr. Giordano and I should have shown more discretion. Please, tell me what you needed."

"These just arrived for you," she says, still beet red, gesturing to a vase overflowing with gorgeous purple irises.

"Oh?" I ask, curious. I pluck the card nestled amongst the flowers and open it.

Thank you again. I look forward to helping you safeguard what matters most to you. —Bryce

Maggie looks at me expectantly.

"They're from Bryce Hoyt," I explain, "thanking us for accepting the security proposal." I pause. "What do purple irises mean?"

"Admiration," Alessandro offers from behind me.

I turn to see him leaning against my door frame, glaring at the flowers.

THIRTEEN

On Saturday morning, after we've finished breakfast, Alessandro leans back in his chair, quiet and contemplative.

"You're not still mad about the flowers, are you?" I ask warily.

I'm not a fan of moody, pouting Alessandro. The sex with him is decidedly not as good, and I'm on the verge of kicking him out for the day if he insists on continuing to sulk around my apartment.

He glances sidelong at me. "What if I am?" he asks.

I pick up our plates and put them in the kitchen. I contemplate trying to seduce him out of his funk again, but it didn't work last night, so I brush the idea off.

"I thought you *wanted* me to consult a security expert?" I remind him.

"Yes," he allows grumpily, "but an old, fat one."

I laugh unreservedly.

"Okay, that's not helping my hurt ego over here," he points out, and I'm startled out of my amusement.

I approach him and settle into his lap, wrapping my arms around his neck. "You have nothing to worry about from Bryce Hoyt," I promise. "I'm yours, dummy, in case you hadn't noticed." I look seriously into his eyes, letting my words sink in.

He strokes my cheek with his thumb. "Okay," he says.

I blanch in shock. "Okay?" I echo. "That's all it took?"

He laughs and shrugs. "What can I say? I believe you," he replies.

I pout a little and run my hands down his chest. "But I didn't even get to use my feminine wiles to convince you of my affections."

"Well, you know I'll never say no to that," he teases. His lips brush my jaw and he nuzzles into my neck. "But I have other plans for the day. Rain check?"

"That's not how feminine wiles work," I sigh, feigning exasperation, and he laughs.

"You'll have to show me tonight," he murmurs, kissing my neck.

"Mmmm," I respond. "Are you coming back here, or should I meet you at your place?"

"I'll pick you up at seven," he replies, still pecking at my neck.

"Why are you picking me up? That seems inefficient." I frown, confused.

"Well, my little efficiency monitor," he laughs, "I'm picking you up because I'm taking you out tonight. And before you ask, no, you don't get to know where."

And I don't know whether to pout or to protest, so I go for Option C and kiss him goodbye.

A FEW MINUTES AFTER SEVEN THERE IS A KNOCK ON THE DOOR. I give myself a last glance in the bathroom mirror, and I can't help but feel nervously excited. My hair is pulled back into an elegant chignon and I'm wearing my favorite red, silk halter dress. Its sweetheart neckline both compliments and contains my full chest, and it floats away from hugging my torso at the waist, falling in graceful waves to my knees. The floaty material is every little girl's dream — it's a dress that simply begs to be twirled in. Grinning playfully, I allow myself one small spin before answering the door.

I open the door to find Alessandro looking especially dashing in a dark blue suit with a buttoned vest over a crisp, white shirt open at the neck. He's been keeping the beard lately, which I approve of, especially as well-manicured as it is this evening. His dark brown hair is just long enough to really run your fingers through, though it is a bit too well-coifed now to invite such treatment. *Later, perhaps,* I think to myself, smiling coyly.

"*Ciao*," I greet him. "Would you like to come in?"

His full lips settle into my favorite sideways smile that suggests all manner of naughty things that may be going through his mind.

"Thank you, but I think it best that I don't. You look *magnifico*," he says, eyeing my dress appreciatively.

"*Grazie*. Okay then," I concede, grabbing my clutch. "Let's go."

∾

WE ARRIVE AT A RESTAURANT HIDDEN BEHIND ONE OF downtown Seattle's towering skyscrapers. It doesn't look like much from the outside and has a faded sign that says "Rossi's."

"What is this place?" I ask reticently.

Alessandro takes my hand and squeezes it gently. "It's an Italian restaurant."

I laugh. "An Italian restaurant that meets the standards of an actual Italian?"

He smirks. "Marco's family owns it," he explains. "They've been here about twenty years now. Best and most authentic Italian in Seattle."

"Will Marco be here?" I ask, my eyes widening.

"And Giovanni, and Francesca, and Maria," he replies. "And a good many other people."

I pull his hand, stopping him just outside the door. "Do they know about us already?"

Alessandro laughs. "Well, if they didn't before the other night when you showed up and I kicked them out, they do now," he smirks, and I cover my face, embarrassed. "It's fine. You worry too much."

"Comes with the package," I remind him.

He laughs and kisses me briefly before holding the door open for me. Stepping in, we are greeted by a raucous chorus of "*Ciao*!" Taking it all in, I count no fewer than thirty people, all seated around a series of tables pushed together in the center of the dining room.

Marco approaches us with a woman I presume is his wife, and they each embrace Alessandro in turn, exchanging quick pleasantries in rapid Italian.

Marco smiles brightly and folds me into an unexpected hug. "Serafina, I'm so glad you're joining us," he says warmly. "This is my wife, Angela." She shakes my hand kindly.

"*Piacere*," I say.

She looks pleasantly surprised. "*Tu parli Italiano*," she replies, smiling.

"*Solo un po*," I respond. "I fear I'll get lost quickly tonight, though." I smile disarmingly.

Marco laughs. "Yes, it's a full house! Hey!" he calls to the room, approaching the table. "Everyone, you know Alessandro. This is Serafina Evans. Serafina, you know Giovanni, Francesca, and Maria" — they each give me a "ciao" as he points them out — "that's Maria's husband, Raffaele; my father, Pietro; my mama, Gianna; and more uncles, aunts, and cousins than you can probably remember," he says waving his hand vaguely at the rest, and everyone laughs.

"*Benvenuto*, Serafina," Gianna says warmly, offering Alessandro and I seats. "*Per favore*, sit, sit."

"*Grazie mille*," I say shyly. As Alessandro has noticed before, my Italian is only so-so and, while I understand a good deal more than I can speak, even that is limited.

Maria sits next to me and she leans in close, so I can hear her. "I'm glad to see you out of work for once," she says, smiling. "It looks good on you." She laughs, and I join in.

"What can I say, Alessandro has been a good influence on me," I reply.

She smiles knowingly and gives me a wink. "And you on him."

Alessandro touches my elbow and I turn my attention to him. "If you're hungry there's some *antipasti* still on the table," he offers, gesturing to the remaining *insalata caprese*. "But the next course will be served soon."

"Where are all the other customers?" I ask, glancing around the restaurant.

Alessandro waves his hand dismissively. "It's just family tonight. One of Marco's cousins, Maria, just got married," he points to a young woman with sable hair and a pink dress. "They've had the wedding all day, and this is the family dinner after. It'll be great fun, you'll see."

I flush with embarrassment. "I wish you'd told me," I hiss. "I would've brought a present."

He laughs. "No need," he assures me.

I regard him skeptically. "Did you go to the wedding? Is that where you disappeared to today?"

He frowns at my accusation. "No, Serafina," he says crossly. "I had to work. You think I wouldn't have jumped at the chance to show you off? Besides, I wasn't invited."

I don't know which surprises me more — his annoyance or the fact that he's that proud to be with me, but it softens my attitude considerably.

"I'm sorry," I apologize, kissing him softly.

His lips melt into mine, and he prolongs the kiss for a moment before letting me pull away.

"*Va bene, bella*," he assures me. "Just relax and enjoy the food. It's going to be amazing, if Gianna has anything to do with it."

And he's not wrong. The first course — *primo* — is served shortly. "*Fiori di zucchini farcito*," Gianna declares triumphantly as Marco's cousins distribute plates.

I know I'm going to need to pace myself, so I sample a small bite of the cheese-stuffed zucchini flowers laid out beautifully on the plate and practically melt into my chair. I contemplate the rest of the portion warily.

"How authentic of a meal are we talking here?" I ask Alessandro.

He covers his laugh as he swallows the food in his mouth.

"Fully," he replies. "You're still in for *secondo, contorno, dolce, caffe, e digestivo*." I'm sure I look alarmed because he wraps his hand around mine and kisses my fingers. "Don't worry, Serafina. Eat. Enjoy. Don't think so much. Live like an Italian for a night."

Eyeing the rest of my plate, I decide he's right and tuck in until the plate is clean. Between each course, the alcohol and conversation flow freely. Thankfully, Marco's cousins mostly speak English, so it's only the older generation that sticks to Italian, and I'm delighted to find I'm able to participate fully.

Well, when I'm not distracted by the parade of succulent dishes, that is. The *fiori di zucchini farcito* is followed by a melt-in-your-mouth *pappardelle e sugo di carne*. For good measure I circle back to the *insalata caprese* that still sits on the table. It is light and amazing with over-the-top flavorful heirloom tomatoes, freshly made *mozzarella di bufala*, and fragrant just-picked basil.

Alessandro was not kidding about the food. Not that Italians kid about food, as I'm learning. As the *dolce* is served — a delicate *panna cotta* with berries — I decide that this procession can't possibly be called a meal by any standards I've ever known. It's more like a food orgy where each course is a new lover seducing you with its unique wiles. That is, until the next comes along to pleasure you in a whole new, exciting way.

After the *panna cotta* I am sated and sleepy. I watch in awe as another hour or two passes and they all continue to consume espressos and small shots of *limoncello*.

"How do you drink caffeine this late?" I ask Maria in awe.

"Lots of practice," she jokes, tossing back another. "Besides, we don't do this every night."

"I should think not," I reply. "I'm going to need the rest of the weekend to recover."

She laughs a laugh that I'm coming to learn from all of them translates roughly as "silly Americans."

I chuckle softly. They may have a point. I look around at the camaraderie and laughter and decide I could get used to this.

As the drinks run out, the crowd begins to thin and soon we are saying our thank yous and goodbyes. As we emerge into the cool night air, I feel the effect of the food and drink weighing on my senses.

"Ready to go home?" Alessandro asks, opening the car door for me.

I nod sleepily. "Your home?"

"If that's what you want," he replies, smiling tenderly at me.

"Yes, please," I say sleepily, settling in to the passenger seat.

✌

I MUST HAVE DRIFTED OFF AS SOON AS WE DROVE AWAY, because the next thing I know Alessandro's strong arms are lifting me out of the car and carrying me into the elevator.

When he sees that I'm awake, he allows my legs to fall gently to the floor but holds me up with an arm around my waist.

I'm able to manage getting into his apartment, though by the time we enter the bedroom I'm barely conscious. Alessandro undresses me tenderly and helps me into bed. I watch him start to remove his own clothing and something stirs in me briefly before I'm lost to sleep once again.

WHEN I WAKE IT'S STILL DARK OUT. I GLANCE AT THE CLOCK, and its glowing numbers tell me it's just after four a.m. I reach for Alessandro and find his side of the bed empty but warm. I sit up and see him standing by the window. Slipping out of bed, I approach him from behind and wrap my arms around him. He turns and envelops me in his arms, kissing the top of my head.

"I didn't mean to wake you," he apologizes.

"It's okay," I reply. "Have you been up this whole time?"

"No, I just woke up a few minutes ago," he murmurs.

I look up into his eyes. His expression is serious but veiled.

"Is everything okay?"

"Very," he assures me, kissing me lightly. I shiver, and I'm not sure if it's being out of bed or his kiss. "Come, let's go back to bed."

I crawl in beside him, nestling myself in his arms. "What were you thinking about?" I ask.

He brushes my hair from my face and his fingers linger on

my cheek. He takes a moment to respond, as if he's struggling to express himself.

"How much I want to make love to you," he breathes finally.

And his warm mouth locks on mine, his strong hands pulling me tightly against his body. I sink into him, warmth spreading through me as my body wakes under his touch.

I roll onto my back and he slides on top of me, his mouth and hands working me into a frenzy. I eagerly part my legs, allowing him to slip into me. Our mouths break apart as we both sigh in pleasure at the sensation. He places my arms around his neck. "Don't let go," he urges me, staring into my eyes as he begins to move.

The intensity of his gaze, the full length of our bodies touching, and his firm yet gentle thrusts send waves of bliss rolling through me. The pleasure is connected to a deep joy I feel in his arms, our bodies connected on a level deeper than I can describe.

I feel a tear slip from my eye and he holds me tighter, dropping his lips to my ear.

"Don't hold back," he urges softly.

And I know this isn't commanding Alessandro who is fucking me for pleasure. This is something different.

"Not any more," I reply, drawing my knees up to urge him deeper into me, to allow him to lean in closer.

His breath quickens and his pupils dilate. His mouth descends hungrily once more upon mine, and I thread my fingers through his hair, pulling him into me in every way. His pelvis rocks rhythmically with mine as we join, and instead of the tightening I usually feel heading toward climax, my body relaxes and tears start to flow freely from my eyes.

Alessandro kisses them, kisses me. He holds my face in his hands and looks deeps into my eyes as his pace quickens.

"I love you, Serafina," he breathes softly, urgently.

I half sob and half laugh in relief. "I love you, too, Alessandro," I confess.

And my relaxed muscles spring back together to concentrate all the emotions he's made me feel in these last weeks into the center of my body, and they explode out of me as I climax in his arms. I grip him tightly, my eyes locked on his at the moment the orgasm floods through me. As he watches my climax, he spills himself into me, pressing his forehead against mine and calling out my name.

With one last, deep thrust, he settles into me and stills. I hold him, loosely wrapped in my arms and legs, as he breathes heavily, resting his head on my shoulder. It's a long while before either of us moves.

When we finally extricate our entangled bodies, he stretches himself out next to me, laying inches away, and it's as if we are staring at each other with new eyes.

"I meant it," he says softly. "It wasn't just one of those things that accidentally happened in a moment of pleasure. I mean, it was pleasurable …"

I put a finger to his lips and laugh. "I know," I assure him.

"I haven't said that to anybody in a very long time," he admits. "I didn't expect to say it tonight."

"Neither did I," I agree. "When was the last time?"

He ponders the question for a moment. "I can't say for certain. Years. Maybe two?" He shakes his head slightly as if trying to dislodge a memory. "What about you?"

"I've only said it to one other person, more than ten years ago," I reply, and fresh tears spring to my eyes.

"Shhh, *bella*," he whispers, wiping the tears away. "We don't need to say any more tonight. Let's just rest now." He folds me in his arms again and pulls the sheet over us. His mouth finds mine one last time, wiping away any memories and thoughts of past hurts that were lingering.

With a hand on his chest, I feel his breathing settle into a rhythm, and I drift off to the steady tempo created by its combination with the beat of his heart.

After a long, peaceful sleep I wake alone to early afternoon sunlight streaming through the window. I stretch my limbs out, feeling the looseness in my body, unable to remember the last time I was this relaxed. My stomach rumbles, and I suppress a laugh. I didn't think I'd be hungry again for days.

I slip out of bed and look around the room for something to wear. I chance a look through Alessandro's dresser and manage to find a white T-shirt and a pair of boxers. The loose shorts hang off my hips, but at least they stay on.

I venture out of the room, into the living room, but Alessandro isn't there, nor is he in the kitchen. I find him in his office, drinking a cup of coffee and reading the newspaper at his desk, wearing only a pair of old sweats.

"Well, don't you look ridiculously sexy," I say from the doorway.

He looks up in surprise and smiles widely. "*Buon pomeriggio*, sleepyhead," he greets me, beckoning me to him.

I cross the room and settle into his lap, placing a gentle kiss on his lips.

He nuzzles my neck and his hands slide up my thighs and begin exploring. "Aren't you a nice distraction?" he murmurs appreciatively.

"I hope I'm not keeping you from anything important," I tease. "What's on the agenda today?"

He rubs my nipple with one thumb over my shirt absent-mindedly as he considers the question. "Well, I need to pick up a few things, go grocery shopping, and other various errands," he replies. "Or I could spend the rest of the day making love to you." He slips his hand under the shirt and holds my breast in his hand while kissing my neck.

I groan in pleasure and protest. "As wonderful as that sounds, I'm actually starving," I admit. "After last night I didn't think I'd eat for the rest of the weekend, but there it is."

"A quick fuck then?" he asks huskily.

Before I can respond, he stands, laying me on the desk, pulling at my shorts. I lift my backside off the desk, helping him slide them down, and kicking them away from me as he pulls down his sweats just enough to take me roughly and urgently on the desk.

FOURTEEN

On Monday morning I wake before Alessandro's alarm. I shift quietly in bed so that I can turn myself to face him. His arms are flung over his head, his long legs splayed out over the large bed. He looks extremely content, and I momentarily check the urge to run my hands over his naked body. Until I remember the nipple alarm clock incident.

Grinning idiotically, I lick my finger and run it over his nipple. As it hardens, I roll it between my fingers and feel him start to shift. He opens one eye slightly and regards me sleepily. I blow on the nipple lightly, then sink my mouth onto it, sucking hard. Both of his eyes fully open and he moans deeply.

"I see what you did there," he rumbles.

I let go slowly, running his nipple through my teeth one last time, and then pull away laughing. "Good morning, sunshine," I tease him.

"I'll show you a good morning," he replies, and rolls on top of me, his erection pressing into me.

I give a small gasp of surprise before he covers my mouth with his and we proceed to wake each other up in every way possible.

❧

Early morning exploits aside, I still make it into work before my normal arrival time. It gives me a few minutes to collect my thoughts and prepare for the slew of meetings that will consume my day. Between meetings with Bryce, Eleanor Roberts, my senior lead project manager, and Jackson to hand over the reins on the Sutton Developments project, I won't have much time for preparation, and I'm glad for the quiet.

I'm set up in the conference room for the morning, and eventually Allie pokes her head in about fifteen minutes prior to our meeting time.

"Sera! You must be as eager to get this show on the road as I am," she remarks, settling into the chair next to me.

"I am," I admit. "Good weekend?"

"Wonderful," she gushes. "David and I hiked to Heather Lake. It was a bit cold, but stunning."

"That sounds like a lot of work," I remark drily.

"It's totally worth it," she assures me. "I'd ask how your

weekend was, but judging by the gossip tearing around the office this morning, I can guess it was pretty good and likely involved a lot of time with our favorite Italian client."

I roll my eyes. "Well, that took about five minutes," I lament.

She raises an eyebrow.

"Maggie caught us kissing in my office on Friday afternoon," I explain.

"Well, aren't we throwing caution to the wind these days?"

"We are," I reply, grinning stupidly. "He told me he loves me."

Allie's jaw drops in shock. "Holy shit, Sera, that's huge! What did you say?!"

I smile shyly. "I told him I loved him too," I admit.

She leans over and gives me a bone-crunching hug. "Really? Oh, Sera, dear, I'm so happy for you," she says ardently.

"Really? Because you seemed pretty worried before," I ask skeptically.

"If you're not worried, I'm not worried," she responds. "You're a big girl. And if anyone knows how much those three words mean to you, it's me. I can't imagine you jumping in without all the facts."

Her words give me pause, but my thoughts are interrupted by Maggie at the door.

"Mr. Hoyt is here for your meeting," she says. "Are you ready for him?"

"Yes, send him in please, Maggie, thank you," I reply.

Allie and I both rise as Bryce strides into the room, handsome as ever in dark slacks and a sky-blue button-up shirt that matches his eyes. I can feel Allie's eyes bugging out of her head next to me, and I realize I forgot to warn her.

"Bryce," I greet him warmly, "so good to see you." He grasps my hand genially. "This is Alison Kramer, my head of human resources."

"Ladies, good morning," he responds. Turning his dazzling smile on Allie, he shakes her hand as well, and they exchange pleasant greetings.

As he takes a seat Allie goes to sit next to me and whispers in my ear on the way, "Holy hot security advisor, Batman!" I press my lips together to suppress a smile and shoot her an exasperated look. She shrugs and beams at me beatifically.

Thankfully, Bryce is all business and before long the table is covered in papers, the whiteboard a scrawl of procedural editing. We go over all the topics Bryce had us prepare for and then some. Within a couple of hours, Allie has a large document of changes and actions.

"So, from now on you can implement your own background checks on new clients if you'd prefer," Bryce recaps, "but my assistant is already pulling together the two sets of files for your current major accounts with Buone Case and Sutton Developments to give you an idea of the kind of depth of check we can provide you, and to help minimize surprises going forward. Knowledge is power, and given your recent power struggle with Sutton, especially, you should learn everything you can about his company before moving forward on anything."

"Makes sense," I agree. "But why Buone Case? Their deal is done end of next week."

"Yes," he replies. "So, you still have time to throw up a red flag if you find anything that will affect your participation in this deal, or at the very least inform you further if you consider continuing your business with them."

"Fair enough, I suppose," I concede reluctantly.

"These are big accounts for your company," he reiterates. "I'm here to make sure I do everything in my power to help things go smoothly for you from now on. You won't need to do the level of background check we'll be providing on every client, but even for the smaller accounts you'll want to know who you're getting into bed with."

Allie coughs quietly next to me and I kick her under the table. "If that's all for me, I'll take my leave now," Allie interjects.

"Absolutely, it was a pleasure to meet you, Mrs. Kramer," Bryce responds, shaking her hand again across the table.

Allie leaves the conference room, and I can hear her chuckling to herself on her way down the hall.

"I've arranged for a separate meeting with finance and IT after lunch," I say, pressing on. "Perhaps we can go over some of the other matters at hand?"

"Absolutely," Bryce agrees.

He proceeds to walk me through selecting security cameras, and, finally, going over my personal security needs.

"I'm fairly satisfied with the access control here and at your condo. And based on our preliminary research on Ms. Stanwood, we have no reason to believe she poses any kind of physical threat to you. But as we don't know who else she's working with, or the 'why,' I would be most comfortable with your checking in with me each morning," he requests. "Otherwise, we have armed security personnel standing by at all times. If you encounter anything that concerns you, contact this number," he hands me a card, "and someone will be at your side in minutes. Program it into all your devices. Even a blank text or missed call will bring someone running. If you need to arrange for personal security for a meeting, event, or outing, or decide you would be more comfortable having it on an ongoing basis, just let me know."

"Boy, you really take your job seriously," I murmur, turning the thick card over in my fingers.

He catches my eyes and holds me pinned with an intense expression. "And I need you to take this seriously, Sera," he says, his voice a soft contrast to the heat of his gaze. "All of this," he gestures at the papers and whiteboard, "is to protect you. All the plans, all the care, is for naught if you won't help me safeguard the most important thing in this whole company — you."

I smile wryly at the fatefulness of his warning. Little does he know I've spent most of my life safeguarding myself from everyone, everything. And now, just when I'm learning to let that go, I'm being asked to re-embrace it. The irony is delicious.

"You have my full cooperation in this process."

My assurances help relax his stance, and he sighs, relieved.

"I'm glad to hear it," he replies. "Now, what's good to eat around here?"

AFTER LUNCH WE START ON IT SECURITY. AS I EXPECTED, Will takes immediate umbrage with Bryce's homebrewed software security concerns. Bryce, sensing his reaction, steps lightly, but does not back down. It's quite a dance to watch. Thankfully, we're able to press through and make an action plan for Will to work with Hoyt Corporate Services' network security division on evaluating all our systems and software fully.

Nick, on the other hand, almost immediately starts worshipping the ground Bryce walks on. He eagerly documents every suggestion and bounces out of the conference already eagerly anticipating implementing the various training and compliance programs and starting his risk management matrix. Even Bryce laughs in amusement — after he's sure that Nick is gone, of course.

"Well, that was a mixed bag," I laugh.

"That's normal," Bryce replies easily. "Some people take this stuff very personally." He shrugs. "Doesn't bother me."

"Good," I reply teasingly. "You'll need a thick skin to survive us."

He smiles timidly at me. "I don't know, I'm rather enjoying myself," he replies. I blush, and he clears his throat, rising and gathering his things. "I know you have another meeting coming up. I'll see you tomorrow first thing to file that police report. And my assistant should be sending the two client background packages by courier by the end of the day."

I extend my hand to him, and his shake is reassuringly firm. "Thank you," I say sincerely. "I can't tell you how grateful I am for everything."

He winks slyly. "You're most welcome, but we're just getting started." And with a small wave, he's gone.

I slowly stack the papers in the conference room to return them to my office before the next meeting.

∽

RETURNING TO THE CONFERENCE ROOM I AM, ONCE AGAIN, slightly early. I check my phone and see a text from Alessandro.

Morning sex makes me miss you more. Hope your day is good, amore.

I smile blissfully, remembering his embraces. *Miss you too. See you tonight? <3*

His response is immediate. *Working late again. I can come sleep at your place when we're done?*

I'm glad he's not here so I don't have to hide my disappointment. After a pause I reply. *Boo. Maybe tomorrow night then. I doubt there would be much sleeping, and I have an early meeting tomorrow.*

When Ellie and Jackson enter, Alessandro still hasn't responded, and I flip my phone back to silent. I take in Ellie's tall, thin frame and note that her already tan skin seems even more deeply browned, providing quite a shocking contrast to her pale blond hair.

"Ellie!" I greet her, hugging her tightly. "We've missed you! You look like you had a nice, sunny vacation!"

"It was fabulous," she trills. "I'll show you the pictures later. But more importantly, I hear you've got something big for us to sink our teeth into!"

I laugh appreciatively. Ellie has been with me from the start, and her eagerness never fails to impress. "Absolutely. I hope you guys like big piles of research, because if you do, it's your lucky day!" Everyone chuckles appreciatively.

It takes us several hours to work through the framework of my research and go over a plan for our meeting with Sutton Developments on Wednesday morning, but by the end I'm confident that not only will we be prepared, but that Ellie and Jackson will be able to work together productively. As I wish them a good evening and head back to my office, I'm feeling pretty good about our turnaround.

Heading into my office, I catch Maggie packing up for the evening. "Good night, Maggie," I greet her. "Thanks for everything."

She smiles warmly. "My pleasure, Ms. Evans," she replies. "The delivery from Hoyt Corporate Services is on your desk."

"I'd completely forgotten about that, thanks," I reply. "It'll make good after-dinner reading, I'm sure."

She laughs and waves as she heads home for the night. I gather my things and head home on time, for once.

AFTER DINNER, I DECIDE TO LOOK THROUGH THE SUTTON Developments brief first in case there are any major showstoppers. The format of the report is helpful — a summary page at the beginning lists a table of contents and status of each report, color-coded green for completed reports, red if they contain any potential flags.

There is a red flag on their past litigation, so I jump ahead. Skimming the text, it turns out to be an issue between Sutton Developments and the City of Seattle for a building code violation. Sutton refused to acknowledge the code violation, as the laws had changed over the course of the project. Foreseeably, fighting the City of Seattle in a City of Seattle court, they lost, incurring a hefty fine and, highly likely, a matching hefty bill to bring the issue up to the new code.

Everything else looks clean as a whistle, and that's saying

something given the exhaustive pile of research with five-year histories on the company's financials, personal background checks on all its executive officers, Better Business Bureau files, the works. I set the thick file aside for further examination another time.

The Buone Case file looks slim in comparison, which is unsurprising as, with not quite five years incorporated and only twenty or so employees total, they have less than a quarter of Sutton Development's staff and only one executive officer — Alessandro.

As I expect, there are no red flags in Buone Case's report. While he hasn't always heeded my advice, I've never seen Alessandro be anything but completely forthright in his business dealings. And in this business, that's saying something.

A quick glance over his background check doesn't bring any surprises. No criminal record, not even so much as a speeding ticket, no lawsuits, no litigation.

I yawn widely and glance at the clock on my phone — its only just after nine. My weekend exploits must be catching up with me.

As I go to close Buone Case's file, something on Alessandro's background check catches my eye. Under the address history section there are four addresses — two in San Francisco, with dates indicating that he moved from one to the other, and two in Seattle, both for the full six months he's lived here. One I recognize, his apartment. The other I don't.

With a furrowed brow I plug the address into the maps app

on my phone. University District. A rental maybe? I go to the King County Assessor's webpage and call up the property detail. The owner name is listed as GIORDANO ALESSANDRO VITTORIO. He's the sole owner, so that lends weight to the rental theory.

Still perturbed, I pull up the home's stats through my real estate agent portal. Three bedrooms, two baths, almost two thousand square feet. It's a hot neighborhood, and the home value estimate has increased a small amount even from such a recent purchase date. I check all the usual property listing sites but can't find any rental listings for the property since Alessandro purchased it.

I run a search on the address and one of the names jumps off the page. Peyton Giordano, 26, female. Previous residences include several cities in California, including San Francisco, current residence Seattle. Previous names used include Peyton Chadwick. My throat constricts as the logical conclusion forms in my mind.

I frantically search social media and find only one site with an account for a Peyton Giordano. Her profile picture is a snapshot of two people kissing, with the Space Needle looming in the background. I click to expand the photo for a closer look. The woman in the picture, presumably her, is short, athletic, and blond. The other is, unmistakably, Alessandro.

My dinner rises in my throat, and I drop my phone and run to the bathroom.

FIFTEEN

When I'm sure I won't be sick again anytime soon, I clamber back to my phone to explore Peyton's profile, but it's locked down. There are only two other public pictures of her, both alone, and lots of pictures of woods and mountains and the like. Her profile lists her as married. The profile picture is dated three months ago.

I already know Alessandro doesn't do social media, but I search for his name again and come up empty. My head spins, attempting to craft theories that explain what I've found.

I'm briefly tempted to create a profile and send her a friend request, but just as quickly dismiss the thought. It would be incredibly difficult to get any real answers online.

I poke around the internet a bit more to see if she has any other public accounts, but there is nothing else for her in either

her married name or what I presume her to be her maiden name.

I realize I'm chewing my fingernails to the quick when I yelp in pain on biting flesh. I bury my face in my hands and try not to cry.

I could just ask him. Couldn't I? I laugh out loud as I imagine my opening salvo. *Hey, Alessandro, I know I just told you I love you, but I realized I may not actually know you as well as I thought I did. You aren't, by any chance, married, are you?*

How would he even respond? There are only two answers to that question. Yes and no. If the former, certainly there could be a million explanations — or excuses. But the evidence is staring at me from my phone screen. How could he possibly deny it? Does it even matter why?

I can't decide, but regardless I need to know if it's true. And if it is, I need to know how I could go so wrong, again.

A banner notification appears over Peyton's profile page — a text message. From Alessandro.

Buona notte, amore. Dream of me.

My gut wrenches and my phone falls to the floor. Burying my face in one of the couch pillows, I finally release the sobs and let the tears go.

∽

I wake screaming and gasping for air in the predawn hours. I look around the dark living room and realize I must have passed out on the couch in my hysteria. The nightmares that woke me flood back — a small, blond Peyton chasing me out of their home, yelling loudly that he belongs to her.

Their home. A dangerous idea possesses me. I have to see their house. I have to see her.

⁓

I'm not able to get back to sleep, so I email Allie and Maggie that I'm taking a sick day. I text Bryce the same excuse, asking to reschedule our police department trip.

As I stare morosely at the dark outside, I must fall asleep again eventually as when I wake abruptly once more it is fully light outside. I have emails from Allie and Maggie wishing me good health and telling me not to worry, everything at the office will be taken care of. I can sense the concern in both of their messages.

Bryce has similarly sent his best, asking that I let him know when I'm back on my feet. I get the sense he thinks I took his advice to try taking a step back occasionally. I'm slightly uncomfortable with the deception, but if that's one less person worried about me today, so much the better.

I head to the bathroom to ready myself for my excursion. Upon seeing my disheveled and ghastly state in the mirror, I decide to shower before leaving.

Clean and presentable once more, I dress carefully in plain khaki slacks, and a black tunic top that suits my black mood. I tie back my long, wet hair into a braid, not wanting to bother about styling it.

I ignore the kitchen, unable to even contemplate eating, and pick up my keys and bag and head to the car to make the short trip.

∾

IN NOT QUITE TWENTY MINUTES I'M PARKED ACROSS THE STREET from the two-story, modern home of the Giordanos. Glancing at the dashboard I see that it's almost ten. There are no cars in the driveway and nothing else to indicate anyone is home.

I watch the comings and goings of the neighborhood for a while, occasionally checking my email on my phone. I can't remember ever taking a sick day, and it's making me incredibly nervous on top of my already-shot nerves. I lean down to stick my phone in my bag in an attempt to let it go.

As I'm sitting back up, a car pulls into the driveway. It's a gorgeous, sleek black coupe. German. Definitely very expensive. A short, slim, and stunning blond woman exits, clad in workout gear.

Before I can stop myself, I'm climbing out of my car and calling to her. "Mrs. Giordano?"

She stops on the doorstep and eyes me suspiciously. "Yes?"

My heart sinks as she responds to the name. She stares at me expectantly, and I call on all my powers of improvisation.

"I'm sorry if I scared you," I smile disarmingly. "I'm Claire Adams." I extend my hand.

She shifts her gym bag and takes my hand. Her perfectly manicured fingers squeeze mine limply. "Are you from immigration?" she asks warily.

I seize upon the opportunity. "Yes!" I exclaim a little too enthusiastically. "I apologize, I was told you'd been informed of my visit. Is Mr. Giordano at home?"

She looks relieved, probably because now at least she knows I'm not an axe murderer or something. "No, he's not, but you're welcome to come in. I hope you haven't been waiting long," she says kindly. "Nobody told us you were coming."

"It's okay, it happens all the time," I reply. I realize suddenly that I've left everything in the car, and I imagine I look suspicious without anything in my hands. "Oh, I'm so sorry, I forgot my papers. Let me go grab those from my car."

She nods, and I dash back to my car, grab the folio and pen out of my bag, and slip my phone in my pocket after putting it on silent. Returning quickly, I find Peyton waiting for me on the doorstep, her gym bag inside the entry way.

"Please come in," she invites me. "I'll just go throw on a sweater. You can look around if you like, or have a seat, whatever you prefer. I'll be back shortly."

She disappears up the stairs and I step down into the living room and take a deep breath.

If she assumed I was from immigration, that must mean they've either been here before, or they were possibly expecting a visit at some point. I knew that Alessandro had a conditional green card, but I realize now that I didn't even think about why that was. Perhaps part of the process is a visit verifying the authenticity of their marriage? I'm guessing, but I'm no citizenship expert. In any case, I'm confident I can steer clear of outing myself.

Thankfully, if I were an immigration agent here to check on them, she wouldn't expect me to feed her the answers to the questions I'm meant to verify their responses to. I smile, grimly realizing I have the license I need to ask her for all the information I'm looking for.

Getting into the role, I stroll the living room, examining the furnishings and photographs. There are dozens of framed pictures, mostly of the two of them. I turn slowly, looking around the room for a specific picture, and spot it over the larger of two couches. Their wedding photo.

Alessandro looks younger, his hair is short, and he's clean shaven. But he's every inch the man I know, handsome as ever in a black tuxedo. Peyton glows in the photo, beaming up at her man, a vision in her pure white mermaid gown. I want to retch again, but I know if I'm going to get what I came for I'm going to have to bring my acting game.

Becoming a real estate agent has given me a good start.

Years as a property manager hasn't hurt, either. I've had my fair share of training in the art of bullshitting my way through a tough situation.

Peyton suddenly reappears. "Handsome, isn't he?" she asks wistfully.

I clear my throat and take a seat on the couch, opening my folio and poising my pen. "Yes, I suppose he is," I reply. "How long have you been married?"

She sits somberly on the smaller couch next to me, crossing her slim legs and folding her perfectly manicured fingers over her knee. "Four years next month." I stare at her expectantly. "June 30th," she adds.

I nod and make a note. "And what is Mr. Giordano's profession?" I ask. I need a chance to react to information I know.

"He owns his own real estate development company," she says proudly. "We moved here six months ago from San Francisco because he said it was a hot market, and I was able to transfer to the University of Washington."

"I see," I reply. "And what are you studying?"

"Nursing," she responds.

"That's a great field," I respond warmly, hoping to win her over.

She takes the bait, beaming under the praise. "I think so! I really enjoy taking care of people," she replies.

"How long do you have left before you graduate?"

"I'm supposed to be done with my degree by the end of the

year," she says. "It's hard to get a job as a new nurse. I'm already nervous!"

"I'm sure you'll find something fantastic," I say encouragingly. "So, you're planning on staying in the area then?"

"Oh yes, we love it here. We go hiking and boating all the time," she gushes enthusiastically. "Are you from here?"

"Yes," I reply shortly. I tilt my head and give her a tolerant look, hoping to discourage further questions about me. It seems to work, and she stares at me expectantly.

"Owning his own business must be difficult. Do you see your husband much, Mrs. Giordano?" I inquire.

For the first time she looks more than a little uncomfortable. "He's my husband, we see each other plenty," she replies testily, but pauses before admitting, "He does have an apartment downtown, though. He stays there when he has to work late or be in the office early."

"Downtown? But you're so close here," I press.

"He doesn't like traffic, and even though the distance is short, it can be a tough commute," she explains.

"That must make your marriage difficult at times," I reply.

She shrugs. "It gives me time to do my homework," she says simply. "I see him often enough."

"When was the last time you saw him?" I push. And I can't tell if I'm feigning the suspicion in my voice or if it's real.

"Last night," she says a little coldly. "As I said, I see him often enough."

Working late, my ass. I suppress my reaction, but also sense I'm wearing out my welcome.

"I'm sure you do," I reply kindly, making a fake note. "There's only one more thing I'm supposed to ask for — do you have a recent picture of the two of you?"

"Sure," she says eagerly, clearly ready for this to be over. She gestures for me to follow her and leads me to the kitchen. Plucking a photo from the front of the refrigerator, she hands it to me.

"We went to a friend's wedding in San Francisco week before last," she explains.

I look at the picture and compare the Alessandro in the picture to the Alessandro in my memory who had just returned from San Francisco. He had a newly grown beard, which you can just see budding in the picture of them beaming and embracing on the dance floor of a large ballroom, surrounding by happy partygoers. The photo is a wedding keepsake, etched with the bride and groom's names and date in one corner. The Thursday he was in San Francisco.

"I see," I say softly. "Thank you. May I keep it?"

"Sure, yes of course, I have another copy," she accedes.

I stare for a moment at the blank space on the fridge where the picture hung, somehow saddened by the emptiness. My eyes are drawn to a black and white image just below the bare spot. She follows my eyes and smiles delicately.

"Yes," she says in response to my stare. She pulls the sono-gram picture from the fridge. "I'm pregnant."

My heart is frozen in my chest and I will myself to speak. "Congratulations," I manage. "You must be thrilled."

"We are," she replies. "Alex is going to be a great dad."

"Yes," I agree, "I'm sure he will be. I think I'm done here."

∽

How I manage to make it home I'll never know. All I know is that when I do, I crawl in bed and cry until I'm too exhausted to stay awake, then surrender myself gratefully to blackness.

∽

I wake midafternoon feeling like I've been hit by a truck. My eyes are puffy and swollen, my face red and streaky. My head pounds from the trauma and lack of food. I make myself a cup of tea and nurse it contemplatively at the kitchen bar, also managing to choke down half of a plain bagel. Even the small amount of sustenance makes a big difference, and my head begins to clear.

And I find my despair slowly being replaced by anger at all the lies he must have told me. The betrayal feels like a hot, iron fist in my gut. I'm angry with myself as well, for letting my guard down and falling in love with him. And at him again, for having an affair on that poor, unsuspecting young woman, who also happens to be *pregnant* with his child! I stand furiously and pace the living room.

Okay, Evans, get a grip. I stop and close my eyes, taking a series of deep breaths. Too many people are counting on me for me to go to pieces over this. And I'm not one to wallow. I'm a doer. *So, what am I going to do?*

End it, obviously. But how?

I don't want to be the insecure mess I was when Tom left me. But I'm not the one being left this time. I consider how Alessandro will react.

I can't see calling or texting him that we're through going over well. He'll want to hear it straight from my lips. And if I try to end it with no explanation I already know he won't let it go. So that's not an option. I just don't want to hear his excuses, don't want to give him an opportunity to convince me to come back to him.

So, don't give him the opportunity.

I retrieve the photograph Peyton gave me from the table next to the door. Giving it a sorrowful glance, I return it to its spot, face down, and pick up my phone. I have a few emails, none of them urgent, and three missed text messages. All from Alessandro.

At six forty-five this morning — *Buongiorno, mio tesoro. Miss you. x*

And again, at eleven this morning — *Everything okay? Busy day?*

And just about half an hour ago — *Getting worried. Call me please? I'm working from home today.*

And my next action demonstrates that, while usually a creature of logic, deep down I'm as impulsive as any woman scorned, because I grab the photo and stuff it in my purse, slamming the door behind me on my way out.

∾

I START TO QUESTION MY ABILITY TO SEE MY RASH COURSE OF action through when Alessandro answers the door shirtless and out of breath, headphones dangling around his neck. He glistens sexily, his lean, muscular torso covered in a sheen of sweat.

"Sera," he greets me in surprise and relief, holding the door open. "I was worried about you. I'm glad you're here."

I step in, and he closes the door, leaning in to kiss me. I sidestep and shake my head silently. He regards me curiously as he takes in my appearance, my expression. Thankfully, my eyes aren't as puffy, but I'm sure I still look a frightful and somber mess.

"What's wrong?" he asks, slowly realizing something is amiss. "Why aren't you at work?"

I take a seat in the chair next to the couch, and he perches himself on the arm of the couch.

"I took the day off," I finally say. He furrows his brow and I can't handle shirtless, concerned Alessandro. "Will you put a shirt on, please?"

He looks at me levelly then saunters to the treadmill in the corner. Slinging his headphones over the handle, he pulls his shirt off the side table next to it and slides it on, then reseats himself on the couch. "What is going on?" he demands.

I lean forward in the chair. "I don't know how to say this, so I'm just going to say it," I preface, and a look of terror crosses his face as he realizes what I'm about to do.

"No, Sera," he starts to protest.

I put my hand up. "Please, just let me get this out," I plead.

He pushes on, clearly understanding where I'm going and horrified. "Don't do this," he says anxiously, falling to his knees in front of me. "What can I do?" He stretches his hand out, seeking mine.

I sigh heavily and pull the picture out of my purse and place it in his open palm.

"You can go back to your wife," I say simply.

SIXTEEN

Alessandro's horrified expression is enough to settle the question of his betrayal of both women he's promised his love to.

"Where did you get this?" he finally asks.

"From Peyton," I respond evenly, averting my gaze to the ceiling and blinking back the heavy tears that have started stinging the back of my eyes.

"How did she find you?" he asks, dumbstruck.

I drop my head forward again to give him a questioning look. "She didn't; I found her. And it's not like I needed the confirmation, but it's satisfying to have it," I reply gravely.

"No, Sera, please listen to me," he insists. "I don't know what Peyton's told you, but I was going to explain every-thing." He sits back on the couch and buries his face in his hands.

"What's to tell? You're married. This," I gesture between us, "is over."

"Please hear me out," he begs, tears filling his eyes.

And this, exactly, is what I didn't want. Excuses. Explanations. Time for him to talk his way out of responsibility for his actions. Time for him to convince me out of my convictions.

"There is no explanation you can give me that will fix this. Why would I even believe you after you lied to me? Which is just as much of a problem, by the way," I reply. He goes to open his mouth in protest. "And please don't insult me by saying you never said you weren't married."

"That's not what I was going to say," he asserts. "You're right, I lied to you. But not the way you think."

I rub my temples. "I can't do this, Alessandro," I say tiredly. "I can't argue about this, and I don't want to hear excuses. It's over. Please, just let go. Your deal closes next week, we won't ever have to do business with each other again. I'll move on, you'll go back to your wife." And it sounds so simple coming out of my mouth, though I know it will be anything but.

"I don't want to move on," he says as tears threaten to spill down his cheeks. He squeezes his eyes closed and roughly wipes the moisture from his face. "I love you. And I think if you listened to me you would understand. My marriage is a sham."

"Okay, so don't go back to her, I don't care," I interrupt, exasperated. "But I'm not going to be with a married man.

Under any circumstances. But before you decide your marriage is over you might want to think about what's best for the baby."

"What?" he asks blankly.

"Cheating on your wife is one thing, but leaving her while she's pregnant? I didn't think you were capable of such selfishness," I elaborate. "But then again, I didn't see this coming either." I gesture at the photo in his hand.

He slowly sets the photo, picture side down, onto the coffee table and stares ahead, clearly utterly shocked. "Peyton is *pregnant?*"

I give him a look of disbelief. "You can't seriously expect me to believe you didn't know that."

"I didn't," he says tightly. "That does change things."

I'm dismayed by the confused expression on his face, then distracted as I remember something else he said. "You asked if she found me. Does she know about us?"

"Yes, more or less," he says.

"Which is it, more or less?"

"She doesn't know about you specifically, but she knows I'm involved with other women," he replies. "I told you, it's not what you think, we …"

I put a hand up. "Stop. Please. I've already told you it doesn't matter. I don't want to hear any more."

"Even if it changes your mind?" he asks persistently.

"Especially if it changes my mind," I concur. "Because at the end of this conversation, you're still married." *And you still lied to me. After I told you I trusted you.* And for the first time my calm, collected demeanor slips and I feel the anguish inside spilling out with the tears that fall down my cheeks.

"Yes, that is, unfortunately, true," he admits forlornly.

He reaches out to wipe away my tears, and I wave his hand away.

"Please don't make this any harder than it is."

He looks tortured and drops his hands impotently in his lap, staring down at them. "Serafina," he says softly before raising his eyes to meet mine. "I didn't want to hurt you. I thought I could wait and perhaps never have to tell you. But obviously that was selfish, and I ended up hurting you anyway. I'm sorrier than you can possibly know."

"I'm sure you are," I acknowledge, rising. "Goodbye, Alessandro." I don't wait for his reply to leave.

∽

As soon as I'm home I snap into my old standby defense mechanism — work mode. I call Bryce and reschedule filing the police report for the following afternoon, and I settle in to answer emails and touch base with Ellie and Jackson ahead of our meeting with Sutton Developments in the morning.

Once I'm caught up, I make a quick dinner and bring it back to the coffee table, choking it down mechanically while I go through my backlog of less urgent matters I've had on the back burner. I settle into a soothing rhythm and the night passes quickly.

W̲EDNESDAY FLIES BY JUST AS RAPIDLY. O̲UR INITIAL MEETING with Sutton Developments goes extremely well, and Mr. Sutton takes to Jackson particularly, validating my decision to allow him to shadow Ellie on the project. The execution now in their hands, I'm pleased to pass the project to Ellie and Jackson, so I can monitor our security plan adjustments and focus on some general, high-level business planning for once.

I meet Bryce after lunch at the police headquarters on 5th. He looks as handsome as ever but keeps his distance physically and verbally, as if he senses my inner torment.

I note with some amusement that, even in a building packed with hunky men in uniform, Bryce still turns heads. But I'm grateful for his calm presence as he walks me through the procedure and makes sure everything is fully documented.

I return to my office with a sense of relief at having put on record the events that upended my company's stability. It's given me back a measure of control, as have all the other procedures and changes Bryce recommended, of which I'm especially appreciative given recent events.

I delve back into work, blocking out everything but the spreadsheets in front of me.

WHEN MAGGIE KNOCKS ON MY DOOR AT THE END OF THE DAY, I'm surprised at how much time has passed. I stretch widely as she enters.

"Ms. Evans," Maggie says in way of greeting. "Mr. Giordano is here to see you."

I fold back in on myself abruptly, clenching my jaw to hold back a frustrated noise. "Please tell him I'm busy," I instruct her in a tight voice.

But he's already strolling in past her. "Come now, is that any way to treat your favorite client?" he teases, his smile directed toward easing the tension on Maggie's face at my reaction. He's forcing me to play nice for our audience.

"Of course not, please have a seat, Mr. Giordano," I gesture to a chair. "Thank you, Maggie."

She closes the door behind her on her way out, and I curse internally.

"What can I do for you, Mr. Giordano?" I stare at him coolly.

"Do you want to hear what I did today?" he asks, leaning forward in his chair.

So, it's not work related. My anger flares.

"No. I thought I made myself perfectly clear," I state firmly.

"As did I," he replies, imploring me with his eyes. "I'm not giving up."

"Unfortunately, you don't have a choice in the matter," I reply.

He runs his finger under his chin and I shift uncomfortably.

A smile tugs at the corners of his mouth. "Don't I?" he asks.

"No," I reply, but my tone is uncertain at best.

He regards me thoughtfully for a moment. "I'll go," he concedes. "Another time, perhaps." He pauses at the door. "Is there any hope, Sera, for you and me?"

I press my lips together to suppress a sad smile as I can't help but give the response I'm not sure he'll even understand. "There never was much hope," I answer. "Just a fool's hope."

I sit at my desk a long while after he leaves, staring into the ever-darkening void outside my window.

◦⁓◦

I DECIDE TO SKIP THE WEEKLY TAG-UP WITH BUONE CASE ON Friday, for my own sanity. Jackson seems fine with it. He's much more confident these days, and it's reassuring. I'm comforted, at least, to know I still have employees I can trust.

I wander into Allie's office in the afternoon, as I realize I haven't talked to her since our security meeting on Monday.

She's texting on her phone when I walk into her office, and she looks up guiltily, then with relief as she realizes it's just me.

"You know, you shouldn't look relieved," I kid. "I am still your boss."

"Psshhh," she replies. "Go ahead and fire me." She smiles widely as she finishes her message and puts down her phone. As soon as she's gotten a good look at me, she stands up and closes the door. "Good lord, Sera, are you still sick?"

"No, but that's an interesting way to greet your best friend," I reply, collapsing tiredly into one of her chairs.

She sits in the chair next to me, turning it so we're face to face. "Come on, Sera, it's me," she urges.

I look up at the ceiling and blink back tears. When I think I'll be able to keep control of myself, I look at her squarely. "You know the background checks Hoyt Corporate Services provided? Well, they led me to a rather nasty discovery," I say delicately. "Alessandro is married. To a very lovely — and pregnant — young woman named Peyton."

Allie gasps in shock. "NO!" she protests. I nod morosely. "Do you want to talk about it?"

I shake my head vehemently and she envelops me in a hug. We embrace for a good solid minute before she releases me. I wipe the dampness from my eyes and compose myself.

"I should've known better," I lament.

"Oh, Sera, don't," she admonishes me. "Don't do that to yourself. You took a risk. I'm proud of you. And I'm terribly sorry it didn't work out."

"That's a lovely way to frame it, thank you, Allie," I say sincerely. "But I still think I'm going to need quite a lot of alcohol this evening. Game?"

"I'm all yours," she replies without hesitation. "Let's blow this pop stand."

I laugh, and we pack out for an evening of booze and dancing, the only proper sendoff for crushed dreams and a broken heart.

Around two a.m. I stumble out of the elevator onto my floor, mostly just tired, though still decently buzzed. I'm so busy fumbling with my keys as I walk down the hall that I don't notice Alessandro leaning against my doorframe. He wears his favorite linen, navy trousers that skim his taught legs perfectly, with a crisp, white button up shirt, the top few buttons of which have been undone. His dark hair is mussed and sexy, his expression tired but intense.

My keys fall to the floor as our eyes lock. He silently steps forward and retrieves them, handing them to me. "I told you, I can't give up," he says in response to my perplexed expression.

I push past him and open my door. I drop my things on the table, kick off my heels angrily, and make to close the door in his face when he puts a hand out to stop me. He stands in front of me, his breath hot on my face.

"Please, Serafina," he breathes. "I need you to understand."

He reaches out and touches my face. His fingers leave a hot trail down my cheek and I let out an involuntary sigh. I realize it's been nearly five days since we last touched, and the thought lights a fire inside me, my brain taking a backseat to the heat I feel this close to him.

"It's still a no," I reply, my voice a soft sigh. But even I hear the "yes" in my "no."

He steps in and closes the door behind him, pressing me

against the wall. "Then maybe less talking, more showing," he says, and his mouth descends upon mine.

My brain wants to protest, but my body shoves it in a deep, dark room inside me and locks the door. Dizzy with alcohol and lust, I respond to his touch, twisting my fingers in his thick hair, pulling myself to him.

After a few moments of feverish kissing, he scoops me up and carries me to the bedroom. It takes us mere seconds to liberate ourselves of our clothing before we're wrapped in each other once more on the bed. He pins me under him, working his way between my legs. I allow him in eagerly, my back arching off the bed as he enters me. One of his hands finds my breast and works my nipple as he starts to move in me. I'm writhing in pleasure and torment, simultaneously furious at allowing this to be but desperately wanting more.

His tormented cries join my own and his mouth finds mine once again, his tongue wreaking havoc with my senses as he drags me toward climax. He lays his arms over mine, pinning me with his whole torso as he kisses my neck and chest, pumping into me all the while. His mouth drops to my ear.

"I can't live without you, Serafina," he groans. "I need you."

I groan loudly in protest and enjoyment. His words touch me in a way I can't guard against while he's inside me, and my need for him is just as strong. I press on his chest until he pulls back so I can climb on top of him.

I ease him inside me and sink onto him so that our bodies

are fully connected as I start to work my hips. He runs his hands over my back, moaning in pleasure. I snake my fingers into his hair and kiss him deeply as I move. He pulls my face up with his hands, staring deeply into my eyes. His stare is so open and vulnerable my heart can't take it.

"I love you, Alessandro," I breathe, tears of anger and confusion threatening to spill over my cheeks.

The ferocity of his response knocks me onto my back. He hovers over me, pressing his forehead to mine. "*Ti amo*," he whispers to me, our eyes locked once more, and he slides into me, thrusting furiously until we both climax loudly and collapse in each other's arms.

The bliss I used to feel after our lovemaking is notably absent. The confused tears finally leak out of the corners of my eyes, and I lay still and quiet in his arms until I'm sure he is asleep.

I shift quietly out of bed, twisting my pillow next to him hoping it helps delay his noticing my absence. I stand at the window for a long while, considering my moment of weakness as I fully sober up.

I can't shake feeling like I should tattoo a large "A" on my chest in penance for knowingly fucking another woman's husband. The deep conviction that I simply cannot do this settles over me. I can't be with him. But I can't resist him either. And he can't seem to let go.

I pack a bag slowly and quietly and, as dawn approaches, I slip into the living room to finish my preparations.

Standing as far from the bedroom as I can manage, I place a call and wait for an answer on the other end. After many rings, my mother finally picks up, sounding very sleepy.

"Hi, Mom, I'm sorry to wake you," I say quietly.

"Is everything okay, dear?" she asks, her voice filled with concern.

"No, Mom. Can I come stay with you for a while?"

Her pause is, thankfully, short. "Of course, honey. I'm always happy to see you," she responds.

"Thanks," I sigh in relief. "I'll be home in a couple hours." We say our goodbyes and I write a note for Alessandro.

I wish I could say I'm not sorry that you managed to seduce me once again, but I am. As you once promised we would, I'm ending this on my terms. I love you, Alessandro, but I can't be with you in good conscience. Unfortunately, since you won't give up so easily, I'm left with no choice but to remove myself from the situation. I hope you'll understand and respect my decision, but then you wouldn't be the man I fell in love with. Nonetheless, I am gone.

—Your Darling Serafina

Before he can wake, I place the note on the nightstand. I resist the urge to kiss him, touch him one last time. Toting my luggage as quietly as I can, I manage to slip out of the apartment with no sign of having woken him.

SEVENTEEN

Driving up I-5, I feel the best I have in days. A weight lifts from my shoulders the farther I get from Seattle, and I'm able to enjoy the rolling, green landscapes that splay out around me. On my way through Mount Vernon, I hit up a drive-through for a quick breakfast and manage to finish all of it as I drive.

I make it to my mother's house in record time, the sun still rising in the sky. My mother greets me at the door, helping me settle my luggage into my childhood bedroom. She uncharacteristically doesn't press me for information, making small talk about the changes to the neighborhood since my last visit.

When she's run out of small talk, we sit quietly at the small, round dining room table, sipping coffee.

Throwing caution to the wind, I break the silence. "You were right, Mom," I offer. "I'm in love with Alessandro." It occurs to me for the first time that I may have had feelings for him all along, and my mother simply noticed before I did.

She nods and puts her cup down. "I know, honey," she responds. "What happened?"

I smile grimly. "I found out he's married." I take another sip of coffee, hiding my expression behind the mug so I can privately enjoy her reaction.

She doesn't disappoint — she gasps loudly as her hands fly over her mouth. "That son of a bitch!" she exclaims loudly, and I have to laugh. She puts her hand on my arm. "I'm sorry, Sera."

"It'll be okay," I say, trying to convince myself as much as her. "He tried to persuade me not to leave him, but I can't be the other woman."

"No," she agrees. "You're made of better stuff than that."

I eye her speculatively. "Thanks," I reply. "He didn't exactly make it easy to stick to my guns."

"Then I'm all the prouder of you," she responds sincerely.

"Thanks, Mom."

~

THAT AFTERNOON I SETTLE INTO MY ROOM TO COME UP WITH my game plan. The first order of business is to call Allie. As I pick up my phone I notice a text message from Alessandro.

I'll settle for trying to be better than the man you fell in love with and hope that you change your mind. Until then I'll do my best to give you space. Ti amo.

I close my eyes briefly and push my reaction into a place in my mind where I can deal with it later. For now, I need to focus. I scroll to Allie's cell number and place the call.

"Sera, dear," she greets me. "Did you still want to go shopping tomorrow?"

"Hey Allie," I respond. "No, there's been a slight change of plans."

"Oh? Do tell," she replies curiously.

"When I got home last night Alessandro was waiting for me," I admit.

"Omigod," she gasps.

"Yeah," I agree. "I should've known he would do something along those lines, but I wasn't thinking about it. I was so taken by surprise …"

"That you fell onto his penis?" she accurately guesses.

I laugh joylessly. "Something like that," I concede. "I regretted it immediately."

"Naturally," she replies.

"So, once he was asleep, I left. I'm at my mom's."

"You *left*?!" she cries. "As in, you left him sleeping there at your place, by himself? And then went to your *mother's* house? Holy shit."

"I know," I agree. "But I needed to put some distance between us, since it seems like that's what it's going to take. He says he'll give me space, but I kind of don't believe it."

"No, you absolutely did the right thing," she agrees. "I'm just surprised you went to your mom's house."

"Yeah, me too," I laugh. "But I guess sometimes you just need your mom." I pause. "I think I'm going to move and rent out my condo."

"Wow," Allie responds. "Do you feel like you need to do that to shake him off?"

"Yes," I reply honestly. "But I also think it's time for a change."

"You know, most people just get a new hairstyle when they break up with someone," she jokes.

"Well, I'm not most people," I reply. "I'm going to work from here at least through this week. Buone Case's deal closes on Friday. There might be some follow-up, but that's all Jackson, and it won't require them to be in the office."

"Sounds like a plan," she agrees. "I'm proud of you, Sera."

"Thanks, Allie," I reply. "Talk soon."

Once we're off the phone, I send an email to Maggie letting her know I'll be remote for personal reasons indefinitely, with instructions not to notify anyone outside of the company without my permission. I also send a very vague email to everyone in the office instructing them to call or email me with any questions, and, finally, set an out-of-office message to the same effect.

I also realize I need to call Bryce immediately and notify him of my location, as I hadn't checked in this morning.

He picks up on the first ring. "Sera, thank God, I was just about to call you," he answers, his voice filled with concern.

"I'm so sorry, Bryce. I had a rather unexpected morning and forgot to call until just now," I apologize.

"It must have been something outrageous. You're usually so punctual," he teases, obviously relieved.

"That's one word for it," I agree drily. "I'm at my mother's house now, in Bellingham."

"Oh? Finally needed a break, huh?" he asks.

"You got me," I admit. "I'll be working remotely from here through Friday at least. I was also wondering if you could recommend a secured, temporary living space for when I return?"

"Did something happen that I need to know about?" he asks sharply.

I consider the question. "Something happened, yes, but not what you're thinking," I reply slowly.

"The Italian?" he asks matter-of-factly.

I'm aghast. "How did you know that?"

"If it was business-related, you would have told me earlier this week when you'd gone all quiet," he says pointedly.

"I guess you don't work as a security consultant if you're not highly observant," I allow, and he laughs.

"Nope," he replies. "He didn't do anything to you, did he?"

"God, no, nothing like that," I reply quickly. "It's just over. And he's having a hard time accepting that."

"I see," he says. "So, you're not concerned for your safety?"

"Not at all. I think it's just best if I remove myself as an option for him," I say delicately.

"I'm with you one hundred percent," he agrees enthusiastically, and it causes me to raise an eyebrow. There's that hint of interest again.

"At any rate, I plan to buy a new place. It was time anyway. It was the first place I ever bought, years ago. I'll rent it out eventually, but in the meantime, I could use some help getting my things into storage and setting up something temporary while I secure a new living situation."

"Absolutely, I'm happy to arrange all of that," he replies. "I'd ask if you need help securely purchasing a new place, but I imagine you know how to do that, given your line of work."

"Yes, that I do," I agree. "All of my properties are each held in their own LLC. I've been operating that way for ages."

"Smart woman," he says.

∽

ON SUNDAY, MOM AND I SPEND THE DAY SETTING UP MY OLD room to suit me for my stay, grocery shopping, and preparing food. We chat pleasantly throughout, and it almost feels like a normal relationship. She makes the occasional snarky comment, of course, but since there's nobody here to embarrass me in front of, I'm able to brush it off and we fall into a mellow rhythm.

Come Monday morning we establish a new routine of breakfasting together, then she heads to work, where she does bookkeeping for a large accounting firm. I spend my mornings dealing with the normal ebb and flow of work issues, and as much of my free time as possible looking for a new place. After spending so much time in Alessandro's spacious apartment, I'm ready for something bigger, with a view to match.

On Tuesday afternoon I get an email from Allie. The subject line reads, *So much for that.* I open the email curiously.

I just caught Alessandro trying to wrest your whereabouts out of Maggie. Does three-and-a-half days count as "giving you space"?

I shake my head and reply.

I'm surprised it took that long. How's everything?

Her reply comes quickly.

Five by five, boss. Keep doing what you gotta. We've got this. ;)

With a chuckle I return to my hunt for a new condo.

⚬

I'M SHOWING MY MOTHER SOME LISTINGS THAT EVENING WHEN Bryce calls.

"Bryce!" I answer, surprised. "You're working awfully late."

"Comes with the territory," he replies. "I just wanted to let you know your things are in storage and I've secured you a place, ready whenever you are. How's the apartment hunt going?"

"Not bad," I respond. "There are several places I think I'd like to check out once I get back."

"Well, if you need someone to go with you, I'm happy to help," he responds. While friendly, his response takes me by surprise.

"Isn't that a little outside of your job description?" I tease him.

"For you? Nothing's out of my job description," he replies seriously, and I'm taken aback. "But really, it's not. I'm happy to check it out with you. You know, from a security perspective."

"Boy, you really go above and beyond for your clients, don't you?" I reply edgily.

"I'm sorry if I seem forward, Sera," he says, sensing the reticence in my voice. "I just feel very strongly about helping you as much as I can."

"Is that the only reason?" I probe bluntly.

"Sort of," he admits. "But it's not what you're thinking. I'm not trying to hit on you or anything, I promise. I can't even explain it. I just feel very protective of you."

I frown, weighing his words. I have an independent streak a mile wide, so I'm naturally resistant to anyone trying to treat me like I'm incapable of taking care of myself. On the other hand, there is an ex-employee with an unknown partner, unknown motives, and a knack for sabotage out there hating my guts at this very moment. So, a handsome security expert with a yen to be at my beck and call probably isn't the worst thing in the world.

"Thanks, Bryce," I capitulate. "I'll do my best not to take advantage of that."

He laughs heartily. "Hey, I'm the one who put it out there," he replies. "If you do, it's on me for offering."

"You're a good guy, Bryce."

"Thanks, Sera. I'm honored to be working with you, really. You're a special woman."

∽

On Thursday, I find it. My new home. It's a gorgeous, recently renovated, luxury four bedroom, two-and-a-half bath, sprawling condo in one of the older sections of downtown. It has gorgeous views of Elliott Bay and amenities galore, including a bevy of security features in the unit itself. At around three thousand square feet it's more than twice my current square footage. Normally I'm not one for excess, but the place just calls out to me with its simple, clean lines and lack of fussiness.

I call the seller's real estate agent immediately and am pleased to discover that, having just come on the market, there aren't any offers in. Nor are there likely to be many on this level of real estate, but I know in my gut that this is where I want to live, so I offer at asking.

"You realize it's just under four *million*, don't you, dear? Not four hundred thousand."

I've been condescended to enough in my career to not take the bait. "Absolutely," I respond as sweetly as possible. "I prefer to finance my investments for tax purposes, but if the seller needs a quick close or would prefer cash I'm happy to oblige."

"Are you sure you wouldn't rather see the property first?" she presses, clearly skeptical.

"Quite," I respond. "I'll email you the offer paperwork shortly. Please let me know where to send the earnest money."

"Ohhkay," she sighs, and I can tell she still doesn't believe I'm for real.

I confirm her email address from the listing and end the call. After I've submitted the paperwork I forward the listing to Bryce. I title the email *Home, sweet home.*

∽

First thing Friday morning I call Allie.

"Mrs. Kramer," I greet her. "Good morning to you."

"And to you, Ms. Evans," she responds just as formally. "What can I do for you today?"

"I checked with Jackson yesterday, and it looks like everything is still greenlit on the Buone Case deal to close today. I'd like you to get in the loop on that and revoke Buone Case's access credentials as soon as that's wrapped," I instruct her.

"You've got it, boss," she replies. "How much longer will you stay in Bellingham?"

"Not long," I reply. "I've found a place, and as soon as my offer is accepted I'm going to order an inspection. So, I'll need to be there for that."

"Oooh, exciting!" she exclaims, and suddenly I hear voices in the background. "Hey, gotta go. Talk soon!"

JUST AFTER NOON I GET AN EMAIL FROM JAN ROGERS, THE condescending real estate agent, that my cash offer has been accepted with a twelve-day close. I do a little happy dance before calling my inspector.

"Hey Rich, it's Sera Evans."

"Sera! My favorite real estate mogul! How the heck are ya, kid?"

I laugh. "I could complain, but I won't," I joke. "Do you have time to inspect a downtown condo at three thousand square feet early next week?"

"For you? Without a doubt. I can get you in Monday afternoon or Tuesday afternoon," he offers.

"Monday afternoon," I respond immediately. I'm eager to get in there and see if it's everything it seems to be. I provide Rich the details and follow on with an email to Jan. And as an afterthought, I email Bryce to see if he's available to join me. What the hell, why not?

∾

I RECEIVE TWO MORE CALLS THAT AFTERNOON, THE FIRST FROM Jackson gleefully sharing that Buone Case is now the proud owner of their new land parcel, for which they plan to break ground the following week after a few standard preparatory checks. The second is from Allie informing me that the Buone Case team's access has been revoked. I breathe a sigh of relief all around.

∾

THAT EVENING, MY MOM TRUDGES IN THE DOOR, COLLAPSING IN her favorite chair dramatically.

"Hey, Mom, how was work?" I ask warily.

"A disaster," she replies affectedly. "We have a new client — a mom-and-pop ice cream shop. I went in to their office to go over their books with the owners, and they had boxes upon boxes of receipts. Nothing had been organized or cataloged. I'm going to be piecing together their books for *ages*."

"Well, I have just the thing for you then," I reply, smiling. "I'm taking you out to dinner!"

"Yay!" she exclaims, brightening. I laugh at her sudden change in mood. "Where should we go?"

"Your choice, Mom," I reply. "But no Italian."

∾

WE DECIDE ON CHINESE FOOD, OUR OLD STANDBY. IT'S NOT fancy, but there's a great dumpling restaurant not far from the house. As we get seated, the waiter asks if we're celebrating anything tonight.

"Oh!" I say, remembering suddenly. "Yes! I just bought a new place."

The waiter offers his congratulations and takes our drink orders.

"Sera, you didn't tell me you'd found a place already," my mother chides after he's gone.

"Sorry, Mom, it slipped my mind. It was a busy day, and then you were all," I pull a melodramatic face, "when you got home."

She smacks me playfully on the arm. "Tell me about it," she insists.

I resist the temptation to pretend like she's asking me to describe her dramatic entrance this evening and fill her in on the specs of the new condo. When I tell her the price, her jaw drops.

"I just … how do you even …" she's having trouble finding words.

"It's a lot of money, I know," I concede. "But it just looked like home."

"Well, crap, for that much money it better do a whole lot more than that," she grumbles.

"I can afford it, Mom," I assure her.

"Goodness, Serafina. I knew you were doing well for yourself, but I had no idea how well," she admits.

"I am, but I couldn't afford that on the salary I draw from ERS, Mom. That money comes from the investments Grandma and Grandpa Tyler left me," I say.

"You're not using up everything they left you so quickly, are you?" my mother asks in horror.

"God, no! The cashflow from the properties they left me is more than enough to cover anything I could possibly need for several lifetimes," I promise. "I know what I'm doing."

Our waiter interrupts to deliver our drinks and takes our dinner orders before whisking efficiently off.

My mother huffs quietly, and I already know she's been biting back a snappy retort based on both the subject matter and her tight expression.

"I suppose that's why my parents left the bulk of their holdings to you instead of me," she finally grumbles.

I bite back the urge to snap back with a biting agreement of her assessment. As if my knowledge magically appeared but had been denied her. She never had any interest in Grandpa's empire while he was alive. But I lived with my grandparents while I went to college and eagerly learned everything I could from Grandpa. And after I graduated, I spent years proving that I could manage his holdings before he bequeathed them to me.

I roll my eyes at the reactiveness and oversimplification of her resentment, and change the subject instead of rising to the bait.

"Alessandro's deal closed today. So, our contract with them is officially complete," I offer.

"Well, that's a blessing," she replies, taking the bait. "Now he has no reason to darken your doorstep ever again."

I grimace. "Something tells me he doesn't need a reason. But with my moving and him not having access to our offices anymore, there are no more doorsteps for him, anyway."

"Good. Once a cheater, always a cheater," she says in a vicious tone.

Perhaps following the touchy subject of being passed over as heir to her father's legacy with the even touchier subject of my perfidious ex-boyfriend wasn't the smartest tactic.

"I'm sure he has his own story, Mom," I defend him. She looks sharply at me and I put my hands up. "Hey, I'm not saying what he did was okay. I was certainly not prepared to be a part of it." I pause thoughtfully. "But I've seen him in difficult ethical situations and he never disappointed me before. So, he may have his reasons here."

"There is *never* a good reason to cheat on your spouse. *Never.*"

"Geez, Mom, okay, I hear you," I say, trying to defuse her feisty tone.

My mother contemplates me carefully for a moment. "I think it's time you knew why your father really left."

EIGHTEEN

I spit out the sip of soda I just took. "Excuse me?" I ask, aghast, mopping up the mess with a napkin.

"Sera, your father left because I kicked him out. For cheating on me. On us," she says matter-of-factly.

"And you're only just now telling me this? Seventeen years later?!" I'm appalled at her revelation. "What do you mean he was cheating on *us*?"

My mother sighs and folds her hands in her lap. "I didn't tell you before because I thought it would hurt too much. But given recent events, I think it's time you knew. Your father had another family. He was married to another woman — not legally, obviously — and had a child with her. He would frequently disappear," she explains. "And until I found out the truth, he never had any explanation for his behavior. I put up with it for years, and I kick myself for it to this day."

I sit there dumbstruck, unable to wrap my head around what she's told me. She sips her water primly and sets it down with an exasperated look.

"I shouldn't have told you," she says. "It was too much."

"No, Mom," I say, quietly furious. "You should have told me *much* sooner."

She looks like she's about to say something nasty in return, but before she can her face crumples. "I'm sorry, darling. I thought I was protecting you. You're right, I should have told you sooner."

"So, tell me now, Mom," I prompt.

The waiter returns at just that moment with our dinners, laying the dumpling and rice steamers around the table. When he's gone, my mother quietly fills her plate, so I do the same, trying to contain the flood of emotions I'm feeling.

After she's eaten a few pork dumplings, she puts her chopsticks down.

"When you were four years old I found out I had uterine cancer," she says. My jaw drops and I start to respond, but she motions for me to let her continue. "I never told you because you were so young. And by the time you were old enough to know, well, things were hard for our family, and I had enough to worry about."

She exhales heavily and slowly consumes another dumpling. I eat hesitantly, waiting for her to continue, wondering what other bombshells she's about to drop.

"It's why we never had more children," she begins again. "I

was deeply depressed for several years, and even after I sought help at your father's behest, I still struggled. It's not something you just get over as a woman." She sniffs delicately, and I reach out and cover her hand with mine.

"I'm so sorry, Mom," I say.

She flips her palm over and gives my hand a squeeze, then withdraws to pick at her rice.

"When your father started working more and going on 'trips' on the weekend, I thought he was just tired of dealing with me," she explains. "But then, one day, when you were twelve, your father was at work, and she came to me. His other wife. She begged me to free him. He'd been telling her I knew about her and their child and was refusing to let him get a divorce, so he could truly be with her."

"How old was their child?" I ask.

"He was five, at the time," she replies.

"So, what did you do?" I probe.

"I called him every name in the book. I threw things. I threatened him. And then, when nothing I said or did got a reaction from him, I told him to leave and never come back," she admits.

"So, it wasn't Dad's choice to leave us?" I ask.

"Really, Sera, after all that I've told you, *that's* your response?"

I hear my own words in my head and my eyes pop. "No, Mom, I'm sorry, I'm not saying it was your fault," I explain. "I completely understand why you did what you did. I'm just trying to wrap my head around it."

She gives me a sideways scowl. "What else was I supposed to do? Pretend like it never happened? Tell him it was okay?" she demands. "If I hadn't kicked him out, he would have left eventually."

"It doesn't matter what he would have done," I concede. "I would have done the same, in your shoes."

My mother grabs my hand and leans in earnestly. "Yes, Sera," she says urgently. "That's exactly why I'm telling you this. You'd do the same. You've done it. Now stick with it. Men that do this to women — they're no good."

"Mom, Alessandro is nothing like Dad," I reply, pulling my hand away.

"Why are you defending him? He may be handsome, Sera, but don't let that distract you from his actions. He's showed you who he is. Don't forget that," she insists.

I shake my head. As angry as I am with Alessandro, I can't put him in the same class as my father, especially given this information.

"Everyone makes mistakes, Mom. Some mistakes are unforgivable," I agree. "And I'm sticking to my decision — I have no intention of going back to Alessandro. But despite his issues, I can't see him ever saying what Dad said to me when he left."

My mother looks at me blankly. "I don't remember your father saying anything to you that night," she responds slowly.

"Seriously? You were standing right next to me. He said," I have to reach deep to say this calmly, "nobody could ever love me. Who says that to their kid? Or to anybody, for that matter?"

I may has well have just slapped my mother. Her face turns red and splotchy and she is utterly flabbergasted. I put down my chopsticks and push my plate away.

"Your father didn't say that to you," she manages after a moment. "He said that to *me*, Sera. He was talking to *me*. All these years, you thought your father didn't love you? That you are unlovable?"

I can see in her eyes that she now understands so much more about my relationships with men, or lack thereof. And through her admission, she's shown me a good deal about why she is the way she is too.

As my brain processes her correction I want to protest, to say she's wrong, but my adult eyes look through my childish understanding of those events that unfolded at such a tender age, and I know she's right. And the tears that threaten to spill out of my eyes are for all the years that we never spoke a word of that day.

⸺

I LAY IN BED THAT NIGHT, STARING AT THE GLOWING PLASTIC stars I affixed to the ceiling when I was nine. My mother and I talked late into the evening about why she kept my father away from me after that, and in turn I told her more about what happened with both Tom and Alessandro. She wouldn't back down from lumping Alessandro with Dad, though, and my continued defensiveness at the comparison has been troubling me.

Alessandro did cheat on his wife with me. And he did claim that Peyton knew about us, though from my knothole it seemed like she was clueless. So why is my gut rejecting the link? It can't just be my love for him. Even while head over heels, before I knew, I was aware of his shortcomings. His arrogance. His penchant for moodiness. His hot temper.

But having personally witnessed his adherence to his own internal, strong moral compass, I have a hard time reconciling the depth of deceit in his actions to the Alessandro I thought I knew.

Exhausted from a tumultuous day, I file the issue away under "doesn't matter anyway" and fall into a fitful sleep.

My phone pings around seven, so I stop trying to sleep in and pick it up. Even with a crappy night's sleep I don't think there's any chance I'll be able to ignore the bright morning light peeping around the blinds.

It's a text from Bryce. *I have business in Vancouver this evening, can I stop by and take you to lunch on my way up?*

I contemplate the offer for a moment. I doubt he asks all his clients to go to lunch on a Saturday, hours from home.

But I'm not planning on returning to Seattle until Monday morning, and I'll need the keys for my temporary living quarters.

Okay, bring my new keys? I type quickly.

You got it. See you around noon.

I shuffle out of bed and into the kitchen where I'm greeted by the smell of freshly brewed coffee and bacon.

"Mmmm," I say, grabbing a slice of bacon that's drying on a big, yellow plate next to the stove. "Thanks, Ma."

She smirks as I steal another piece. "You're welcome, dear. What's on the agenda for today?"

"I have some work to do this morning, and then apparently I'm having lunch with my security consultant," I respond. "But I'm open this afternoon if you still need helping to clean out the garage."

"Your security consultant is driving all the way up here just to have lunch with you?" she asks archly.

"No, Mom, it's not like that," I respond to her unspoken accusation. *Except it probably is like that, for him, anyway,* I think to myself. "He's got to be in Vancouver tonight, he's just passing through."

"Okay," she replies skeptically. "If you say so."

"Yeah yeah yeah," I respond. I switch to a mocking falsetto, "'When I was your age, when a young man went out of his way to take a young woman to lunch it meant something,'"

She blushes, confirming that that was *exactly* what she was just thinking. "So, he's young, hmmm?" she counters.

"Compared to you? Yes," I tease her, and flounce out of the room with a freshly poured cup of coffee.

⁓

Bryce, punctual as ever, pulls up exactly at noon. I attempt to meet him outside before my mother can get her claws in him, but I'm no match for her handsome-man-approaching radar and find her already outside watering the flowers.

Bryce unfolds his tall frame from the car and my mother eagerly appraises him as he approaches.

"Ms. Evans," he greets my mother. "It's a pleasure to meet you."

She shakes his hand warmly. "I'm afraid you have me at a disadvantage," she coos. "Sera didn't tell me your name."

"Oh, I'm terribly sorry," he says sincerely. "Bryce Hoyt, ma'am."

Her smile slips a little at the "ma'am" and I hide a grin behind my hand.

"Well, it was nice to meet you," she replies a bit stiffly and takes her leave.

"I made her feel old, didn't I?" he asks sheepishly after the front door has closed behind her.

"Yes. That was amazing," I laugh. And I smile brightly, realizing I'm genuinely happy he's here. "Hey, Bryce."

He grins widely. "Hey, Sera. Ready for lunch?"

"You betcha," I reply.

⌇

We grab some sandwiches, chips, and sodas at a local sub shop and eat on the benches outside in the uncharacteristically sunny and dry morning.

I happily polish off my sub in record time and Bryce chuckles. "You're easy to please," he remarks.

I shrug. "I guess so," I agree.

"One of the many things I like about you," he replies, smiling.

I internally sigh and attempt to redirect the conversation. "Anything I need to know about my interim accommodations?" I ask.

"Nothing that I can't show you on Monday," he replies.

"Oh," I say in surprise. "I didn't know you'd be personally helping me get settled. Guess you didn't need to stop by to drop off the keys then."

He brushes the remnants of his sandwich from his hands. "Since I'll be going with you to see the condo after lunch anyway, I figured I might as well," he responds. "Besides, I think we both know I was going to come here today anyway."

"Bryce," I start, a caution in my voice.

"Sera," he replies calmly, grinning. I shake my head and laugh. "I don't want to make you uncomfortable. But to be completely honest …"

"You *are* trying to hit on me?" I interrupt teasingly.

He laughs. "I did say before that I wasn't trying to do that, didn't I?" he allows.

"Yep," I agree.

"Yeah, that's not really my usual style," he says. "I guess what I'm trying to say is, I feel a connection here. And I want to know if you feel it too. I know this isn't the most professional proposition or the best timing, and you have a lot going on. But being upfront about what's on my mind *is* my style. And I don't want to keep it to myself if there's a chance you feel the same way. And if you don't, all you have to do is say the word, and I'm back in my consultant box."

I consider for a moment. "I appreciate your honesty," I say slowly. "And I'm absolutely for saying what's on your mind. I just wish I knew my own a little better right now."

He smiles tolerantly. "I get it," he says. "A lot has happened in a short amount of time. You don't need to respond now. Just, maybe think about it?"

I nod. "Definitely," I agree. I stand, encouraging our departure. "Thanks for lunch, Bryce."

"Anytime, Sera," he replies, offering his arm to me on the way back to the car.

I slip my hand through the crook of his elbow and we walk comfortably side by side.

∽

I wave to Bryce as he pulls away and return to the house to face the inquisition.

"That handsome young man has a thing for you," my mother comments as soon as I sit down next to her on the couch.

"Yes," I reply matter-of-factly. "Yes, he does."

"How do you feel about him?" she asks curiously.

I sigh heavily. "He's …"

"Hot?" my mom offers, and I laugh.

"Definitely. And he makes me feel safe," I admit. "But he's a security consultant. That's kind of his job."

"Does he take such good care of all his clients?" she asks pointedly.

"I don't know," I reply, starting to get slightly aggravated.

"We don't have to talk about this anymore," she says backing off. "You've got enough on your plate."

"It's not that," I respond. "I think I could like him. Or I would. If it weren't for …" I don't even want to say his name, but my mother nods in understanding.

"I know, honey," she says kindly. "Give it time. You might be okay sooner than you think."

"I hope so," I say softly.

NINETEEN

As rush hour winds down on Monday morning, I begin my trip back to Seattle, and reality. The drive flies by, and before I know it I'm pulling into the extended stay facility. It's close to Boeing Field, which means a longer commute than I'm used to, and I note a loud airplane flying low overhead as I enter the building.

Bryce is waiting for me in the lobby. "Good morning," he says, his smile warm as sunshine.

"Hey, Bryce," I reply, smiling back. His upbeat mood is infectious.

"Ready to see your new digs?" he asks.

"Roger dodger," I respond. "Lead the way."

"There's a concierge at the front desk at all times," he tells me, pointing toward reception. "You can pick up your mail there. There's also a gym and indoor pool down that hallway," he points behind me and I turn to look. "There are complimentary newspapers and hot breakfast daily, and laundry and dry cleaning on-site, which the daily housekeeping service can tend to for you."

"Wow," I reply, impressed. "I may never leave."

"I looked at the listing for that condo. I think you will." He winks, and gestures to a nearby elevator. Once inside he hands me a parking placard and an electronic key. At the third floor, the highest, we exit, passing three doors until he gestures to door number 321. That will be easy to remember.

Looking skeptically at the drab, grey hallway, I put my key in the slot and push the heavy door open. As I enter, I'm pleased to find that it's not the same dreary color as the rest of the building. Everything is in warm earth tones.

Two big, chocolate brown microfiber couches fill the small living room. A small, square tan dining table with four medium-brown upholstered chairs sits beyond it next to a very beige, efficient kitchen.

As I walk around I notice my personal effects scattered throughout the suite. "Did you do that?" I ask, pointing to a picture of mom and I at my college graduation.

"Sort of," he admits. "I asked our relocation techs to transfer some of your things from storage, so we could make it feel homier."

"That's sweet, Bryce, thank you," I reply, somewhat relieved that he hadn't personally been rifling through my belongings.

Bryce hangs back to let me complete my inspection. I stand by the living room windows and note that the noise of the airplanes passing overhead is low and muffled. Bryce approaches and taps on the window.

"Triple-paned," he assures me.

Continuing through the suite, I find two bedrooms connected by a large bathroom off the side of the living room opposite the kitchen and dining areas. They are both decently sized, one set up as a bedroom, the other as an office. More of my things have been set up in the bedroom, including all my clothing and shoes.

Returning to the living room, I find Bryce has settled himself on one of the couches.

"This thing is comfortable," he informs me, bouncing on it a bit like a sugared-up three-year-old.

I can't help but laugh at his enthusiasm. "Good to know," I reply. "How about we go get some lunch?"

He springs up eagerly and gestures for me to lead the way.

◈

WE GO TO A BURGER JOINT MIDWAY BETWEEN MY OFFICE AND the new condo. Being out with Bryce is somehow both familiar and comfortable. Our conversation over lunch flows easily as he fills me in on the progress to date for all the changes we've been making.

"So, you're not going into the office today, I take it?" Bryce asks, wiping the last crumbs from his plate.

"No," I reply, still picking at my fries. "I took a personal day. Tomorrow, though."

"How are you doing, Sera?" I look up in surprise at his concerned face.

"Unexpectedly good," I reply. "In a way, this break has been really great for me. I've been able to focus on some strategic planning, which isn't something I'm able to do much of amid the day-to-day needs of the business." I pause. "What made you ask me that now?"

"The thing about my business," he explains, "is that I usually get to know people at the most tumultuous times in their lives." He considers his next words for a moment. "In the past month you've learned that an employee stole from you, that that employee was also sabotaging you, and that there is likely more treachery afoot. *And* you've gotten out of what seemed like a fairly serious relationship. And now you're uprooting yourself to move to a new place. Yet, with all that, you seem so normal. Focused. Happy, even, to be using this as an opportunity to propel yourself into the next thing." He shakes his head in disbelief. "It's just hard to believe someone can be so resilient. I'm in awe of you."

I blush at the compliment. "I'm sure it'll all hit me one of these days and I'll do my share of crying alone, in the dark, under a blanket," I joke. As if there hasn't been crying already.

"And don't think I'm going to let you off for using the phrase 'treachery afoot.' I'm filing that one away for later."

"You do that," he says, smiling and leaning back in his chair. "Now, are we going to visit your new palace, or what?"

"Absolutely," I respond, reminded of the task. I rise, and he follows me out of the restaurant.

We go to Bryce's car, which is parked on the street in front of the restaurant. As he opens the door for me to get inside, someone across the street catches my eye. They are stopped and gawking at Bryce and me.

It only takes me a moment to process the sexily disheveled shock of dark brown hair, the strong shoulders, and the intense gaze. It's Alessandro, with Francesca and Giovanni at his side, looking at him curiously, clearly trying to figure out why he's stopped. As our eyes lock, I stop breathing and my heart pounds ferociously against my rib cage. Bryce notices that I've gone still and follows my gaze.

Alessandro tears his forlorn gaze from mine and fixes Bryce briefly with a fierce look before abruptly turning and continuing on with his team. The whole thing happened in less than ten seconds, but it takes me much longer than that to catch my breath.

Bryce stands by me, quietly, clearly waiting to make sure I'm okay. When I've recovered enough to move, I slide into the car and Bryce shuts the door. He rounds the vehicle and drops into the driver's seat. He looks straight ahead for a stretch, gripping the steering wheel tightly. As my pulse returns to normal, I try not to think about Alessandro.

"Are you okay?" I ask Bryce tentatively.

His hands drop from the steering wheel and he turns to me, his expression veiled. "I should be asking you that," he replies evenly.

"I'm fine," I assure him. "Seeing him just took me by surprise."

"Me too," he admits. "I'm glad he was across the street or I would have ..." he squeezes his fists and shakes his head. "Never mind."

"Bryce," I say with caution in my voice. "I'm not mad at him. And you shouldn't be either."

He smiles ironically. "You wouldn't be," he says. "You're too nice. But I saw you, after. And let's just say I hope for his sake that he and I never meet when you're not around." The anger in his voice surprises me.

"Did I look that bad?" I ask curiously.

"You looked fragile," he admits. "Broken. And with what you're already going through, it made me want to hurt him. I don't know what he did to you, Sera, but you deserve better." He tries to keep his face impassive, but I can see his anger in the tight corners of his mouth, the flare of his nostrils.

"I know," I concede. And I feel the need to explain. "We weren't together very long. It was just intense. I don't trust easily, but somehow, when I'd just managed to, it all blew up in my face."

He smiles wryly. "Yeah," he says softly. "Been there." He gives my hand a squeeze, starts the car, and pulls into traffic.

⸻

"THERE ARE A FEW MINOR ISSUES," RICH SAYS, SHOWING ME the notes on his list, "but no showstoppers. The only thing I'd even bother asking them to repair is the second bedroom cracked window frame. This high up you don't want to leave it like that."

I take the report from him, skimming it skeptically. Bryce elbows me gently. "If it's too good to be true," he says in a singsong voice and I laugh.

"It would only be too good to be true if the price tag was about a million less," I joke back.

Jan the Condescending Real Estate Agent huffs quietly in her chosen corner and I turn away, rolling my eyes.

Bryce catches me and laughs quietly. I shrug, shooting him a conspiratorial smile, and slip the report in my bag.

"I'll look for your formal response to the inspection, Ms. Evans," Jan says, leading us out. "But in the meantime, please do let me know if there's anything else you need."

"Thank you, *Jan*," I reply pointedly, stepping into the hall. "Presuming your clients will agree to have the window frame repaired I don't see any further obstacles to closing."

"Oh, I'm sure they'll be happy to," she assures me, locking

the door behind us. Her phone rings and she steps away to answer it, waving dismissively at us.

"Thank God that's over," I say under my breath and pull Bryce into the elevator.

He starts to laugh, but his foot catches the gap in the floor and he tumbles forward into me.

He catches himself, bracing his arms on either side of me, leaving me pressed between his tall, muscled frame and the elevator wall as the doors slide closed behind him. I look up into his sparkling blue eyes and my breath catches in my throat, the heat between us palpable as his eyes drop to my mouth.

He slowly lowers his face to mine and, unconsciously, I rise on my toes to meet him. Our lips touch, warm and soft. It's nice. A gentle, tentative kiss, and I find I don't mind it at all. Surrendering to the moment, I allow him to deepen the kiss, his lips parting, his breath hot in my mouth for a moment before he gently releases me and pushes the button for the first floor.

As the elevator begins its long descent, he wordlessly takes my hand, pulling me smoothly to his side. I slide under his arm and he holds me there, nestled in his warm, soothing embrace, and we complete the ride down in comfortable silence.

∽

As Bryce drops the last of my bags in the suite's entryway, I hand him a bottle of water.

"It's all that was in the fridge," I lament. "Thanks for your help."

He waves a hand at the bags indifferently. "You didn't have that much stuff, but you're welcome," he replies.

I smile and settle into the overstuffed couch. "Not just for that," I say. "For everything. I don't know how I would have managed without you."

He sits next to me, his arm brushing against mine. "Sera, I don't think there's anything you couldn't do if you decided to," he says confidently. He pulls away to look in my eyes. "But I'm happy to help you however I can, all the same."

I contemplate him for a moment. "I don't know what I did to impress you so much." My tone is skeptical.

He laughs and smiles his bright-as-sunshine smile that always ends up mirrored on my face, then shrugs. "I don't think it's something you did, per se," he replies. "I have a superpower." He waggles his eyebrows and I laugh.

"You can make women melt into your protective embrace using only your boyish charm?" I tease.

"No," he says, blushing. "I'm just really good at reading people."

"Oh. That makes sense too," I agree.

He smiles and rises from the couch. "I should go and let you get settled in," he replies. I see him to the door and he hesitates before leaving. "I enjoyed spending the day with you, Sera."

"Me too," I reply shyly.

"Can I take you on a real date sometime?"

"I think I'd like that, Bryce," I say honestly, and his smile is back in full force.

"How about I pick you up Friday at seven?" he offers.

"You don't waste time, do you?" I laugh. "Okay."

"Talk to you soon, then."

I GO INTO THE OFFICE EXTRA EARLY THE NEXT MORNING TO avoid any potential traffic. It also seems like a good idea since I've been out of the office for so long. Everything looks the same as I set myself back up at my desk. By the time everyone has arrived, I'm sipping my third cup of coffee.

"Ms. Evans!" Maggie's excited greeting causes me to look up in surprise.

She rushes toward me and I stand and hug her, because it seems like the thing to do. I'm a bit shocked by her warm greeting, and I examine her for a moment. A sudden rush of appreciation for this woman who's helped me for so long without complaint washes over me.

"Maggie, you've worked for me for two years," I tell her. "You should really call me Sera."

She smiles brightly. "I'll try," she replies. "Welcome back. Everyone has missed you."

"I've missed everyone too," I respond. "Are we set up for a full team meeting this morning?"

"Absolutely," she assures me. "I've brought in several boxes of pastries from a certain favorite bakery of yours as a special treat."

My mouth fills with saliva. "Ohhhh, Maggie, have I ever told you that you're my favorite person ever?" I say. "You didn't happen to get any coconut cream pie bites, did you?"

"No, they were fresh out," she replies, her face falling. She whips something out from behind her back and presents a clear container with a single slice of the amazing pie. "So, I got you your own piece!"

I jump up and down, clapping my hands and she laughs merrily. "Thank you, thank you, thank you."

"You're welcome, Ms. Evans," she says, then blushes. "I mean, Sera."

Realizing I haven't had anything but coffee this morning, as soon as Maggie is gone I blissfully descend upon the pie.

The team meeting is filled with raucous laughter and enjoyment, both of the incredible pastries and the stories of all that I've missed. It seems there were a lot of things forgotten or neglected that made people really miss my involvement and presence. Their clear relief at having me back is touching.

I'm also extremely pleased with the progress our property management team has made in recruiting new accounts. They've managed to garner nearly fifty new units, significantly bolstering engagement and a general feeling of optimism on the team. I make a mental note to give Ana, our property management lead, a significant raise on her next salary review.

Our project management team is chugging along, busy as usual, and the Sutton Developments project is progressing nicely. Ellie and Jackson have identified three potential sites that they're nearly ready to present to Mr. Sutton. I commend them on their speed and hope privately that we'll be able to make progress rapidly enough to impress Mr. Sutton and keep him from concluding that we lack the resources to meet his needs.

By early afternoon I've fully settled back into my usual rhythms.

But at three p.m. it all falls spectacularly apart when Jackson comes crashing into my office unannounced, pale as a sheet. Ellie tails after him, frantically calling for him to calm down.

"Jackson!" I exclaim. "What's wrong?"

But he's blubbering incoherently, and I can't make out anything from the sounds coming out of his mouth.

"I'm sorry, Ms. Evans," Ellie gasps, out of breath from chasing Jackson. "I tried to tell him that we needed to come up with a solution before we barged into your office."

"A solution for what? Did Mr. Sutton contact you?" I go cold as the blood leaves my face.

"No, it has nothing to do with that," she says. "I heard him on the phone and tried to get him to talk to me about it before he came to you."

"You're killing me here, Ellie," I say through clenched teeth.

Jackson finally finds his words. "It's Buone Case," he moans. "Their land is unbuildable."

TWENTY

"What do you mean, 'unbuildable'?" I demand.

"Giovanni was at the site yesterday as the equipment was being brought in to clear the plot," Jackson explains. "Something about the shift of the soil as the machines rolled in bothered him, so he had some samples taken to compare to the original report. They came back today. The soil composition is completely different. They'll take a full sample set tomorrow, but it appears to be completely unsuitable for their purposes."

I'm speechless as I process the ramifications of this. Buone Case is not a large company. An issue this big could sink them if their investors get wind of it before we can fix it.

At the terror of this thought, my brain finally snaps back and straight into problem-solving mode.

"What about underpinning?" I ask. "Or anchors?"

"He's talking to Marco, but that would require a fairly extensive redesign based on the existing build plan," he replies. "Which could take months."

"Can they dig down? Replace foundation soil?" I press.

Jackson shrugs. "I don't know," he says honestly. "It was Marco who called, I think they're still reacting to the situation."

"Reacting or panicking?" Ellie mutters.

"I'm so sorry, Sera, I don't know how this happened. I can go look through the paperwork and try to figure out what went wrong."

I stop Jackson by holding my hand up. "That can wait. I'm sure they're doing what they can to see if there's a way to move forward on the plot they purchased, but weren't there other options?" I ask.

"Yes, three," he replies. "We offered on one as a backup but withdrew when we put the preferred parcel under contract."

"Find out which of those, if any, are still available and get me the selling agents on the phone as soon as possible," I instruct. "In the meantime, I want both of your sets of eyes on those alternatives checking every detail. Be ready to assist their team with whatever paperwork they'll need to move forward on another site."

"Sure thing, boss," Jackson replies. "I have copies of the permits they pulled. I'll create the applications and grease the wheels for anything still available."

Jackson and Ellie start to leave.

"Oh, and Jackson?" I call after him. He pauses at the door. "When did they get the soil samples back?"

"This morning," he replies.

I nod grimly, and they scurry off to begin damage control. I take a deep breath and pick up the phone to call Alessandro.

"Serafina," he answers on the first ring. "You've heard." His warm, rough voice bears no trace of anger, just gloomy exhaustion.

Hearing him again stirs something deep inside me, but I suppress it and try to focus. "Yes," I reply, my voice cracking anyway. "I can't imagine how busy you must be right now, but I wanted to let you know that we'll do everything we can from our end to get you back on schedule. And then we'll figure out how the hell this happened."

He doesn't respond for a moment. "I appreciate that," he finally says, and I let out my breath.

I stop myself from asking all the questions that are running through my brain and ask simply, "What do you need?"

He sighs heavily. "I don't suppose 'you' is an acceptable answer?"

I want to laugh and cry in equal measure, but I stay silent, holding back tears.

"I didn't think so," he mutters. "I don't know, we're still in discovery mode. Marco and Giovanni are doing everything they can. I don't have anything to share with our investors yet, and even if I did I don't want to breathe a word of it to them until I have a plan. I feel pretty useless right now."

"I'm so sorry," I reply, blinking the moisture from my eyes. I clear my voice. "Jackson tells me there were alternative parcels. We're looking into their current statuses and starting the paperwork across the board to push forward on whatever we can lock down as soon as possible."

"I'm not sure that's necessary until we know the full situation here," he replies doubtfully.

"I'm not leaving anything to chance," I insist. "I am going to make sure you have every option available to you, to your investors. You are not going to take this hit alone while I'm here. We are going to aggressively pursue every path to get you back on track as soon as humanly possible. Or faster, if I have anything to do with it."

"*Grazie mille*," he responds. "We'll have additional members of our team here by this evening, so we should have the bandwidth to keep you better informed soon."

"We'll throw everyone we've got at this too, whatever you need, just ask," I assure him. I chew on my last question for a moment before uttering it. "Alessandro, why didn't you call me when you found out?"

He takes a while to reply. "Because nothing was worth hurting you over if you didn't want to hear from me," he responds.

The depth of his regard for my feelings slams into me like a brick wall. He'd stake *millions* of dollars and his company, his reputation, on not disturbing my emotional state? Part of me wants to shake him for his lack of consideration for his employees, for himself. But mostly it cracks the door open on the well of anguish I've locked away deep inside. And it reminds me how much he really had worked his way into my heart.

Because even though I've done everything I can to erase our time together from my mind and heart, in this moment I realize I love him more than I ever have, and I miss him so completely that I can't contain the tears any longer. They spill over my cheeks, mourning what can't be.

"Serafina?" he asks after a moment. "Are you okay?"

I laugh wryly. "I'm fine, Alessandro," I reply thickly. *And by FINE, I mean Fucked up, Insecure, Neurotic, and Emotional.* "Talk to you soon."

∾

JACKSON, ELLIE, AND I WORK LATE INTO THE EVENING FILLING out forms and reviewing data. At eleven p.m. I call it for the evening and thank them for their help.

Sitting at my desk, I shuffle through the stack of papers, reviewing our progress so far. Given the enormity of what's at stake, even the considerable progress we've made just doesn't feel like enough. While we have verbal acceptance on the two properties that are still available, even a fast cash close could take as much as a few weeks. And that's assuming the site inspections that we've preordered confirm our previous data with no additional surprises. And the stack of permits is all completed, but even with our usual contacts in the appropriate places, getting through bureaucracy in a hurry is a crapshoot.

I turn away from the stacks, staring into the night and trying to find peace in this storm. The challenges in front of us are not insurmountable. I'm not even all that concerned about the potential further damage to our company's reputation. I think we've demonstrated our resiliency at this point.

The pile of cash I'll be personally doling out for this doesn't even faze me. I've always known if it came down to it I'd use every penny I had to save my company. And if I can't save our relationship, it's the least I can do, I suppose.

And like a flash, I finally realize what's really bothering me most of all. Alessandro is hurting. And I can't be there for him. At least, not in the way that we both yearn for. I shake the thought from my head, fighting my natural instincts to try to save us. These are the repercussions of his choices. He's made his bed, and now he gets to lie in it alone.

First thing on Wednesday I transmit the offers and permitting paperwork, and arrange for all the necessary same-day wire transfers. I wait patiently and am rewarded with offer acceptances by lunchtime. This is where the real work begins.

For the remainder of the week I have all twelve of my project managers working on coordinating with Buone Case, the selling agents on inspections, the title company on paperwork, the city and county on permitting, and the chasing of countless other details. Everyone is bustling in a full-court press, working against the clock to help re-secure Alessandro's company's future.

After lunch on Friday I get a text from Bryce. *Can't wait to see you tonight. Hope your week is good.*

Shit. Amidst the scramble, I had completely forgotten our date, and we have so much more to do before I can even think about going home, much less anything else. My fingers fly over the keys, texting him back.

Bryce, I'm so sorry, I completely forgot. We've had a major issue this week that has occupied my full attention. Rain check?

My phone rings a moment later, and Bryce's concern is apparent in his greeting. "Hey, you okay?" he asks.

"Mostly," I reply. "I'll explain it all later. It's just a mess, and we're under a time crunch."

"Don't forget to take care of yourself, Sera," he reminds me gently. "Have you eaten anything today?"

I have to think about that for a minute, and I realize the answer is no. "I'll eat when I get home," I reply impatiently. "I really am sorry. It would've been nice to take a break from all of this."

"Hmmm. How about this? I'll come to you and make you dinner while you work. You can take a few minutes to eat, and then I'll get to see you and I'll know you at least got one square meal in this week," he offers.

I can't help but chuckle appreciatively at his persistence. "You can cook?" I ask skeptically.

"Hey, I'll have you know I make a mean bowl of spaghetti," he jokes.

"How can I say no to that?" I tease. "I'll tell you what. If you can wait until nine I'm all yours. You're right, I do need a break. And a low-key dinner at home sounds perfect."

"I can't wait," Bryce says eagerly, all sunshine and cheer once again. "See you later, Sera."

Amazingly, by eight we've done everything we can do for the day anyway, so I send everyone home. I shut everything off and wearily trudge home myself.

∾

ONCE I'M BACK IN MY SUITE, I DECIDE TO TAKE A QUICK shower before Bryce arrives. As the heat soothes my tired body, I try to clear my mind of all the stress of the week. The hot water runs out before I'm able to achieve that goal, though.

I sigh resignedly and step out to dry off and dress.

As I'm sliding on a long-sleeved, red shirtdress over black leggings, the doorbell rings. I pad quickly to answer it, opening the door to Bryce and his usual sunshine-smile.

"Hey, Bryce," I greet him, grabbing one of the bags he's carrying. "Come in, let me help you."

"Thanks, Sera." He grins, and we deposit the groceries in the kitchen.

"I need to finish getting ready," I admit. "You okay here?"

"You bet," he assures me. I turn to leave, and he calls out, "Hey, Sera?" I turn, and he quickly closes the short distance between us, leaning in and kissing me briefly, sweetly. "Hi."

I smile. "Hey," I reply.

He laughs and returns to the kitchen, and I head off to dry my hair.

As we finish the remnants of our meal, I sigh contentedly. "This was exactly what I needed. Thanks, Bryce." I polish off my wine and push back my plate.

"I'm glad you liked it," he replies, taking the dishes to the kitchen.

"Hey," I protest, "you cooked! I'm supposed to do that."

He comes back wagging a finger at me. "Not tonight. You've had a hard week." He offers me a hand, which I take gladly, and uses it to lead me to the couch. "Why don't you tell me more about it?"

I flop down next to him, eyeing him skeptically. "You really want me to bore you with all that?"

"I couldn't be bored around you if I tried, Sera."

I shrug. "Okay," I reply.

As he rubs my shoulders, I spend the next fifteen minutes giving him more than the brief highlights I'd mentioned over dinner and answering the occasional question. He's very attentive and interested, and it does feel good to process things verbally with someone who doesn't have an emotional stake in it.

As I finish my story, he strokes my hand with his thumb thoughtfully. "You really just have had all manner of bad luck lately, haven't you?" he asks, frowning.

I laugh drily. "That's one way to put it," I reply. "But when it rains, it pours I guess, right? Tell me about your week."

"My week was pretty dull," he says. "Mostly just meetings, filing briefs, that sort of thing. I thought about you a lot."

He squeezes my hand gently and I blush. He moves his hand to my chin and turns my face toward his. I look up into his eyes nervously. They are a deep, glittering blue and fixed intently on my face, eyeing my lips hungrily. I can read the desire in his expression, feel it in the heat that has suddenly sprung up between us, and I suddenly realize I'm not ready for more. Not yet.

I pull away gently, scooting back into the couch and out of his embrace. His expression shifts quickly to embarrassed understanding.

"I'm sorry," he offers softly. "I didn't mean to …"

"No, please, don't. It's not …" I stop myself from saying, *It's not you, it's me.* I take a deep breath and start again. "You have nothing to apologize for. I appreciate that you care about me. I care about you too. It's just been a shitty time. And I'm easily overwhelmed these days." It's mostly true, anyway, and the kindest way I can think to keep him at a safe distance.

He studies my face intently, chewing on his bottom lip. "I don't want to overwhelm you," he finally says. "Why don't we call it a night?"

He starts to rise from the couch and my gut twists unpleasantly at the thought of leaving things like this. I grab his wrist, pulling him back down to sit next to me.

"Stay, please," I plead. "Let's just watch a movie or something."

His sunshine smile appears, crinkling the corners of his eyes. I smile back, relieved, and sink gratefully into the crook of his arm as we settle in to find something *else* to entertain us.

TWENTY-ONE

I'm woken by the sun filtering in the living room windows behind us and the muted sound of a jet overhead. As my eyes adjust, I realize I'm lying against Bryce, who is slumped back into the couch, legs up on the ottoman in front of him. His face is peaceful in sleep, and his long, heavy arm is draped around me. The TV plays lowly still, and I gingerly stretch my limbs, trying to shake out the sore stiffness of having fallen asleep in such an awkward position.

Contemplating how best to extricate myself, I'm somehow drawn back into thinking about my situation. Bryce was right about one thing last night — it's been a shitty time for me. I've been stolen from, sabotaged, lost a major client, gained another under shaky terms, and now I've somehow failed someone I care deeply for in a career-ending way. It's almost too much to be chance.

My heart jumps into my throat as a realization hits me. As if my brain had been working on the connection all night.

It's not a coincidence. It's more sabotage.

I shake Bryce awake. He stirs sleepily and cracks a broad smile.

"Good morning, gorgeous," he greets me, stretching widely and releasing me from being pinned next to him.

"I realized something," I say urgently, sitting up. My tone shifts his mood and he sits up beside me, alert. "It was sabotage, Bryce. Somebody tampered with that soil report."

He scratches his neck and considers me, clearly unconvinced. "That's a big leap, Sera," he replies slowly, clearly still waking up. "What makes you think that's the case?"

"A million reasons," I say, my words toppling quickly out. "It's just too much of a coincidence, this all happening in such a short time. Those reports would be easy to fake. Ms. Stanwood had full access to our systems, and her last week there was when we were pulling all the due diligence reports for Buone Case's deal. But most of all, I just know it, Bryce. I feel it."

He studies me carefully for a minute as he adjusts his rumpled shirt. "Okay," he says. "I'll investigate it."

"Thank you," I reply, grateful that he's finally taking me seriously.

He laughs and musses my hair. "You know I trust you," he says, and I cock an eyebrow skeptically. "If you think this was sabotage, you're probably right. I'll find the evidence if it's there. First thing Monday morning we'll get our digital forensic experts on it. We'll probably need your help, of course, but they should be able to determine if that was the case."

I hug him tightly. "Thanks, Bryce." Pulling back, I look hard at him, wishing I wasn't in this place. Wishing I'd met him some other time.

My cellphone rings, interrupting my thoughts. I grab it from the side table. It's Alessandro.

"*Buongiorno*," I greet him, simultaneously signaling to Bryce who my caller is.

He grimaces but takes the hint and heads to the bathroom.

"*Buongiorno*," Alessandro greets me. "I just wanted to let you know that we concluded negotiations with our second choice this morning. They're going to allow us to do all our preparatory work ahead of closing. Assuming all goes to plan, we may only start two to three weeks later than planned."

I sigh in relief. "That's great news, Alessandro," I reply. "And please assure your investors that we will cover any additional costs due to the delay."

"What's that going to do to your company, Sera?" His voice is filled with concern. "Do you have that kind of cash?"

I realize I never told Alessandro about my inherited empire. "My company does not," I admit. "But I do. Don't worry about it."

He's quiet as he processes that I'm personally paying to save him. *Yes, you jackass, that's what you screwed up.*

"You've been amazing through this, Sera," he responds, his

voice full of affection and sorrow. "I don't know how I would have handled this without you."

I bite my lip, unsure of how to respond. "You wouldn't have been in this mess if it weren't for me," I finally reply.

"Don't," he protests. "It was a mistake. I'm sure we'll figure out how it happened."

"I'm pretty sure I know how it happened," I interrupt.

"What do you mean?"

"I've been so busy fixing it, it only just hit me," I tell him. "It was more sabotage, Alessandro."

He takes merely a beat to process that. "Fuck. You're right," he breathes.

His innate trust causes a wave of grief to pass through me. "We're going to prove it, and we're going to stop these bastards," I promise him. "But in the meantime, please be careful. I'm not sure what else the saboteurs may have up their sleeve and I could never forgive myself if anything happened to you."

"Sera, I…" the rest of Alessandro's words are drowned out as Bryce steps out of the bathroom.

"You don't happen to have an extra toothbrush, do you?" he asks.

I facepalm internally and gesture fiercely at the cupboard next to the bathroom door. Bryce retrieves his quarry and disappears back into the bathroom.

The line is silent.

"Are you still there?" I ask timidly.

"I'm here," Alessandro replies tightly, and I know he's heard Bryce. "I didn't know you were occupied. I'll let you go. Take care, Serafina."

I start to protest. But he's already gone.

∽

On Sunday afternoon Allie and I stroll through the mall, lugging our retail spoils. Between stores I've just managed to fill her in on the events from Friday night into Saturday morning.

"God, Sera, I don't know which issue to unpack first," she says, slumping down on a bench and releasing her bags.

"Yes, you do," I tease, sitting down next to her.

"You're right," she replies. "Are you sure you're ready to date this guy?"

I inhale deeply. "No?" I admit. "But I kind of am already." I groan dramatically. "What do I doooo?"

"Geez, Sera, what a conundrum," Allie mockingly ponders. "Yet *another* gorgeous guy beating down your door — one who's *not* already taken — who is willing to take it as slow as you want. What's the problem again?"

"I know, it sounds ridiculous," I allow. "I *do* like him. We get along well. I'm totally comfortable around him. But I'm just not ready. It's only been a few weeks."

"I guess," she responds. "But you and Alessandro only dated for, what? Like a month? So, a few weeks is more than half of the relationship and you know the rule." She smiles teasingly.

I smile back wryly. "You mean the 'It takes half the length of the relationship to get over it' hypothesis? Aside from that being complete, fabricated bullshit, I've never been one to pay much attention to the rules anyway," I remind her. And some people affect you more deeply than others. I sigh deeply and come to a decision. "I'm just not ready. And I don't want to string Bryce along."

"No, that wouldn't be very nice," she agrees.

We sit silently for a moment as I suppress the urge to run through the consequences of that decision. The potential for losing Bryce altogether. Thankfully, Allie interrupts my reverie before I can get too far.

"So, you really think Megan and her crew are still messing with you?"

"Well, *still* may be an overstatement. That report would have been tampered with ages ago, and it's only now playing out," I explain. "But it does make me scared of what else she might have done."

"Good thing you've got a hunky security guy ready to jump in and help you fight your battles," she remarks. "Maybe you *should* wait to break up with him."

I shove her lightly. "That wouldn't be very nice," I reply mockingly, and she laughs.

On Monday morning my first priority is investigating what happened with the original soil report for Buone Case's deal. We jump in eagerly, sending Bryce everything we have. I push from my mind when and how I will let Bryce down easily. For now, I need to focus, and I need to see if I'm right about what happened. Not that it matters much with Alessandro's next deal moving forward, but I have a foreboding sense of unease, and I need the facts.

After a brief review with my team, we decide that we'll need to request both a digital and hard copy of the original report from the engineering firm, so I have Jackson place the request immediately. The evidence now under examination, there's not much to do but wait for the results of the investigation.

On Tuesday I get a call reminding me that my condo purchase closes the next day. In all the turmoil I'd completely forgotten, and I realize I'll need to have my things delivered this weekend, so I call Bryce to arrange it, even though I still haven't decided how to break things off with him.

"Hey gorgeous," he answers. "How's the day treating you so far?"

"Not bad, you?" I ask.

"Better now that I'm talking to you."

A twinge of guilt wrings in my gut. His being adorably smitten with me is not going to make it easy to dump him.

"Hey, so, my condo closes tomorrow," I say, opting for avoidance.

"Oh? That's quick," he replies.

"Cash purchase," I remind him. "Can we arrange to have my items in storage delivered this weekend?"

"No problem," he assures me. "How about I take you out to celebrate tomorrow night?"

"Okay," I agree reluctantly. A little more than a day to find the words and work up the courage. I swallow hard.

"Great, I'll pick you up at seven?"

"Sure thing."

"Bye, gorgeous," he says brightly.

"See ya, Bryce."

THE NOTARY FROM THE TITLE COMPANY LEAVES MY OFFICE around four p.m. on Wednesday, leaving me with a pile of papers, keys, and a yearning to leave work early to go do cartwheels in my new condo.

After attempting to press through it for another twenty minutes, I give in and pack up for the day and head to my new home.

I lean my head on the warm glass, watching the sun glitter on Elliott Bay. Standing alone in the empty condo, I feel desolation where I expected joy. Something about its barrenness, with the gorgeous views of the city sprawled out around me, just makes me feel isolated and adrift.

The events of the last weeks finally seem to be weighing heavily on my shoulders, and I feel myself spiraling into dangerous territory, as if I'm floating into a tempest. Bryce is supposed to pick me up from my extended-stay suite in two hours, but the thought brings me no pleasure because of what I know I must do.

I pull out my phone, contemplating whether or not to rip off the bandage. I start the call before I can chicken out.

"Hey, gorgeous." Bryce's sunshine radiates through the line.

"Hi," I say softly. "Listen, I can't make dinner."

"No problem," he says smoothly. "Rain check?"

I sigh. "I'm sorry, Bryce, but I think it would be best if we didn't date," I lay it out bluntly.

"Ah."

"You're a great guy," I say, feeling like a cliché, "but I just can't right now."

"I see," he says quietly. "I'm disappointed. But I understand." Something in me senses the lie, but I'm still relieved, beyond belief. "Thanks for giving it a shot." His tone, while wry, is also laced with sadness.

"How could I not?" I muse out loud. He makes a noncommittal noise and, feeling like an ass, I decide it's best to end this conversation as quickly as possible. "See you, Bryce."

"See you, Sera."

Hanging up, I slide to the floor and wrap my arms around my legs. All the feelings I've been suppressing wash through me, and I let the tears flow freely for a few minutes without interference.

When they stop, I wander out of the building, and decide to walk aimlessly for a while. It's rush hour and the bustle of the city around me is strangely calming, my own cares and concerns a drop in the ocean of humanity around me. Cars whiz by, café patrons sip coffee at covered tables along the sidewalk, a street vendor yells loudly to draw people in.

I feel less alone observing the activity around me. I walk past a construction site and manage a fond smile as I watch the workers clean up for the day, their behemoth starting to claw its iron talons toward the sky as the materials come together, magically creating a new economy where once there was none.

After a while my feet stop, and I examine my surroundings. I am not surprised to find myself standing in front of Alessandro's building. I think I knew I was headed here all along, though to what end I cannot say. My mind hasn't changed.

As I exit the elevator I wonder what I hope to accomplish. I'm already angry with myself that I'm asking to make things worse for us both, but my subconscious overrides me and I move forward.

I knock at his door, hoping he doesn't answer. Hoping he's not home.

But the door swings open to reveal him standing there in his black sweats and a black T-shirt, his wet hair longer than it was when I last saw him, his beard thick and overgrown. We stare at each other wordlessly for a moment before he steps back in invitation.

I enter silently, and he closes the door behind me. I turn and he's there, next to me, his dark eyes sad and imploring. Being here with him, I realize it's a lost fight. I need him. He's worked his way in now, and his absence has left a gaping chasm that I've filled with work and other distractions. But ultimately never replacing my need for him. I let out a small, strangled sob and he closes the gap between us, wrapping me in his arms.

I rest my head on his chest and wrap my arms around him. "I'm sorry," I sob quietly. *For being here. For torturing you like this. For saying one thing and wanting another, and somehow expecting you to accept both truths.* And another part of me is riddled with guilt and disgust knowing I'd asked the same of Bryce, and in doing so I might have lost him too.

Alessandro seems to understand my unspoken torment, because he shushes me and holds me tighter, resting his chin on my head as I release my anguish.

After a few minutes he frees me from his arms and slips his hands in mine, pulling me to the bedroom. I resist, fear tearing a hole through my chest, and I shake my head.

"Just to rest, darling," he whispers soothingly.

Reassured, I follow. We lay down next to each other, face to face, and he holds me in his arms, singing softly in Italian. Exhaustion rolls over me and I pass out in Alessandro's arms.

⁓

I'M WOKEN SOONER THAN I'D LIKE BY THE SOFT CARESS OF Alessandro's hands moving along my face.

"Time to wake, *mio tesoro*," he whispers. "If you sleep too much now you won't sleep tonight."

My eyelids flutter open to his deep eyes searching for mine. I can't help but smile sadly, and he smiles back.

"Hi," I say simply.

"*Ciao*," he offers.

And we both laugh.

"I miss you," I say.

"I can tell," he replies, stroking my face. "I miss you more than I can say. But something tells me this isn't our reunion."

"No," I say sadly. "I wish it were, but you know I ..."

"Shhhh," he admonishes me. "I know." He holds my face in his hand. "I can be patient."

I shake my head sadly, and say, "I wish patience was all it took."

"You'll see, *bella*," he assures me. "I think you need me as much as I need you."

I consider denying it, but it's pointless. I'm here. My need for him is obvious.

"I didn't think you'd be happy to see me," I admit.

"Why? Because you're dating the giant?" he asks baldly.

"I'm not dating the giant," I reply crossly.

"Aren't you? I've seen you together with my own eyes," he says darkly. "And you spent the night together."

Again, his accusation is undeniable, but not in the way he thinks.

"I wanted to want to date him," I admit. "But in the end …" — I resist saying, *It's only you I want* — "moving on is more difficult than I thought it would be." He looks at me like he knew exactly what I was going to say anyway, and I pull away, sitting up abruptly. "I shouldn't have come."

"All the same, I'm glad you did," he replies, sitting up next to me. "I told you, I'm not giving up."

"Why not?" I ask, turning toward him earnestly. "You know how I feel."

"Because I know something you don't know," he admits, a smile playing around his lips. "But you've told me you don't want excuses and explanations."

"No, I don't," I agree, angry at only myself. "Believing the words of an eager lover is what got me into this situation."

He laughs at my summary of him. "An eager lover," his tongue caresses the words and he runs his finger along his chin as he considers them. "Yes, I suppose I am that. For you."

He fixes me with his intense stare, and I feel the heat rising inside me.

"Come, I think it's time you go before I can't resist you any longer," he prompts.

I give a small smile of agreement and follow him to the door.

"You know I'm here for you, whenever you need me," he promises.

"I know," I respond. I give him a last, lingering look.

He grabs my hand and pulls me into one last hug, kissing the top of my head. Goodbye too painful a word to utter, we part in silence.

TWENTY-TWO

"Show me the counteroffer," I instruct Ellie and Jackson. They hand me the stack of papers and I scan through them. A few lines catch my eye and I look up at Ellie. "This reads like they have another bidder."

Ellie shifts uncomfortably. "Yes, we think they do," she admits.

"You know that's a whole different ball game," I chide. "Why didn't you mention that up front?"

Ellie shrugs. "I wasn't sure," she replies. "And I didn't want to give more than we had to."

I rub my neck, frustrated. For all of Ellie's knowledge, she often lacks tenacity.

"Ellie, we don't have room to dick around here," I say, cutting to the chase. "I'll have a serious conversation with the seller's agent and will find out if they have another bidder and, if I can, who it is. You guys need to ask Sutton what their limits are if you don't already know." I pause, frustrated. "This is a very important account, and this is the only property that Sutton is interested in. So next time, if you need help, don't wait so long to ask."

I pick up my handset, dismissing Ellie and Jackson, and make the call.

$\backsim$

AS I'M WRAPPING UP A PHONE CALL WITH THE REAL ESTATE agent representing Sutton's competing bidder, Jackson pokes his head back into my office and I gesture for him to sit while I finish.

"Well, if that's their plan, I think I'm able to see that we both get what we want, Jake," I say.

"How's that?" he asks, curious.

I've known Jake Roberts for years and he's never one to turn down a deal.

"I have a client that recently purchased a property that meets your client's specs, but they ended up going with a different site," I reply. "I guarantee you that he will wholesale you that property if you'll withdraw your bid. Everyone wins."

"Send me the paperwork," he responds. "And if it lines up, we've got a deal."

"You got it, Jake," I reply. "Pleasure doing business with you. Talk soon."

"Bye, Sera."

I hang up the phone and yelp triumphantly.

"Did you just do what I think you just did?" Jackson asks, his eyes wide.

"If you think I just baited the competing bidder out of being interested in the same property as Sutton Developments and into buying the property Buone Case won't be able to use, I sure as fuck did," I say matter-of-factly, and Jackson laughs. "You can let Mr. Giordano know when you're done here. Now, what can I do for you, Jackson?"

"Well, I had Mr. Sutton's bottom line figures for you, but it sounds like that may be moot now," he offers.

"Indeed," I agree. "And once I've locked down Jake's client, I think we should play hardball on Mr. Sutton's offer." I grin mischievously, enjoying the mounting victories.

⌒

BY THE END OF THE DAY ON FRIDAY, JAKE'S CLIENT IS LOCKED into a purchase and sale on Alessandro's original property with minimal loss, and the offer paperwork has been submitted for the plot that Sutton Developments is after. With things shaping up nicely, I call it a day and head out to start moving into my new condo.

⌒

On Saturday the relocation techs move all my old furniture in. Moving into twice the space, everything I have looks small and inadequate in its new setting, and I realize I'm going to have to do some major shopping to make this place feel like home. Rather cheered by the thought, I call Allie and ask if she wants to go with me to the local big-box furniture store.

"Seriously?" she asks when I make my proposal.

"Yes, Allie, I happen to appreciate fine, build-it-yourself Swedish furniture," I reply.

"Really?"

"Actually, yes. I know it's silly, but I find it extremely satisfying to put a piece of furniture together," I admit. "Plus, walking around that place is practically a workout. Two birds, one stone!"

Allie laughs. "All right," she concedes. "But I might have a hard time convincing David he can't come. He loves that place."

"The more, the merrier," I respond.

"Okay," she agrees. "Pick us up in half an hour?"

"You got it."

"So what kind of look are you going for?" Allie asks, turning a blue throw pillow in her hands.

"White," I respond immediately. "Lots of white." The color of perfection.

Allie raises her eyebrows. "Clearly you aren't planning on having children," she jokes.

"Not any time soon," I reply. "Missing one key element to make that happen."

David waves a hand airily. "Aren't there places to take care of that part these days?"

I give him a funny look. "Like a bordello?"

Allie laughs. "I think he meant like a sperm bank. Do they even have bordellos here? And do bordellos even have dudes?"

David shakes his head. "Forget I said anything. I'm not touching any of that with a ten-foot pole."

"I bet they have those at bordellos too," I joke, and Allie whacks me with the pillow, rolling her eyes.

"Seriously, Sera, you should think about the future," Allie presses. "Even if you don't have kids, maybe you'll want to get a dog or a cat or something. Pets and white furniture don't mix either."

"Allie, you know I'm not prone to ostentatious displays of wealth," I reply. "But given my finances, I think I could probably afford to replace a houseful of this furniture without too much trouble."

"That's not the point," she persists. "It's about having the *option*."

I stop in front of a display of potted plants. "I suddenly get the feeling this has nothing to do with me," I say suspiciously. "What's up, Allie?"

Allie looks askance at David and he shrugs. She looks back at me and presses her lips together. "I'm pregnant, Sera," she admits, beaming.

I freeze for a moment, my eyes wide. She looks at me curiously, waiting for me to react.

I shriek loudly and throw my arms around her. She shrieks too and suddenly we're jumping up and down together, laughing.

"Congratulations, you guys!" I scream, pulling David into the huddle.

He begrudgingly joins our hug. "But I'm not jumping up and down," he protests, and Allie and I laugh.

Releasing them both, I hold her at arm's length. "You look happy," I decide.

She nods excitedly. "We're *so* happy," she gushes. She and David share a loving look and a small stab of pain radiates through my chest, causing my smile to disappear.

I turn away and start walking again to disguise my reaction. "Well, don't worry," I assure her. "Your baby can come mess up my white furniture anytime."

"Gee, thanks," Allie replies sardonically. "That won't make me feel like a jerk at all."

"So, should we be looking at baby stuff while we're here?" I ask, plastering a smile back on my lips and facing her.

"Oh no, it's way too early for that," she responds. "But if

you want, we can start talking about the new paid maternity leave program I'm thinking of implementing." She winks slyly at me and loops her arm through mine as we continue our shopping.

∾

THAT EVENING I SIT AMONG PILES OF BOXES, THOUGH I'VE long since lost the will to unpack. I decide to give up and collapse into the lone armchair I've pointed at the wall of windows in the living room. I turn the lights off, grab a glass of wine, and sink into the chair to watch the glow of the city out the window.

As I sip my wine I recall the look that Allie and David shared, their love and connection on full display to the world. I wonder suddenly if Alessandro used to look at Peyton like that. If knowing she was pregnant has changed anything between them for the better.

And for the first time I wonder what the story is there, and why he's so convinced it would make a difference. Because if David ever did to Allie what Alessandro has done to Peyton, I'd kill him.

But the fact remains that Alessandro fills my thoughts more than I like. And that moving on from him might be nearly impossible. That I might get sucked right back in, despite my deep moral objections. It seems like an irresolvable conundrum.

I drain my wine glass and look around my spectacular new

apartment, at the gorgeous view of Seattle sprawled out at my feet, realizing it's a hollow enjoyment without someone to share it with.

∽

EXHAUSTED AND DISHEARTENED, I SPEND SUNDAY IN A FOG, allowing myself a day of wallowing while I assemble and arrange my new furniture. But Monday morning I am determined to get back on the horse.

Thankfully, the day starts well, with the acceptance of Sutton Development's offer. I've decided to take a more hands-on approach in supervising Ellie and Jackson to ensure that Mr. Sutton is nothing less than fully satisfied with our performance.

"I want to personally deliver the earnest monies to the title company," I instruct Ellie and Jackson.

"So, are all three of us going to Sutton Developments, then?" Jackson asks, confused.

"That might be a bit much," Ellie remarks, and I have to agree.

"Just one of us is fine. I'd like to personally reassure Mr. Sutton anyway, so I can handle it," I reply.

As I leave my office I find Lucy seated at Maggie's desk, peering expectantly at me as I exit my office. She must have heard us talking.

"Lucy!" I exclaim in surprise. "Where's Maggie?"

"Hello, Ms. Evans," she replies. "Maggie's off today, remember? She put in for it a few weeks ago."

"Oh," I reply. I did not remember that, but then with everything going on, that's not surprising. "Okay, thank you for reminding me."

"Of course, Ms. Evans," she replies, smiling. "There are only a few things she asked me to look after today. I'll be in reception most of the time, so if you need any help you can find me there."

"Thanks, Lucy," I respond. "I'll be back in a bit."

"Sure thing, Ms. Evans," she responds.

∽

MR. SUTTON IS IN A FINE MOOD, AND HE'S DROPPING compliments like candy. I hand him his copies of the completed offer paperwork.

"Ms. Evans, against the odds, you've impressed me," he admits, taking the papers and handing me the earnest money check in turn. I take it, trying not to show my disapproval — despite my trying to convince him to use electronic transfer, he's simply a creature of habit. "Your redirection of Puget Sound Realty's interest not only garnered us the parcel but also at a lower price than we'd expected to commit to."

I slip the check into a zippered compartment in my folio and zip my folio into my bag.

"It was my pleasure, Mr. Sutton," I respond, straightening

up. "I'm glad we've exceeded your expectations and sincerely hope that we continue to do so."

"Indeed, young lady," he replies. He extends his hand, and I shake it cordially. "And it was a pleasure seeing you again."

"Thank you, sir, you as well," I respond. "We'll be in touch soon."

∾

It's almost noon when I arrive at the title company to find that their escrow officer has taken lunch. Unfortunately, there's nobody else to accept the deposit, so I return to my office until I'm able to come back in the afternoon, cursing Mr. Sutton's insistence on using a physical check.

Thankfully, the afternoon passes in a blur of spreadsheets and meetings, and I'm able to just escape in time to make it back to the title company before they close at five. Handing the check to the escrow officer gives me a great sense of relief and accomplishment, and I head straight home after, more exhausted than usual.

∾

A good shower and a hot meal have left me relatively relaxed and calm, so when my mother calls I find I'm actually pleased at the opportunity to catch up.

"Hi, Mom," I answer.

"Sera, dear, how are you?" she asks.

"It's been an interesting week, but I'm okay," I reply. "How are you?"

"Good, good, honey," she replies vaguely. "I just wanted to make sure you are okay. I enjoyed having you home, but you hadn't visited in so long. I'm worried about you is all. And with everything I told you, I just wanted to check in."

"Thanks, Mom, I appreciate it," I respond tiredly. "Is that all?"

"No," she says nervously. "After we talked about your dad I did a lot of thinking. About how mad you were that I didn't tell you sooner, and how I kept him and your brother away from you for so long."

My interest piqued, I scoot anxiously into a sitting position. "I'm not sure where you're going with this," I reply nervously.

"I know where they are, Sera," she finally says plainly. "And how to contact them. If you wanted to reach out."

I'm shocked into silence. With everything going on I hadn't even thought about it, and I'm not sure what to say.

"Are you still there?" my mom asks.

"Yes, I'm here," I whisper. "I just don't know what to do with that."

"It's okay, honey, I just wanted to tell you that it's okay with me if you do want to try to get in touch," she replies.

My brain starts to catch up. "How do you even know where they are?"

"After your father left, his mother, your Grandma Evans,

would still call occasionally," she explains. "We never talked about your father, just you mostly. So, I called her after you left, and we finally had the chat we probably should have had years ago as well."

"Wow, Mom," I reply, stunned at the continued fount of new information. "Are you okay?"

I'm also more than a little awed that my failed relationship has somehow led my mother down this path. I've never heard her so selflessly concerned about me, and she's more than scaled back on all the nastiness that's had me keeping her at arm's length all these years. At least something good seems to be coming out of it.

"Absolutely, Sera, don't be ridiculous," she says. "This is all for you. I've made my peace with it years ago." I roll my eyes.

"Whatever you say, Mom," I respond.

"Anyway, she was happy to tell me what your dad and brother have been up to, where they are, the whole nine yards," she explains.

"And you're suddenly magically okay with me talking to Dad?" I ask skeptically.

She takes a moment to respond. "I can't say I'm thrilled about the prospect, no," she admits. "But if it's what you want, then I'll learn to be. I don't want us to go backward, Sera. I feel like we've started to mend things between us, so this is me showing you that I want to be in your life, on your terms."

My eyes fill with tears. Despite the years of difficulty

getting along with my mother, she's still my mom and I've always wanted exactly this. It's another bittersweet and unexpected positive that's come of the mess that is my life right now.

"That means more to me than you know," I tell her, my voice thick and strained. "But I don't think now is the time. Maybe someday. But it's nice to know I have the option."

"Just let me know," she promises. "Love you, kiddo."

"Love you too, Mom."

TWENTY-THREE

First thing Tuesday morning I call to check in with Bryce, as usual.

"Sera," he greets me, his tone grave.

My heart sinks in my chest. "What's up, Bryce? Everything okay?"

"We need to meet with you today. At our offices," he replies cryptically. "When can you and Will make it in?"

"Will doesn't usually get in until around nine, but pretty much any time after that that you're ready for us," I respond.

"Good, we'll see you at nine thirty then?"

"Absolutely," I reply, mystified and deeply concerned.

∽

WILL IS A BUNDLE OF NERVES AS WE'RE SHOWN TO A conference room next to Bryce's office. Bryce and a slight, sandy-haired man in his mid-twenties are hunched over a laptop when we enter, seemingly hooking it into the projection system.

They both rise as we approach the table.

"Hey, Sera," Bryce greets me, a shadow of his usual smile plastered on his face. "Thanks for getting here so quickly."

"Of course," I reply as calmly as I can, but my stomach is tied in knots.

Bryce gestures to the man next to him. "This is Paul Mullins, the IT specialist assigned to your account," he says.

I extend my hand and Paul takes it, his grip soft and tentative. "Nice to meet you, Ms. Evans," he says politely. "Good to see you, Will."

Will nods to Paul and we all settle around the table.

"Okay, Bryce, you know me," I state. "Let's get whatever is going on out on the table please." I'm not one to show my anxiety, but the tension is killing me, and I'm fidgeting like crazy.

Bryce gestures for Paul to go ahead, and Paul kicks on the overhead projector.

"I'll take you through our findings," Paul begins. "Will has seen some of this, but we have a good deal more to add to our briefing from last week, much of it of key concern ..."

This guy is going to put me in an early grave. I shoot Bryce a deeply impatient look.

"Paul, I'm going to give them the short version first, if you don't mind," Bryce interrupts. Paul shrugs in response and nods his head. "Our initial data seemed to confirm Will's findings, and that all of the tampering originated from one computer — the one in reception. However, that machine is clearly used by most of the staff for various purposes, so that doesn't give us much."

"Have you confirmed that the soil report was tampered with?" I ask.

"Yes," Bryce verifies. "Portions of a report from another file were pasted over the original file. The hard copy and digital copy originals confirm the results showed completely different soil properties. The report was clearly doctored to make that parcel appear as the most attractive option."

"Well, at least we know that's what happened," I reply with a sigh.

"Yes, you were right," he agrees. "But that's not the worst of it." Bryce takes a deep breath. "Last night we found monitoring software embedded in one of your in-house report processes. The process itself was one of several designed to pull data from almost every system you run, from financials to customer reports to payroll, for various metrics and reports. The monitoring software was designed to raw-dump that data through external means."

"Are you telling me that someone still has access to everything we've got?" I clarify.

"That's exactly what I'm telling you," Bryce responds. He glances sidelong at Paul. "But what I haven't told you yet is that the software was installed *after* you fired Megan Stanwood."

Will curses loudly and all the color drains from his face. I try my best not to panic.

"You have a mole, Sera," Bryce says.

"So, her partner is still working at my company?" I'm trying to wrap my head around this.

Will starts shaking his head. "Nobody else in the company could have helped her with the original software sabotage," he says, his voice unsteady. "And she couldn't have written that spyware herself either."

"She has *two* accomplices?" I gasp.

"At least," Paul says. "But this isn't all bad."

"What the hell does that mean?" I ask hotly.

Bryce raises an eyebrow and Paul shrinks back, clearly startled by my vehemence.

"I'm sorry," I apologize quickly, "this is all a lot to handle. Please, go on."

"It means that if they're monitoring you, that gives us an opening to monitor them," Paul clarifies. "It means that we can catch whoever this is red-handed."

"Well, I like that idea," I admit. "But doesn't that mean we have to keep letting them spy on us?"

"Only until they attempt their next data dump," Bryce says. "Once they initiate that, the police will be there to arrest them before it's finished."

"I can live with that," I reply. "Will?"

And nervous, shrinking Will leans forward, his face twisted in anger and responds, "Let's nail the fuckers." We all laugh despite ourselves.

"Paul, why don't you run through the particulars with Will," Bryce suggests. "Sera, I'd like a word with you in my office while they do that, if you don't mind."

"Of course," I agree, secretly pleased to not be subjected to the fine detail but a little apprehensive about being alone with Bryce.

Nonetheless, I follow him out of the conference room and into his office. He closes the door and takes a seat on the wide sofa opposite his desk, gesturing for me to join him. I sit down a careful distance away.

"Do you trust Will?" Bryce asks, getting to the point quickly.

"You think he's helping Ms. Stanwood?" I respond, surprised.

"He seems awfully nervous," Bryce points out. "Is he always like that?"

"Wouldn't you be if you were him?" I scoff. "But yes, he does have a rather nervous personality. He doesn't do particularly well under pressure."

Bryce considers that for a moment. "Has he had any unexplained absences lately?"

I frown uncertainly. "I don't think so," I reply. "What does that have to do with anything?"

"Your inside man or woman is going to be anxious," he

responds. "They're going to be trying their hardest to act normally, but it's a high-stakes situation. They're going to be doing things differently than normal whether they are conscious of it or not. They'll be out of their routine."

"Maggie was gone on Monday," I reflect. "Do you think she did it too?"

"Come on, Sera," Bryce chides. "I'm trying to help."

"Okay, okay," I agree. "You're right, I'm sorry."

"I haven't seen you behave like this. Ever."

My eyebrows shoot together. "Behave like what, exactly?" I ask sharply.

He gestures to me. "Like that. Snappy. Rude."

There he goes saying exactly what's on his mind again. Normally, it's one of the things I appreciate most about him. Right now, it's just annoying. Though I suppose he has a point.

"I don't know who to trust anymore," I admit. "I guess it's getting to me a little. I'm sorry."

"It's okay, Sera, it's understandable. But you do have at least one person. Talk to Allie," Bryce urges. "You trust her beyond the shadow of a doubt, right?"

"Absolutely," I reply unequivocally.

"Good," he says. "But don't talk to anyone else about this. And make sure Will does the same. You don't want them to know you're onto them. Also, ask Allie for the attendance records for anyone who has accessed that computer since this started." He pauses. "I'll be honest, that's more than seventy-five percent of your employees, but if we can piece this together sooner rather than waiting for them to strike again, so much the better."

I take a deep breath and nod in agreement. "Okay, I can do that," I say.

"I've appended all of this to your police report as well," he adds. "Everything is documented. I've been assured that based on the evidence that the police are ready to respond when we notify them that the hacker has triggered another data dump."

"That's great, thanks," I reply, rubbing the back of my neck.

"Are you going to be okay, Sera?"

I smile sadly at him. "I'll be fine," I say softly. "Thanks, Bryce. Are you going to be okay?"

He smiles sadly back. "I don't know," he admits. "Probably."

"You know I wish ..."

He cuts me off. "I know. Me too. Please, don't worry about it. You've got enough going on. I'm still in your corner, Sera."

I shake my head to fight the tears stinging the back of my eyes. "I don't deserve your loyalty, Bryce, but you have no idea how much I appreciate it."

His expression softens, and he grabs my hands, pulling me into a bear hug. "You deserve it, and more," he murmurs into my hair. He doesn't hold me long before letting me fall back into my place on the couch beside him.

"Come on," he says, standing with a menacing scowl. "I'd like to have a conversation with Will about keeping his trap shut long enough to catch these bastards. Think he'll be able to manage it?"

I laugh. "If you keep up that tough act, he'll be too afraid to cross you," I assure him.

"Me? I'm a teddy bear," he smiles his sunshine smile and winks at me.

"*I* know that," I reply. "But I promise I won't tell Will." I wink back, and we head out of his office together.

As soon as we're back in the ERS office, I go to Allie.

"Busy?" I ask, poking my head around her door.

"Nothing that can't wait," she replies, motioning for me to come in. I enter, closing the door behind me, sinking gratefully into a chair. "You look pooped."

"I am pooped," I reply sullenly. "But we're getting closer to sorting out this sabotage bullshit."

"Oh?" she asks. "Do tell."

I explain everything Bryce told me this morning, including describing how the attendance reports may help point us to the culprit.

She looks skeptical. "I can give you all of that by the end of the day, but I don't think it's going to help," she says.

"Why not?" I ask.

She shrugs. "I keep a pretty close eye on things around here, and I haven't noticed any strange comings or goings," she replies. "But if it'll make Bryce feel like we're being proactive, it can't hurt, I guess."

"At this point, Allie, I'll do anything," I respond. "He's right. It's best if we can resolve this before anything else happens."

"You're both right," she relents. "Like I said, it can't hurt. I'll let you know as soon as I'm able to pull the data together."

"Thanks, Allie," I respond. "Will can send you the list of employees."

I leave her to it, going back to my office to distract myself with other work.

But by midnight my eyes are dry and sore, and I'm ready to agree with Allie. There just isn't anything in the attendance reports or employee files that seems out of the ordinary. Unless there's something I'm just not careful enough to notice, we are just going to have to wait for them to make their next move.

⌒

ON WEDNESDAY MORNING I REMEMBER THAT WE SHOULD LET Alessandro know the news on the soil report. I ask Jackson to take care of it, not wanting to stir that pot.

Walking back to my office from Jackson's desk, I can't help but jump at every sound. My paranoia is off the charts, and everyone is a dangerous suspect.

Come midafternoon my nerves are completely frayed, and I wander into the breakroom looking for comfort food. Unfortunately, the usual box of donuts is completely empty at this late hour, and there's nothing in the cupboards. I'm sitting at the breakroom table, resting my forehead on its cool surface when my cellphone rings, causing me to jolt out of my reverie.

"Serafina Evans," I answer without checking the caller ID.

"Ms. Evans, this is Reagan Fuller, the escrow officer for the property purchase of your client, Sutton Developments. I'm afraid there's an issue with the earnest money check."

I sit bolt upright. "What kind of issue?"

"The check was returned by the bank," she says. "And unless we receive the earnest money by close of business at five p.m. today I'm afraid we'll have to inform the seller that they should move on to their next offer."

My frantic brain looks at the breakroom clock and registers that it's not quite three p.m. And secondly that she just said, "next offer."

"What next offer?" I demand, sprinting out of the breakroom to Jackson's desk.

"They let us know that they had another interested party after acceptance, willing to pay more," she explains. "I've emailed you a copy of the check and the return. I would highly recommend you do everything you can to rectify this in time."

Well, no shit, lady. "I'm glad this was caught before it was too late," I reply. "Thank you, Ms. Fuller, I'll be in touch shortly."

Jackson looks at me like I'm nuts as I barrel up to his desk.

"Jackson, we've got a big fucking problem. I don't have

time to explain. You're driving me to Sutton Developments. Now."

We charge through reception and I mash the elevator call button. Lucy looks at us curiously and Jackson shrugs in response. Ignoring them both, I call Charles Sutton.

"Mr. Sutton," I greet him brusquely. "We've got a problem."

"I'm all ears, Ms. Evans," he replies gruffly.

The elevator arrives, and I pull Jackson in behind me. I recount my conversation with Ms. Fuller as quickly as I can while descending in the elevator. The tension on the other end of the line is almost audible when I'm finished, and Jackson looks horrorstruck beside me.

"What's your plan?" Mr. Sutton asks.

Exiting the elevator into the parking garage, I cross my fingers that the call doesn't drop. "I'm heading to meet you now. We need to get your closest bank branch and cut a cashier's check for the earnest money. They won't accept a regular check anymore and we don't have time for a wire transfer."

"5th and Weller," he directs. "I'll be there in less than ten minutes."

"We'll be there in five." I turn to Jackson. "5th and Weller."

He nods tightly and steers us out of the parking garage. The usual downtown traffic doesn't allow us to go quickly, but thankfully it's only a mile or so away, and Jackson pulls up to the curb in front of the bank in just over six minutes.

"Keep the engine running, we're going to the title company after this," I tell him.

As soon as I'm at the doors, I start scanning the area. I don't see Mr. Sutton, so I go inside and do a quick scan of the lobby for him. As soon as I realize he's not inside either, I return to the front to wait for him. I'm waiting less than thirty seconds when another car pulls up behind Jackson and Mr. Sutton emerges from the back.

"Ms. Evans," he greets me tightly. "Let's get this taken care of." He holds the bank door open for me.

"Certainly, sir," I respond as I walk through.

We accompany each other in tense silence. He speaks only to the teller, and through his unique combination of presence and intimidation tactics, we walk out of the bank less ten minutes later with a cashier's check for seventy-five thousand dollars in hand.

"Let's take my car," he barks as his driver opens the door for him.

I nod, calling Jackson as I climb in. He answers immediately.

"Jackson, I'm riding with Mr. Sutton to the title company. You can return to the office," I direct.

"Yes, ma'am," he replies, his voice shaking.

As I hang up I nervously note the time — it's three twenty-four p.m. I carefully give the address to the driver and Mr. Sutton looks at me uneasily. The address is in Shoreline, some twenty miles north. In the burgeoning rush hour traffic that can easily be an hour drive.

I call the title company next and let Ms. Fuller know that we are en route with cashier's check in hand. She wishes us luck. Hanging up, I take in Charles Sutton's sour expression and realize I'm going to need a whole lot more than luck to save this account, even if we do manage to get the check in on time.

"Mr. Sutton, may I see your checkbook, please?" I ask.

Since he used it to confirm the correct account from which to withdraw the funds, I know he has it in his briefcase. He regards me for a moment before opening his briefcase and handing it to me.

I lay it carefully on my lap and scroll through my phone, bringing up the original check image from Ms. Fuller's email. Opening to the book, I hold my phone up and compare the account numbers to verify my suspicion.

"The account number doesn't match," I murmur, confirming my guess. I zoom in on the photo. "The check was doctored." *The mole.*

"Precisely how did that happen?" he asks gruffly.

"Mr. Sutton, I'm afraid your original concerns about my company were not unfounded," I admit. He raises an eyebrow and I sigh heavily. I decide to take a shot on honesty and disclose fully the nature of the situation. "I engaged a security company in our efforts to recover from our mishap. They recently discovered spyware indicating that the employee we fired was not working alone. It seems likely that their accomplice, who we have yet to identify, is still working for me and is behind this."

He considers that for a moment, his graying head leaned forward, fingers steepled under his nose.

"You knew you had a leak and you kept a check for seventy-five thousand dollars laying around?"

"No, sir," I respond vehemently. "I was only informed of the leak yesterday." I resist explaining why I had to take the check back to my office at all, unwilling to sound like I'm making excuses. And I definitely rule out an "I told you so" for using a paper check instead of a wire transfer.

"I see," he replies slowly. "Have there been any other issues I should be aware of?"

"Not with your account, no," I say. I consider whether to disclose the Buone Case issue and decide its best to lay all the cards on the table. "We did find one other report they tampered with that impacted another client. That has been taken care of. And so will this."

"How can I be sure of that if you have a traitor in your midst?" he asks shrewdly.

"My security company advised me to let them use the spyware to trace back to the culprits," I respond. "I have full confidence that will put an end to this matter in short order. But I understand if the uncertainty is too great for you, sir."

Mr. Sutton stares at the traffic zooming the opposite direction on the freeway for a while.

"I knew your grandfather well once," he says. He turns toward me, a sad look in his eyes. "I was terribly sorry to hear of his passing."

Of all the responses I expected, that wasn't even on the list. It takes me a moment to recover my wits, but I'm unsure of how to respond.

"Me too," I finally say softly.

He turns back to looking out the window and says nothing for the rest of the drive, nor when we arrive. He simply follows me in and, at four forty-two p.m., hands the check to Ms. Fuller.

TWENTY-FOUR

The silence on the drive back to Seattle is deafening. I use the time to read my email discreetly, wondering how long this freeze-out will last.

When the car stops in front of my office, he finally turns to me with a deeply contemplative look and says, "Let's let things settle for a day. I'd like to talk to you first thing Friday morning at my office."

"I'll clear my schedule," I assure him, and, exchanging farewells, I exit the vehicle.

I watch the car drive away, then slowly make the journey back to my office, not sure how to feel.

As I exit the elevator, Jackson and Lucy are deep in tense conversation at her desk. They both look up, startled by the soft ping heralding my arrival. I'm not sure if it's my slumped shoulders, clenched jaw, and dead expression or just their general worry over the situation, but they both look petrified.

"Did you make it?" Jackson asks tentatively.

"Yes," I reply. And I just manage to stop myself from saying "But we're probably fucked anyway."

"Then why do you look like your best friend just died?" Lucy asks.

Jackson shoots her an angry look.

"Sorry," she mutters, rolling her eyes.

"No, it's okay," I sigh. "I'm just not sure it did any good."

"What does that mean?" Jackson asks.

I shrug. "There's a quick exit clause in the contract. It means he's probably on the verge of exercising that at any minute," I say grumpily. "It's a problem for another day. Go home, guys, it's late. Thanks for your help today, Jackson."

I feel both sets of eyes following me as I trudge past.

I BARELY SLEEP AT ALL THAT NIGHT, WHICH DOESN'T HELP MY increasingly bad mood. I shut myself in my office most of the day Thursday, and my employees obligingly avoid me the few times I venture out.

The tone in the office is morose at best, but even Allie leaves me to hide in my cave. At six o'clock I step out of my office to find everyone gone. I feel like the shittiest boss ever because I know that all the cash influx in the world won't save my company if Sutton pulls out of his contract. My carefully built reputation will be completely ruined.

Before I leave, I slowly walk the full circuit of the office, taking note of all the family pictures displayed at people's desks and the messy appointment calendars that clearly show lighter loads all around.

So many futures in my hands, including my pregnant best friend's.

I've rarely questioned my ability to keep pressing forward, but in the dark, silent office, I feel weakened by the continuous attacks seemingly from all sides. And I don't know where to find the strength to keep going.

$$\backsim$$

I WAKE TO A LOUD POUNDING NOISE REVERBERATING OFF THE walls, and it takes me a moment to realize it's not from my nightmares. It's someone at my front door. I scramble sleepily for my phone to see what time it is. I barely note that it's only just after five a.m. before I notice the string of missed calls and texts.

I scramble out of bed, pulling on a pair of leggings under my sleep shirt, and stumble to the door sleepily. Through the peephole I see Bryce.

"It's me, Sera," he calls. "Open up."

I open the door, letting him in, and he rushes hurriedly in past me. I close the door and turn to find him pacing.

"You weren't answering your calls or texts," he says, agitated.

"I'm fine, Bryce," I assure him. "You didn't have to try to break down the door." I move to collapse onto one of the new, fluffy white sofas, but he grabs me by the arms.

"I *know* you're fine, Sera," he says urgently, and for the first time I really look at his face. He's *excited*. "That's why I came."

My tired brain is having trouble forming sentences. "What is … why are you … give me a minute to wake up, please," I grumble.

He rolls his eyes and shakes me gently. "We've got them," he says eagerly. "Megan Stanwood and her computer expert. They triggered another download in the middle of the night. They've been found and arrested."

His words are like a bucket of ice water poured over my drowsy head, and suddenly I'm fully awake.

"*Holy shit*," I gasp. Bryce laughs and lifts me up, spinning me around. "That's fantastic!" He finally allows me to slump down onto the couch, astonished. "Who was her accomplice? Have they said who in ERS they were working with?"

"They don't have anything from them yet, but they've only been in custody a couple hours," he responds. "We know from checking the accomplice's ID that his name is Christopher Walker, and from his prints they were able to figure out that he works on the college campus where Megan Stanwood was attending classes."

"Then this isn't over," I say, my voice barely above a whisper.

Bryce sits down on the couch next to me and catches my gaze reassuringly. "They're just getting started, Sera," he says soothingly. "They've just barely been booked. They'll need to be given the opportunity to obtain legal counsel, and then they can be questioned. But this will be over, one way or the other."

"But what if they won't give up the name?" I press. My fears and anxieties of the previous evening begin to gnaw at my insides afresh and I bury my face in my hands.

"Hey, look at me," Bryce says, gently pulling my hands down. "I told you, I'm in your corner. I've got a plan."

"Really?" I ask hopefully. He nods and laughs.

"Really," he replies. "I'm here to help you."

"Okay, hotshot, what's the plan?" I ask.

"You're going to call an all-hands meeting first thing this morning to announce that all computers have been taken offline due to a cyberattack," he says. "Now that Ms. Stanwood and Mr. Walker are in custody, if your spy doesn't already know they soon will anyway."

"If they already know, won't they just not show up today?" I ask ponderously. "Or if they don't know, won't that just scare them off?"

"Exactly," Bryce says. "Between you and Allie, you need to record who is and isn't there. And it'll be obvious who it is if they run. And either way, well, problem solved."

"And what if they don't run?" I press. "What if they just wait it out?"

"With their accomplices in police custody, ready to be questioned at any moment? Not likely."

"So, for argument's sake, let's say they are either that stupid or that ballsy," I push.

He shrugs. "I wasn't kidding about the computers. Paul is there right now installing new features on all of your machines."

"I'm listening," I prompt.

"The computers will be equipped with a two-step login process. The first step can only be satisfied by a unique ID card that will be assigned to each employee at the meeting this morning. The second by thumbprint," he explains. "If anyone leaves their computer idle without locking it for more than a minute, they'll be required to re-log in. Your traitor isn't going to get away with anything else, even if they do stay."

I'm impressed with his plan, but I can see at least one glaring hole instantly. "Bryce, my people all have laptops. I'm sure at least some of them take them home at night," I point out.

"Already covered. Paul already had a list of all your machines and their assignees from Will. He has a list of the six that weren't in the office when he arrived this morning and Will and I are going to collect those as they arrive with their owners," he answers. "Which reminds me, I'm going to need your laptop." My favorite Bryce classic sunshine-smile appears, and I can't help but feel reassured.

"You'll be there too?" I ask in a small voice.

"Just in case," he replies. "It's all downhill from here, Sera."

And for the first time in what feels like a very long time, I feel hopeful.

"Oh!" I exclaim, remembering my promise of the day before yesterday. "I was supposed to meet Charles Sutton this morning."

"Sounds like you have a few calls to make. Why don't you get dressed and we'll go into the office?" he suggests.

∽

By six fifteen Paul, Will, Bryce, Allie and I are all in the office. Paul and Will are working on modifying the computers. Allie is working on calling the leads into a nine o'clock meeting, and having the leads call their teams to pass on the summons.

"Hey, Sera," Allie says, poking her head into the conference room. "Do we need the entire property maintenance team or just Ian?"

Bryce raises an eyebrow. "Do they use the computers here?" he asks.

"No," I provide. "Just Ian. Everyone else is off-site. I don't think they've ever even been here."

"Then just Ian," Bryce replies.

Allie nods and ducks out of the room once more. I look at the two piles flanking Paul and Will. The pile of machines to be processed is slowly, but surely, dwindling.

"Think we'll be ready in time?" I ask Bryce nervously.

"Yes," Paul says shortly without looking up.

Bryce and I exchange an amused look.

"Okay, then I'm going to go call Charles Sutton," I say, and head to my office.

I start scrolling through the names on my phone and make a mental note to change Alessandro's entry, so I don't have to scroll past it every time I open my address book. Even just the passing thought of him feels like a hot, iron fist clutching my insides.

As I hover over his name, like kismet, the phone rings and it's Alessandro calling. I stand gaping at the phone for a moment before I decide to answer it.

"*Buongiorno*," I greet him. "Were your Spidey senses tingling?"

"*Che cosa?*" Alessandro replies, clearly confused.

I smile briefly. "Never mind. What's up?"

"Can we talk?" he asks.

"Now's not really a great time," I reply, wondering where this is going.

"I'm sorry, I'm all over the place," he says. "I don't mean now. I mean, can we meet and talk? Tonight, if you're available?"

"Is it something to do with your build?" I ask, my heart racing for a moment.

"No, no," he assures me quickly. "I have something I need to tell you."

"Alessandro," I sigh. Not this again. "I really can't do this right now."

"Is something going on?" he asks, perhaps finally sensing that the tension in my voice may not be solely about him.

I pause for a moment, not sure if I should say. But he was affected by this too, and I don't see any way it can interfere with our plans. "They caught Megan Stanwood and her associate hacking into our system last night. They've been arrested and we're in the middle of executing a plan to plug the internal leak. So, we're a little busy now."

"That's great news," he replies slowly. "But all the same, if you can, it's important to me that we talk."

And now, even amid my worry about my company, the anguish in his voice strikes a chord deep in me, and I can't deny him.

"Okay," I relent. "Meet me in front of my office building at six p.m."

"Thank you," he replies throatily. "I'll see you then. *In bocca al lupo*, Serafina."

I laugh quietly. "What does that mean?"

And I can hear the smile in his voice when he replies, "I think you'd need to be Italian to really understand. But I suppose what I mean to say is, I hope things go well for you today."

"*Grazie*," I reply softly. "*Ciao*, Alessandro."

"*Ciao*, Serafina."

After he is gone, I stare blankly at my phone screen for a minute before remembering that I was about to call Mr. Sutton.

Perhaps not surprisingly given the hour, when I place the call, it goes to his voicemail.

"Mr. Sutton, this is Serafina Evans," I start, my voice shaking. "Unfortunately, I'm going to need to reschedule our morning meeting. I'm terribly sorry to do this at the last minute, but we've had a development with our compromised security. I'm pleased to share with you that the hackers have been apprehended, but I need to be here this morning to work with our security company to shore up the leak. I'm happy to meet with you this afternoon, or anytime next week of your choosing. I'll be busy with our security team and preparing for a staff meeting this morning, but I'll be checking my messages and email until I go into the staff meeting at nine. I look forward to hearing from you and, again, my apologies."

I drop my phone on the desk and sink into my chair. I turn and stare out the window into the bright blue sky. *At least the weather's nice today*, I can't help but reflect. And the thought makes me laugh until tears well in my eyes. You know you're from Seattle when even amid perhaps the worst crisis you've ever faced, you can still appreciate a sunny day.

TWENTY-FIVE

As the last person files into the conference room, Allie pulls the door closed and slips through the tightly squeezed mass of bodies, dropping a piece of paper between Bryce and me.

Maggie says Mr. Sutton just called and he will see you at 1 p.m.

Only two people are missing — Roberta Oliver (vacation) and Gary Peterson (called in sick this morning).

Bryce points to Gary's name and gives me a questioning look. I use my pen and write "leasing agent" next to his name. After considering for a moment, I write "project manager" next to Roberta's for good measure.

Setting my pen down, I rise and gather everyone's attention. Several dozen pairs of curious eyes stare at me.

"Good morning everyone," I greet them. "I'm just going to skip the bullshit, because I'm sure you all want to know what's going on."

Nervous laughter ripples through the room.

"As you all know, a little more than six weeks ago we fired our part-time receptionist, Ms. Stanwood," I begin. "We have all been suffering from the fallout of the tampering she did while she was employed here. What we did not know until recently was that she has since been spying on us, attempting to continue her sabotage."

My revelation is met with gasps and low rumbles of disbelief.

"Fortunately, Ms. Stanwood and her accomplice were apprehended last night after attempting to extract more information from our computer systems," I share. I try to keep an eye out for particularly nervous glances, but there are so many it seems futile. So, I continue. "All of our computers have been taken offline and modified with new security features. You will receive those back after this meeting, or, for those of you who turned your laptops in upon arrival, a bit later this morning. Will is going to explain the new security features, but first I'd like to pause here and answer any questions you may have."

Karen Quinlan, one of our dedicated real estate agents, raises her hand.

"Karen?" I prompt.

"Has any of our personal data been compromised?"

"No," Allie steps in and responds. "All of our detailed personnel data is stored on a machine that stays locked down in my office and is not connected to the network. The only information that could possibly have been leaked are names and home addresses as shown on your paystubs."

"If anyone is concerned about identity theft issues, I am more than happy to provide credit monitoring and restoration service coverage," I offer.

Karen nods, seemingly satisfied. The next hand in the air is Keith Nystrom's.

"What about our client's data?" he asks.

As head of our contracts, I'm not surprised by his question.

"We've scanned every network-accessible project and property management record, and have found no evidence of any additional tampering," Will offers.

"And the police are investigating what else may have been done with the data received by the perpetrators," Bryce adds.

"It's a situation we will continue to keep an eye on," I assure Keith.

He looks unsatisfied but unfortunately, I don't have anything else to offer him. The room falls silent.

"No more questions?" I ask.

"What about the Sutton account?" Jackson calls from the back of the room.

"I'm afraid we don't know yet, Jackson," I reply. "I'll be meeting with Mr. Sutton this afternoon."

I give the ensuing silence another minute. "Okay, Will, can

you please take us through the new computing security features?" I prompt, sitting back down.

Will rises and takes everyone through the procedure. There are a few questions when he's done, which are easily fielded by Will and Paul. When they've concluded, I rise once again.

"Thanks for coming, everyone. I know this was a lot to take in," I say, my voice thick with the multitude of emotions I'm feeling. "I'm deeply appreciative for the work you all do for this company every day, and I don't want these setbacks to define us. Let's go back out there and keep doing what we do best."

Bryce, Allie, and I step outside the conference room as the team lines up to collect their machines, access cards, and have their thumbprints scanned into the system.

When we are out of earshot, Bryce turns to Allie. "Gary Peterson?"

"Definitely sick. He couldn't even call in himself; his wife had to call for him. I could hear him puking in the background," she replies in disgust.

"She could be in on it," he replies. "He could have been faking."

"What do you want me to do, ask for a vomit sample?" Allie asks, practically gagging at the suggestion.

"No, I'm just playing devil's advocate. The plan still stands. If he is the mole and he was faking an illness, that means he knows."

"Okay, so now what?" I ask Bryce.

He shrugs. "Now we wait and see what happens."

"And do what?" Allie asks. "Just go about our business?"

"Pretty much," Bryce confirms. "I'll be here until Paul is satisfied everything is up and running, likely through the afternoon. So, we'll be here to see if someone bails out before the end of the day."

"And if they don't?" I ask. "What if they just suck it up and stay?" The thought of continuing to employ someone who may still yet destroy my company makes me sick to my stomach.

"One thing at a time, Sera," he says. "The police are still working on Ms. Stanwood and Mr. Walker, and now we know the mole knows that. Let that percolate, and we'll see what happens."

EVERYTHING IS EERILY QUIET LEADING UP TO MY MEETING WITH Charles Sutton. I feel odd leaving at a time like this, but Bryce assures me he'll be my eyes and ears while I'm away. And it's not exactly a meeting I can miss. So, at one p.m. on the dot, I am at Mr. Sutton's office, waiting nervously for his assistant to let me know he's ready for me.

The spacious office still feels closed in by all the dark paneling and sable wood furniture. The air is warm and still, and I can hear his assistant's heels clacking on the dark tile floors as she flits around the office, tidying this or that, offering me a glass of water, answering phones.

My dim mood must frighten her off, because eventually her heels click away and don't return.

"Ms. Evans." I'm startled and look up to see Charles Sutton standing two feet from me, an expectant expression on his face. "I'm terribly sorry if I scared you."

I clear my throat and rise to my feet. "No need, Mr. Sutton," I respond graciously. "I was just lost in thought."

He leads me to his office. "Understandably," he allows. "You must have a lot on your mind."

We enter his office and he gestures for me to take a seat opposite his large, sable desk as he settles in his chair.

"That's putting it mildly," I reply drily.

He smiles humorlessly and leans forward in his chair. "Well, then, I don't want to keep you any longer than necessary," he responds. "Shall we get down to brass tacks?"

"Please," I respond, gesturing for him to continue. I shift in my rigid and uncomfortable chair and briefly wonder if he chose it for that reason. He certainly has me at an advantage, in many ways.

"So, then, have you identified your leak?" he inquires.

"Not yet," I admit. "But our security consultant has implemented measures that would make it impossible to hide the identity of anyone attempting to do further damage. And the police will soon be questioning their accomplices."

"That's good to know," he says contemplatively.

And I don't know if it's his measured responses or having

hit my limit of uncertainty, but I suddenly just can't take it anymore. "Sir, do you plan to cancel our contract?"

Mr. Sutton eyes me levelly. "No, Ms. Evans, I do not."

I'm surprised at both getting a direct answer and having it be favorable. I'd thought for sure we'd lost his business.

"With all due respect, sir," I say tightly, "is there anything else you brought me here for today? Because if not, I think my attentions would be better served ensuring all of the hard work we've done to secure the best interests of both my company and your deal does not go to waste."

"There is, actually," he replies. "I'd very much like to hire you, Ms. Evans."

Again, he surprises me.

"Why?" I can't help but ask.

He chuckles softly. "From the moment I met you, I saw a great deal of your grandfather in you. You're hardheaded, smart, and persistent."

"But what about all the issues we've had?" I protest.

"Ms. Evans," he starts. "In this world, there is very little we can control. You don't get where I am without learning how to mitigate risks and adjust for the rest." He pauses and eyes me appraisingly. "You, young lady, show an immense amount of talent at adjusting. It's one thing to account for the day-to-day challenges of working in our field — red tape, nervous investors, cut-throat competition — the obstacles go on and on. The additional challenges you've been faced with recently are an entirely different sort. And yet, here you are."

I look at him skeptically. Yes, here I am. A complete mess personally and professionally. He smiles indulgently at my confusion.

"I imagine you're feeling rather overwhelmed by all of this," he allows. "I'm sure you've got even more going on than I care to know. I'm not asking you for an answer today. But I would very much like to take you under my wing. I think it would be incredibly beneficial for us both."

"But what would happen to my company?" I manage to ask.

He spreads his hands out. "That depends," he replies. "There are several ways to structure such a relationship. I'm open to negotiation."

I swallow hard, considering his proposal. It's just too much to take in all at once. "How long do I have to think about it?"

"May I call you Sera?" he asks, and I nod. "Sera, my intent was not to make this already difficult time tougher for you. I had hoped it would relieve some of your burden knowing that you can turn to me. So please, take all the time you need. And let me know if there's anything I can do to be of assistance in the meantime."

"I still don't understand," I say, at a loss. "Why?" His offer is too good to be true. I would have far more to gain from such an arrangement than he would.

He steeples his fingers under his nose, as I've seen him do when contemplating in the past.

"Sera, I want you to understand. I would be highly interested in you regardless, as I'm fond of mentoring smart, young people such as yourself," he explains. "But the reason I'm here today is because your grandfather did for me exactly what I am proposing to do for you. Your grandfather mentored me when I was just getting started in this business. He taught me everything he knew. I wouldn't be the man I am today if it weren't for him."

I'm dumbstruck by his admission. "I had no idea," I breathe. "He never mentioned you."

"I'm sure it never came up, as your grandfather mentored a good many young investors," he says dismissively. "And by the time you got to know your grandfather in that capacity I'd long since been running my company here, and he and I had no more than the occasional lunch. But he always spoke very fondly of you, from when you were quite young. He said you would be his finest protégé someday. Were I a less successful man I would have been insulted."

I smile wryly. "That sounds like Grandpa Tyler," I reply.

"He was right. Even apart from the advantage you had as his granddaughter, you stand out," he insists. "I'm not making you this offer because I owe your grandfather, though I do. It's on your own merits." He takes a deep breath. "But I think I've blown enough sunshine up your ass for one afternoon."

I laugh appreciatively at the break in tension. "Yes, I should get back," I agree. "Thank you for your time, Mr. Sutton. And your generous offer. I will consider it fully."

"See that you do," he murmurs speculatively, dismissing me with a nod.

∾

WHEN I WALK BACK INTO THE OFFICE, I FIND JACKSON AT Lucy's desk once again, my exit from the elevator startling them once more out of their tête-à-tête.

While there is no rule against office romances, I do find myself a little annoyed at their obviousness, and I'm sure my expression shows it based on Jackson's guilty look.

"Ms. Evans," he greets me. "How did it go with Mr. Sutton?"

I glance at Lucy and she pretends to busy herself with work. I almost laugh but decide to keep my disapproving expression fixed in place for a while longer to discourage their behavior in the future.

"Well, we haven't lost the contract," I reply, not wanting to admit exactly what happened yet.

"Oh gosh, that's such a relief," Jackson says. "So, he's not mad?"

"Not in the least," I respond. "I don't think you and Ellie will have any troubles dealing with him in the future."

"Excellent," he replies. "I'll go tell Ellie."

"I think that would be a good use of your time," I say pointedly, looking between him and Lucy.

They both look away from each other guiltily and I return to my office, where I allow myself a good chuckle at their expressions before returning to work.

~

Around four-thirty Bryce stops by to let me know he and Paul are done and heading out for the day. He looks utterly exhausted, and a wave of gratitude washes over me for all he's done for me.

"Thank you, Bryce, for everything." I step around my desk to give him a firm hug.

"Anytime, gorgeous," he murmurs into my hair.

I pull away and grimace at him facetiously. He flashes me his sunshine-smile, and I can't help but mirror it back.

"I can't be in a bad mood around you," I tease him. "Time for you to get out."

"Okay, okay, I'm going!" he replies, and I walk with him to the elevator.

As we pass Lucy I'm pleased to see that she appears to be working, Jackson nowhere in sight. I make a mental note to ask Allie what's been going on between those two and for how long.

Bryce pushes the elevator call button. "I'll let you know if I hear anything further from the police."

"Still nothing?" I sigh.

"Hey," he says, locking eyes with me. "That doesn't mean anything. It's still early. Give them some time. Go home, try to relax this weekend."

"I'm not great at relaxing, even under the best of circumstances," I grouse. "I despise uncertainty."

"Sera, there's nothing you can do about it," he replies. "They'll either give up their partner to save their own asses, or they won't, and they'll face harsher sentencing. Odds are overwhelming that they will. And soon. Try to stay positive."

"I'm positive I won't relax this weekend," I joke.

"Fine, have it your way," he replies. The elevator arrives. "Bye, Sera."

"Bye, Bryce," I reply with a wave.

Lucy gives me a nervous smile as I pass her desk again. And on my way by Maggie's desk, I notice her wrestling with her new thumbprint scanner.

"Everything okay there, Maggie?" I ask.

She looks up in surprise. "Yes, I think I just got jam on it," she says crossly, and I can't help but laugh.

But I can hold back on my urge to joke about her "jamming" the new tech. She doesn't look like she's in the mood for humor, and frankly my heart's not really in it anyway.

"I think it's trying to tell you to go home, Maggie," I reply instead. "Really. You guys should all go home. It's been a rough day."

"Really?" she asks brightly.

"Really," I confirm. "Tell Lucy, too, and anyone else that's still here."

"Thanks, Sera," she blushes.

"Have a great weekend, Maggie," I respond.

⌒

JUST BEFORE SIX O'CLOCK I CLOSE MY LAPTOP AND LOCK IT IN my desk. I may not relax this weekend, but I've also decided not to take work home with me. Maybe it'll help. I lock up my office door for good measure, and head to the elevator through the quiet office.

As I walk by Lucy's desk, I'm surprised to find her still working.

"Hey Lucy," I greet her, and she looks up in surprise. "Didn't Maggie tell you I let everyone go earlier?"

"Oh, yeah, she did, Ms. Evans," Lucy replies. "I just got behind today and had some things I didn't want to leave until Monday morning."

"I appreciate that, but maybe in the future you could spend a little less time talking with Jackson and a little more time working so you can go home on time?" I suggest, and she blushes furiously. I make another mental note to have a similar conversation with Jackson later. "I'm not entirely comfortable with you being in the office late by yourself."

"You do it all the time," she replies, then seems to realize her impertinence and hastily adds, "but you're right, I'll go home now."

I check my watch and realize I'm due to meet Alessandro. I push the elevator button, hoping it'll hurry Lucy along.

Thankfully, it does, and as the elevator doors slide open, she rushes out to join me while still stuffing things into her bag.

She follows in behind me and as the elevator doors close, I see her push the button for the penthouse suite four floors up.

"Lucy, I need to go down," I say, confused.

I turn to look at her and realize I'm staring straight down the barrel of a gun.

TWENTY-SIX

"If you make a noise I'll blow your goddamned head off." Lucy's usual casual and irreverent tone has been replaced by a harsh, clipped timbre.

I freeze in place as my brain scrambles to catch up. "It's you," I whisper. She smirks malevolently.

"Took you fucking long enough."

The elevator doors open with a ping, admitting us to the top floor.

"Move," she demands.

As she looks over her shoulder to step carefully out of the elevator, I drop my hand into my pocket, clutching my cellphone as I slowly obey. I glance down and find the "9" and press it. A small tone sounds and her head whips back to me.

"Take your cellphone out of your pocket and drop it on the floor. Now."

I slowly slide my finger to the next position as I raise my hand.

"Don't get cute with me, *Sera*. DROP IT!"

I press down and release the phone. Its hard-shelled case prevents it from shattering on impact, but Lucy, keeping her eyes trained on me, retrieves it and looks at the screen. She holds down the power button to shut off the phone.

"Trying to dial 911?" She shakes her head slowly. "It didn't work, Sera."

That's not who I was trying to reach, but hearing that the call didn't go through makes the blood drain from my face.

"What do you want?" I demand, finding my voice. "Money? Is that what this is about? Or were you just sabotaging my company for your own sick pleasure?"

"Something like that," she responds. "Now turn around and keep moving."

As she guides me into the inner office, I'm finally able to look around. The whole floor appears to be unoccupied and under renovation. She guides me to a chair near the large windows.

"Sit," she commands.

I comply, trying to figure out how to stall her. She tosses me a roll of duct tape that was sitting on the desk beside the chair. The chilling realization that she planned this sends shivers down my spine.

"Tape your ankles to the chair legs."

I stare at her for a moment, agog.

She cocks the hammer of the revolver. "I've been trained to kill, Sera. Don't test me."

I swallow hard and secure my ankles to the chair.

"Now tape your right hand to the arm rest," she directs.

I slowly wrap the tape around my wrist, to the chair, my hands shaking with fear and adrenaline. When I'm done, she relaxes her stance and places the revolver on the desk next to her. She approaches me and snatches the roll of tape, quickly and deftly using it to secure my other wrist to the second arm rest.

"Good. Now I get to explain to you why you're going to die tonight," she rages. "Why you deserve to die."

"Where did you learn how to use a gun?" I ask shakily, hoping to divert her.

"In the military," she replies nonchalantly, stepping back and leaning on the desk.

I appraise her for a moment, realizing I don't know her all that well. I'd put her around my age, maybe a bit younger. Her long, straight black hair reaches halfway down her back, her dark eyes angry and calculating. I've always thought of her as a small person, but on closer inspection I see that she's wiry. I'm not a fighter in the least, so even though I have several inches and easily thirty or forty pounds on her, I realize she's probably a good deal stronger than me. Not that I can fight her off while I'm bound to a chair anyway.

"Yes, look closely, Sera," she says cuttingly. "Not that it

matters. You clearly have no idea who I am. Just another employee. Just another face. Just another casualty of your ambition."

I work to suppress my indignant response, but I'm sure it flits across my face. "Are you going to tell me what I did to deserve this, or are you just going to bore me to death?" I ask tightly. Stupidly. My words make her eyes bulge for a moment. *Great, Sera, taunt the crazy girl with the gun.*

And then she lets out a manic laugh. "You've got balls, I'll give you that," she replies. "Okay. Let's do it your way. Does the name Gabrielle Grayson mean anything to you?"

My heart stops at the name and recognition, followed quickly by anger, wells up inside me.

"You're the crazy bitch who trashed my car and tried to burn down your apartment," I respond.

My Third Deal Disaster. In the flesh. She smiles widely and makes a show of taking a bow.

"Very good, Ms. Evans," she responds. "Though 'crazy bitch' might be a little harsh. Had you bothered to show up for the legal proceedings, I never could have gotten this far without being recognized. At the time it infuriated me, but I suppose I should thank you."

"Are you seriously telling me you've been sabotaging me this whole time, that you plan to *kill* me," I spit, "for pressing charges over your insane behavior?"

And my mouth has finally gotten me in trouble. She

approaches me quickly and reels back, punching me in the face, hard. My head snaps backward and lights pop in my vision. I can feel blood flowing out of my nose as pain shoots through my head.

"*My* insane behavior?" she hisses. "You have no idea what a heartless bitch you are, do you?"

I stare at her, bewildered, and not just from the blow. My brain struggles to make sense of her words amid the pain continuing to radiate through my face.

Admittedly, in my early days of investing I was quite zealous to buy low-income properties, end the leases of the existing tenants, and renovate to put in better tenants, all for better cash flow. Exactly the circumstances that led to our involvement with each other.

But I've never considered myself *heartless*. I've always done everything by the book and worked with people when they came to me with a request that I could reasonably accommodate. I'm no slumlord, but neither can you be a bleeding heart in this business. You'd end up in financial ruin before long.

"Apparently not," I reply quietly, attempting to wipe my nose on my shoulder. "Why don't you educate me?"

I can feel my hands going numb and I hope stalling for time will bring Alessandro looking for me. Except I remember he doesn't have access to the elevator anymore. Fuck. Or maybe he won't even try. Maybe he'll think I changed my mind, and

I'm avoiding him. I try to focus on my captor, hoping she takes the bait.

"Oh, gladly," she scoffs. "I think you already know the little 'lease termination' letter that you sent to me, my deployed fiancé, *and* my roommate clued them in about each other."

I suppress a smirk. "So, it's my fault you got caught cheating?"

"You have no fucking clue what was happening," she fumes, stepping forward to lean in, her face inches from mine. "You don't know me." She takes a breath and straightens up, tossing her hair over her shoulder angrily. "My fiancé was a violent asshole. I wasn't going to stay with him. But my boyfriend? I was protecting him by not telling him. Maybe if you'd bothered to talk to any of us, tell us what you were doing …"

"Seriously? Your boyfriend wasn't on the lease," I retort. "Maybe you shouldn't have shacked up with him in a place your fiancé was legally responsible for. And I sure as hell didn't force you to commit property damage and arson."

She steps forward, livid, and I'm afraid she's going to hit me again, but thankfully she doesn't.

"My life was already ruined. It didn't matter anyway," she responds quietly, leaning back against the desk again. "My fiancé was a high-ranking officer. When he found out, he told me he was going to lie to get me dishonorably discharged. He knew I was counting on going to school on the GI Bill after I left the military. I came from nothing. I had nothing. With a DD and no GI Bill I figured I may as well have a criminal record too. It's just a shame the building didn't actually burn down and ruin you. So, I had to find another way to do it."

"How the fuck did you ever get hired at my company?" I ask in disbelief.

"Seriously?" she replies condescendingly. "Identity theft is easy these days. Well, that is, until you put in your stupid fucking thumbprint scanners. And with Megan gone, there was no one to manipulate into getting around that. Plus, I'm sure she'll be giving me up any minute to the cops."

"If I were her, I'd give you up too," I reply honestly. "You used her as a scapegoat, didn't you? What did you promise her? My money?"

"Your money," she admits. "And she was in love with me. I let her believe I returned her feelings, that we were going to hold your company ransom for millions and then run away together. I tossed her a few pity fucks and had her eating right out of my hand. Until she got her stupid ass fired over a measly four hundred dollars."

"Is Jackson in on this too?" I ask tensely.

She laughs uproariously for a minute. "That idiot? Are you kidding me? God, no," she gasps, wiping tears of laughter from her eyes. "I didn't even need to sleep with him to make him my bitch. A little flirting, a little innuendo, and the desperate loser lets me go through all the Buone Case project files to 'help' him organize everything. He's so trusting, he didn't even notice when I had Megan swap in the altered file."

"And I imagine having full access to my office, the Sutton check wasn't hard to tamper with," I deduce blandly.

She smiles widely in acknowledgement and stands, picking up the revolver. She approaches me with it hanging loosely in her hand by her side.

"So, what now — you're just going to shoot me?" I ask incredulously. "And then what? Walk away?"

"If I can't ruin you like you ruined me, then yes, you deserve it and so much more," she agrees. "But there's no walking away for me. I have nothing left."

So, we're both going to die tonight. And nobody knows where I am. She raises the gun and points it between my eyes.

"Please," I beg, "I'll pay you. Whatever you want. You can go somewhere and start fresh."

Her grip tightens on the gun and I start to feel dizzy from terror.

"You think I want the money you earned fucking over people like me? Ruining people for your greed?" she fumes. "You're an unfeeling monster. You don't give a shit about anyone, just your precious career, your reputation, your *money*." She spits the last word at me. "And your money isn't going to buy you out of justice."

My heart races and I'm desperate to keep her talking. "You're right," I agree, letting my face crumple. She lowers the gun a fraction, and she looks stunned. "I'm a horrible person, I can't even …"

And suddenly there's noise and motion from the elevator, and two people move toward us. Her head whips around, and I use the distraction to try to wriggle out of my bonds, but I just knock myself over in the chair, landing hard on the ground on my left side, smacking my temple against the cold tile floor.

From my sideways vantage point, I see Bryce and Alessandro. They've separated so they're on either side of her, and she's frantically trying to decide who to point her gun at. Only Bryce is armed, and he's looking fixedly at her, gun at the ready.

"Put your weapon on the floor," Bryce commands. "NOW!"

I look at Alessandro to find him staring back at me, desperation and horror on his face.

Gabrielle swings the gun wildly between the two men for a moment, a guttural scream of frustration ripping out of her. "No!"

Bryce advances, raising his gun to point it at her chest. His motion triggers a reflex in her, and before I can tear my eyes away, she places the revolver in her mouth and pulls the trigger. My eyes are fixed in horror as the back of her skull blows apart, and I'm showered with bits of hair, skull, blood, and brain.

The force of the shot topples her body backward, and she lands on the tiles in front of me, the blood quickly pooling around her head and seeping into my clothing, over the exposed skin of my legs. The viscous liquid is warm on my flesh, and I gag, trying to turn my head so I at least don't have to see it. But even with my eyes averted I can smell it — the heavy tang of gunpowder mixed with the sharp smell of her blood. I vomit in the back of my mouth but manage to choke it back down.

I can also hear a low, visceral sound, and I realize I'm making the tortured noise that is somewhere between grunting and crying as tears pour out, mixing with the blood that is still coming out of my nose and dripping onto the floor under my cheek.

Alessandro makes it to me, pulling the chair away from Gabrielle's body and lifting me back into a sitting position. Freed from being pinned against the ground, my shoulders heave, shaking my whole upper body.

Alessandro puts his hands on my shoulders, then moves them to cup my face, his eyes desperately seeking mine. "Shhhh, *bella*," he cries softly. "I'm here. It's over."

I nod fervently, stilling ever so slightly but continuing to sob uncontrollably. As he unwinds the tape binding my limbs to the chair, I see Bryce behind him on the phone.

As the last of my bonds are removed, Bryce ends the call and joins us.

"Sera," Bryce says, his voice strangled and tense. "The police are on the way. You're safe now." He takes my right hand in both of his, using his fingers to gently rub feeling back into my wrist as he looks me over.

Alessandro kneels next to me, gripping my other hand.

"How did you find me?" I ask weakly. My face, wrists, and

ankles throb achingly, and my whole body feels heavy and tired.

"The emergency line rang from you, then cut out," he explains. "So, I traced it. When I saw your phone had connected through the top floor's Wi-Fi I came running. The Italian was standing outside the building and followed me in."

I sigh in relief that the call had, in fact, gone through despite Gabrielle's claim it hadn't. I shudder thinking about what would have happened if it didn't.

Bryce continues his examination, using his hands to lightly skim my limbs and face. "Is it just your nose?" he asks.

I shake my head faintly and touch my left temple gently with my hand. I bring it away and don't see any blood. "I bumped my head when I fell," I manage to whisper. "And she punched me." I touch my nose gingerly and wince at the pain.

"Sera, I'm so sorry," he replies vehemently. "I never should have left your side until we knew who it was."

I shake my head weakly and close my eyes, too exhausted to even respond that I don't blame him.

The elevator pings once more and police officers and medics pour out. The noise immediately makes my head pound harder, and I grab pleadingly for Alessandro's calming touch. He squeezes my hand and wraps his arm around me reassuringly as one of the medics comes to examine me.

I'm barely aware of his inspection; my eyes are fixed on Bryce as he starts to talk to one of the officers. They glance over at me repeatedly. I look away, overwhelmed, knowing I'll have to tell them my story soon.

The medic asks me a few questions, which I answer as shortly as I can, as speaking compounds the pain in my face and my head. He looks at Alessandro and they exchange words, but my hearing is fading, and so is the light. Through a haze I realize that I must be losing consciousness.

TWENTY-SEVEN

When I open my eyes, everything is white and blurry, and I feel like I'm floating. I panic for a moment, thinking I've died, until I turn my head and see through my hazy vision Alessandro, sleeping in a chair next to me. I take a few calming breaths, and my sight comes back into focus as I examine my surroundings.

It's just a hospital room. A very white, clean hospital room. A small, silver machine beeps quietly next to my bed, and a long clear line snakes into my hand. I extend my fingers, checking that I have full feeling back. My wrists are purple and tender, but I don't have any trouble moving them. When I'm satisfied, I stretch my legs, making sure they still work too.

Gingerly, I feel the stiff center of my face and trace the outline of bandaging covering my nose and part of my cheeks. I feel a little cloudy and tired, but otherwise in one piece. And

I'm hungry. So hungry that upon realizing it, my stomach rumbles loudly. Loudly enough to wake Alessandro.

"Serafina," he says softly, clearly surprised and pleased to see me awake. He leans forward and takes my hand in his. His liquid, dark brown eyes are filled with love and concern, his hair and beard long and disheveled. "How are you feeling?"

As I contemplate his question, I take note that he's changed his clothes since I last saw him. I struggle to remember when that was, and suddenly a rush of memories flood me, my eyes filling with tears.

"Oh, *mio tesoro*," he murmurs, quickly moving to sit next to me on the bed.

He pulls me gently into his embrace, and I rest my head gratefully against his chest. He holds me quietly for a few minutes until a nurse walks in. She's middle-aged, with pale red hair pulled into a bun and bright pink scrubs. Her friendly smile helps me collect myself.

"Ah, I see we're awake finally," she remarks. "I'm your day nurse, Beth. How are you feeling dear?"

"A little foggy," I admit, my voice cracking from disuse. I realize I'm hearing my voice as if someone else is speaking. "And a little floaty."

She smiles again, indulgently this time. "That'll be the pain meds," she agrees. "You were asleep a long time. We didn't know if you were hurting, so we didn't want to take the chance."

"How long was I out?" I ask, looking around for a clock.

"It's Saturday afternoon," she replies, and looks at her watch. "Almost four p.m."

I've been unconscious for more than twenty-one hours. My eyes widen, and I gape at her for a moment. I look at Alessandro, still hovering over me on the bed. "Where is Bryce?" I ask.

"I'll call him in a moment," Alessandro replies softly. "Don't worry."

Nurse Beth flits gently around me, checking my pulse, my temperature, my bandages. Alessandro slides back into his chair to allow her full access, hanging off the edge of the seat nervously.

"Well, your vitals look strong," she finally declares. "Physically, you're doing just fine. If the doctor agrees, I think you'll be able to go home tomorrow morning."

"Why not tonight?" Alessandro asks tensely.

"She's just woken up," Nurse Beth chides. "We'll need to observe her for a while longer." She turns back to me. "The police have been asking after you regularly. I think they'll want to speak to you as soon as they can, but I can hold them off if you don't think you're up for it."

I manage a small, grateful smile. Her gentleness is calming, and I take a deep breath to help steady myself further.

"I'd like to talk to Bryce before that, if I can?" I ask. "Then I think if he's here, and Alessandro is here, then, yes. I think I can manage. But I'd also like to eat first, if that's okay?"

She smiles and pats my hand reassuringly. "I'll go get the doctor, so he can clear you for food," she agrees.

Alessandro pulls his phone out of his pocket, punches in the call, then puts the phone to his ear.

I gesture for him to hand me the phone. "Please? I'd like to talk to him," I ask softly.

Alessandro gives me a guarded look, and I wonder if he's offended at my need to talk to Bryce. After a moment he hands me the phone, and before I can even put it to my ear I hear Bryce answering.

"Alessandro? Are you there? Is she okay?" he asks when I manage to get the phone to my ear.

"It's me, Bryce," I say. "I'm okay."

"Oh, thank God," he breathes. "You're awake. I'm coming to you right now, Sera. I'll be there as soon as I can. How are you feeling?"

"I'll be okay, I think," I reply. "Are you okay?"

"God, Sera, what a question." He laughs, and I can hear a car door closing, and an engine starting. "I'm fine, I've just been out of my mind worrying about you all day. I'm in the car, so I'm going to hang up and drive now, okay? I'll see you soon."

"Okay," I agree. "Thanks, Bryce, see you soon."

I hand the phone back to Alessandro. He climbs back onto the bed and holds me in his arms again, and I sink gratefully into his embrace.

"You don't have to talk the police today if you don't want to," he assures me, stroking my hair gently.

"It's okay," I murmur. "I want to. I want to put this all behind me."

As he comforts me I work hard to suppress the memories, to not think about Gabrielle's accusations, not until I must. I need to be strong enough to get through the next little while, then I can go home and hide.

While we wait the doctor examines me and agrees with Nurse Beth's assessment, asking her to bring me food while he removes my IV and a catheter I hadn't been aware of until that moment. Relieved to be freed of both, I tuck into the small plate of applesauce, crackers, cheese, and juice that is placed before me. Alessandro watches me, pleased, while I devour everything.

Bryce arrives shortly after I finish eating but apparently can't tell me anything until I've spoken to the police. When he's assured that I'm physically up to the task, and has my approval, he calls the detective in charge of the case.

Soon after a short, stern man in his late forties, with dense, curly black hair, an olive complexion, and kind, intelligent brown eyes enters the room. A uniformed officer enters behind him, hovering near the door.

"Hello, Ms. Evans," he greets me, settling himself in the chair next to my bed. "I'm Detective Stanley. How are you feeling?"

I suppress the urge to respond that I'm getting a little tired of being asked how I'm feeling.

"Just peachy," I reply with a sardonic edge to my voice.

He smiles tolerantly. "I'm glad to hear it," he responds. "I'll keep this as brief as possible, I don't want to overtax you after your ordeal." He lays a recorder on his knee next to a notepad and clicks it on. "Ms. Evans, can you please describe to me the events of yesterday evening, June 18th, 2018?"

Closing my eyes briefly, I take myself back to leaving my office, and walk him through everything as closely as I can remember it. He asks few clarifying questions, and I'm able to focus on letting it all flow out of me. I try hard not to look at the pained expressions on Alessandro's and Bryce's faces, but instead focus on getting the story out as fully and accurately as I'm able to remember it.

Before I know it I'm at the end of the tale, sharing Gabrielle's accusations, her harsh recrimination, her perception at my murder equating to justice served.

When I stop, Detective Stanley looks at me expectantly. "How did you respond?" he asks, seemingly genuinely curious.

I feel hot tears slide down my cheeks as I answer. "I agreed with her."

His eyebrows shoot up, but he says nothing.

"She didn't expect it, and it made her pause long enough for Alessandro and Bryce to arrive, distracting her from shooting me," I end simply.

He makes a few, final notes on his pad and puts his pen down.

"Thank you for your statement, Ms. Evans," he replies. He turns off his recorder. "I'd like to share a few things with you now, if you're feeling up for it."

Curious, I gingerly wipe the tears from my face and nod faintly.

"Ms. Grayson's accomplice, Ms. Stanwood, gave her up not long after she attacked you," he explains. I give him a confused look that asks how she could give her up when we already knew it was her.

"We thought it best not to share the events of yesterday evening with Ms. Stanwood right away," he clarifies, answering my unspoken question. "We told her there had been a development, and it broke her. She told us everything, completely corroborating what you've just shared with me."

I let out a heavy sigh. But where I should feel relief, I only feel sorrow. Detective Stanley looks at me sympathetically.

"You should also know that Ms. Grayson was a deeply troubled young woman," he says softly. "After serving time for her original crimes against you, she was in and out of trouble with the law and had shown suicidal tendencies at times. At one point she was even under a psychiatric hold for suicide watch. She was unbalanced, Ms. Evans. We knew she was a danger to herself. Unfortunately, there either wasn't sufficient evidence, or it was overlooked that she clearly posed a danger to others. Or, to you, more specifically."

My head dips and I let my anxious tears fall into my lap. "Maybe I did deserve it," I mumble.

"To be kidnapped? Assaulted? Murdered?" Detective Stanley asks reproachfully. "Nobody deserves that, Ms. Evans."

I look up into his kind eyes.

"Maybe not," I accede. "But if it weren't for me …"

Bryce steps forward abruptly. "That's enough for today," he says commandingly. "Sera, you're tired and disoriented. I think you should rest now."

I know Bryce hates it when others criticize me, but I feel a fresh wave of affection for him for his objecting to me criticizing myself.

Alessandro steps up next to Bryce and folds his arms over his chest, in clear solidarity with him. The sight of them both defending me is almost too much to take in my weakened state.

Detective Stanley looks between Bryce, Alessandro, and me.

"Thank you for your time, Ms. Evans," Detective Stanley responds, rising from his chair. "I would tell you to take care of yourself, but it looks like you're already being well taken care of. I'm sure we'll be speaking again soon."

He exits the room, and the uniformed officer follows silently behind him. I look apprehensively between Bryce and Alessandro, unsure of what they're thinking now that they know the whole story.

"I should be going too," Bryce offers. "You really should rest more, Sera, you've been through an awful lot." He hugs me delicately, kissing the top of my head. When he pulls back, he pauses a moment and looks me in the eye. "When you're feeling better, if you need to talk, I'm always here for you." His sunshine-smile breaks across his face and I can't help but feel better.

"Thanks, Bryce," I respond. "For everything. You saved my life." I squeeze his hand.

"Anytime, gorgeous," he replies, winking at me. "See you later."

He leaves, and Alessandro settles on the end of the bed.

"He loves you, I think," Alessandro remarks.

I consider that for a moment. "Yes, he probably does," I agree.

"Do you love him?" There is no accusation in his voice, just curiosity.

"I care about Bryce," I admit. "But I'm not in love with him."

Alessandro nods, trying — and failing — to hide his relief. I look longingly at him, wishing for his body pressed against mine, wanting the solace I used to find in his arms. Despite my exhaustion, despite everything we've been through, seeing him here for me like this makes me want him more than ever, in every way.

I look up at the ceiling, willing the tears that start stinging the back of my eyes to go away. Bryce is right, I am tired, and I'm weary of crying. Seeing my distress, Alessandro moves to my bedside and grasps my hand.

"Do you want me to go too?" he asks gently.

I'm torn by his simple question. The thought of being

without him floods me with all the feelings of gloom and misery I've fought these last weeks. But wanting what can't be is its own special torment as well. In my fragile mental state, the question is more than I can handle, and the tears flow afresh. I wipe them away tiredly.

"I don't know," I admit, laughing a little at myself.

He smiles benevolently and stretches out next to me again, drawing me into his arms. I accept his embrace appreciatively.

"Then I'll stay until you're asleep," he says.

We lay quietly next to each other, and I soon feel myself drifting off.

I WAKE AGAIN THE NEXT MORNING TO VOICES OUTSIDE MY door.

Nurse Beth's voice floats through the crack in the door. "Yes, physically she's just fine," she says reassuringly. "She can go home whenever she likes."

"Then why is she sleeping so much?" Alessandro's voice replies.

"It's likely just a mental coping mechanism," Nurse Beth replies. "She's been through a lot. It would be best if someone saw her home, got her settled in."

"I see," Alessandro says contemplatively. "Thank you. You've been an angel."

"Oh, dear, it's just my job," she replies, the pleasure from his flattery evident in her tone.

As the door swings open quietly, I scoot up into a sitting position.

"You're up," Alessandro remarks, smiling brightly.

I take in the sight of him, noting he's trimmed his beard. And even in simple dark-wash jeans and a black T-shirt he looks ridiculously gorgeous.

"Yes," I agree. "You don't have to take me home."

He cocks an eyebrow. "You heard."

I nod. "I should call Allie anyway," I press. "Or my mom. You've done enough."

He smirks at me. "I'm taking you home, Serafina," he replies firmly. "It's no trouble at all. And Bryce has already spoken to Allie, and I to your mother."

My jaw drops. "You called my mom?" I ask a little more angrily than I intended to.

He drops a bag of clothes on the end of the bed. "No, she called your mobile phone while you were asleep yesterday. I thought it best to let her know that you were okay," he responds impatiently. "I bought you some clothes."

Flipping back the blanket, I swing my legs out of bed and grumpily grab the bag. "Thanks," I reply crossly. I look in the bag to find a blue shirtdress. I raise my eyebrows, and he smiles innocently in answer as he settles into a chair.

∽

THE DOCTOR CLEARS ME FOR RELEASE, INSTRUCTING ME TO avoid any contact sports until my bruised nose has healed fully. *As if I were about to head out for a round of tennis,* I can't help but think snappily.

But I am in awe that my nose somehow wasn't broken and that the swelling has mostly receded, leaving only deep discoloration and tenderness in its place.

Alessandro takes me home, and the secret of my new residence is lost in the process. He whistles appreciatively as we enter the spacious living room.

"Nice place," he remarks. "Needed a change of view?" He walks to the windows, admiring the panorama.

"Something like that," I agree nonchalantly, settling onto the couch. "What are those?" I attempt to distract him by pointing at a vase of flowers in the kitchen.

He gives me a look and strides toward them, plucking a small card out of the arrangement. "Your mother sent them," he replies, looking at me inquisitively.

I can tell that he knows I'm hiding something. He's silent for a beat as he stares at me. Then I can almost see the realization dawn on his face.

"Did you move so I couldn't find you?" he asks pointedly.

"Maybe," I admit sheepishly.

He takes a seat next to me and examines my face carefully. "*Mi dispiace*," he murmurs, taking my hand. "You know the last thing I want to do is cause you pain."

I squeeze his hand. "I know," I reply. "So, we never got to the part where you told me what was so urgent that you had to see me on Friday."

"We don't have to talk about that now," he replies. "You should rest. Are you hungry?" Now I sense *he's* attempting to divert *me*.

"What's going on, Alessandro?" I ask fearfully.

"We can talk about it later," he replies. "You should rest and eat some lunch. I don't think it's a good idea for you to get worked up."

My already overtaxed brain jumps to the worst possibilities, and I feel panic rising in my chest. "I think it's going to get me a lot more worked up if I don't know what's going on," I insist rigidly.

"I …" he starts, pausing to chew on his lip thoughtfully. "Well, to start, I'm not married anymore."

As I process what this means, my panic turns to excitement. And then I remember the baby.

"But … Peyton," I stutter. "The baby?"

"I tried telling you, my marriage was a sham," he replies. "And if she actually is pregnant," his tone makes it clear that he doubts this very much, "then it's not mine."

"So, you're divorced? Since when?" I press.

"Thursday," he admits. "I'd filed the paperwork ages ago, before I ever met you. But she fought me tooth and nail. I think the pregnancy was just another of her tactics."

"So why did she finally agree to a divorce?" I ask.

"I can't go into it right now," he responds, pulling his hand away from mine and stroking his chin absentmindedly. "It's a long, complicated, and unpleasant story anyway."

"Oh," I reply in a small voice.

His reticence makes me wonder if he no longer trusts me. And if he no longer trusts me, perhaps he no longer wants to be with me? I shudder lightly at the thought.

"So, what are you going to do now?"

"I'm going to stay with you today," he says. "Make sure you're okay. I can't think about anything else after that. Let's just focus on today."

His morose tone concerns me deeply. "Alessandro, if you've changed your mind, please just say so," I urge. "But my feelings haven't changed. This past month without you has been awful. If you're not married, it doesn't have to be that way anymore. I want to be with you."

"I can't do this to you now," he says sadly, avoiding my heated gaze.

His words knock the wind out of me. He has changed his mind. My face throbs slightly as the tears well in my eyes.

"You're already doing it," I whisper. "Just get it over with. Tell me you don't love me anymore."

He lets out a strangled cry and runs his hands over his face. "I have to go back to Italy," he says softly. "I'm leaving tomorrow."

"Why?" I demand, leaning toward him, pulling at his arm so it drops away from his face. "For how long?"

"Because I must," he says miserably.

"For how long?" I press, undeterred.

He shakes his head sadly, wrapping his fingers around mine. "I won't be coming back."

TWENTY-EIGHT

"No," I protest. My whole body protests. I wrap my arms around myself as I start to shake. "Tell me why. Please."

Alessandro slides next to me and cups my face in his hands. "It's better if I don't," he sighs. "Not now."

I shake my head. "Do you still love me at all?" I ask pleadingly.

His torment is clear on his face. "Completely," he admits.

"Then talk to me," I plead. "Be with me."

He runs his thumbs down my jaw, dropping his hands to mine. "I want to," he says earnestly. "But I can't. It's better if you don't know everything right now. Trust me, Serafina."

"Does that mean you can tell me later?" I ask hopefully.

He smiles sadly. "Maybe someday," he agrees, "but by then I hope you have moved on. I want you to be happy."

"You make me happy," I insist.

"Do I?" he asks softly.

"It took me a long time to admit it to myself," I reply. "But I've never been as happy as I was when I realized I loved you. When I let myself be with you."

"But you didn't have the full story then," he reminds me. "And I can't give it to you now. I can't lead you into something not knowing — and even if I could, in this case, I wouldn't." Each admission makes his frown deepen, his voice more resolute, and it's terrifying.

"What about Buone Case?" I ask.

He shrugs and turns his palms up. "Marco has already taken it over," he replies simply. "I've walked away."

"I don't understand," I reply, frustrated.

I search his face for clues to the answers he refuses to provide. My brain scrambles for any connection, any bit of information he could have mentioned that would be causing him to cut ties and flee like this, but I come up hopelessly empty. And, for the first time, I wish I'd listened to his story all those weeks ago.

"I know, *bella*," he murmurs. "That's why you have to trust me."

He raises his hand and runs a finger along my cheek as if asking for permission, exactly the way he did the first time only a couple of short months ago. And my answer hasn't changed.

My lips meet his fervently, searching for the answers in his kiss. His mouth moves with mine gently, careful of my injuries.

The familiar feeling of his warm hands skimming my body and his mouth hungrily exploring mine wakens my long-suppressed need for him. I pull impatiently at his shirt, and he allows me to remove it, as eager to be touched as I am to touch him.

I wrap an arm around his neck, pulling myself into his lap, running my other hand greedily over his taut chest as our tongues intertwine. He pulls his mouth away and sighs in pleasure, then nips a trail down my neck.

Suddenly, he lowers his mouth to my breast and pulls at my nipple through the fabric. A moan escapes me, and his hands tighten around my waist, gathering the fabric of the shirtdress and lifting it over my head. Clearly eager to finish undressing me, he pulls at my bra until my breasts topple out, then returns his mouth to my nipple, sucking it deeply, causing me to moan louder. I reach between his legs to find him ready, and I stroke him longingly through his jeans.

He pulls back abruptly to remove them, toppling me back onto the couch. I use the opportunity to shimmy out of my panties and discard them on the floor, as he returns to me, naked and as gorgeous as ever. His eyes fixed intently on my bare skin, he quickly slides into me unforgivingly.

Covering my mouth with his, he begins thrusting roughly, bracing himself with one hand, his other behind my back, pulling me to him with each push. He breathes heavily into my mouth between each passionate kiss, and I'm overwhelmed by his taste, his wine-and-spice smell that I missed so much, and the feeling of his skin against mine.

Surrendering completely to his desirous consumption of my body, I climax, shuddering under him as the gratification tears through me. My tightening muscles pull him in too, and he groans loudly, his orgasm emptying him into me.

As he lays over me catching his breath, I wrap myself around him gratefully. My need for him went so much deeper than I realized. Here, in his arms, I finally feel whole again, the despair of the last day, the last weeks, forgotten.

He looks deeply into my eyes and places a gentle kiss on each of my cheeks.

"You're beautiful," he murmurs.

"I'm yours," I respond.

He shakes his head and buries his face in my hair.

Pulling his head back up, I look deeply into his eyes. "I love you," I insist ardently. "Nothing you've said or done has changed that."

He regards me carefully, as if he's not sure how to reply. "I love you too," he finally says. "But I still have to go."

I bite back the tears and decide against pressing him further. If he won't explain, and he won't change his mind, there's no point in arguing during our last hours together.

"Then let's have some lunch," I reply, yielding for the moment. "And then we'll go upstairs and enjoy what time we have left."

His eyes search mine before he kisses me sorrowfully and withdraws. I quietly put my dress back on, skipping the undergarments. I pad into the kitchen to assemble some simple sandwiches and fruit, taking my time as I process what has transpired between us.

A bittersweet mix of desire and sorrow hangs in the air, as we eat silently, his foot nestled against mine.

After we've eaten and cleaned up, I lean against the counter, staring forlornly out the window. He leans on the other side of the counter, watching me.

"I can't stand to see you so sad, *mio tesoro*," he breathes.

I turn a rueful smile toward him. "I'm sorry," I reply. "I guess I can't help it."

"I can leave now if you'd prefer?" he says. "I'm not good with …"

"Don't," I stop him. "Not yet, please." Rounding the counter, I take his hand and lead him upstairs.

Standing next to the bed, I remove my dress.

"I think we have some catching up to do first," I breathe sensually, running my hands over his still-bare chest, down to the waistband of his jeans. "Off."

He smiles suggestively, and unzips his pants slowly, teasing me with a peek at his nakedness. Focusing all my energy on the task at hand, I bite my lip in anticipation, dropping to my knees to strip him, and then to pleasure him.

THROUGH THE AFTERNOON AND INTO THE EVENING, WE REVEL IN each other, ardently enjoying our brief reunion. As we lay on the bed, spent from our most recent explorations, the sun sets over the bay out the window and the sky is a brilliant blend of orange, pink, and purple.

"When?" I ask softly, breaking a long silence.

"First thing in the morning," he replies quietly. "I'll need to leave by seven."

I consider his response, trying to be grateful that I'll have him all night.

"I know, it doesn't seem fair," he allows, turning on his side to look at me. "But at least we had today. At least I know you'll be okay."

We've broken our unspoken pact for the day not to speak of it, and with the break the flood of emotions fills me once more.

"I wish I could say the same," I reply.

"I'll be fine," he assures me. "After a while, anyway. But never the same without you."

"Will I ever see you again?" I ask sullenly.

He kisses each of my fingers in turn before answering. "I expect we'll see each other in our dreams for a long while," he admits. "Besides that, I can't promise anything."

And it's too painful to speak anymore of it. I cry silently next to him, and he holds me until I fall asleep.

I WAKE AGAIN, SPRINGING UP FROM MY SLUMBER TO A gorgeous purpling sky, but its beauty is lost on me as I gasp for breath, sweat beading on my forehead. More nightmares. I'd expected them, expected a looming Gabrielle threatening my life. But she was nowhere to be found. Only Alessandro was there, distantly, out of reach, fading into the dark.

I turn and find him asleep next to me, and I'm suddenly oddly thankful for the nightmares. Now that they've woken me, I'll have time to say a proper goodbye. I lean over him and lightly kiss his full lips. He stirs slowly, and I run my hands down his cool chest, continuing to press kisses to his mouth, rousing him gently from his slumber.

His eyes open, taking in my face in the dim light. His mouth finally responds, opening to me, meeting my tongue with his own. I slide my leg over his torso, so I sit astride him, deepening my kiss passionately.

His whole body begins to respond, his hands roving over my backside, his breath quickening. I lightly circle my hips over his, and he begins to harden under the stimulus.

"Mmmmm," he moans. "What a nice way to wake up." He finds the wet warmth between my legs and slides slowly and deeply in, hardening fully as he goes.

I let out a gasp of pleasure. "Imagine, if you'd just change your mind, all the many wonderful ways I could wake you like this each morning," I paraphrase him with a smile.

"It's not my mind that would need changing, *dolcezza*," he murmurs.

I kiss him softly. "Hmmm," I muse, sitting up and sinking

fully onto him. He moans appreciatively. "Then I guess I'll just have to remind you what you'll be missing."

Leaning back, I rock my hips, eliciting groans of pleasure from us both. I change my pace and angle every few thrusts, enjoying the altering sensations. Drawing up on my heels, I ride him forcefully until he's loudly enjoying himself, my breasts bouncing in his hands, his thumbs teasing my nipples and driving me pleasantly to distraction.

Before I can bring him too close to the edge, he pushes up, spinning me onto my front, taking me from behind.

"Two can play at that game," he growls, starting to take me hard, and I bury muffled screams into the comforter.

He leans over me, gripping the base of my neck gently, turning my head so he can hear me. It also drives him deeper into me, and before I can hold back the tide, an orgasm floods through me.

As my body relaxes, he flips me onto my back and takes me again, his body pressed fully into mine, his arms pinning mine over my head. His mouth is at my ear, and I can hear his heavy breathing, his low moans of pleasure. I encourage him with my legs, pulling him deep on each thrust, tilting to meet him as he works over me.

I put my mouth to his ear and between moans, trace his lobe with my tongue. The stimulus quickens his pace and he finishes in a frenzy, crying out loudly.

As he relaxes into me, I whisper in his ear, "*Ti amo*, Alessandro."

He pulls up and looks in my eyes. "*Ti amo*, Serafina," he replies.

We stare at each other, perfectly happy, if only for just this moment. He kisses me softly, only releasing me when his alarm sounds a few minutes later.

AND BEFORE LONG HE IS DRESSED AND READY TO GO. HE SITS on the bed next to me, tugging at my shirtdress playfully. "I'll miss these."

I smile sadly, scooting to the edge of the bed so I can walk him out.

"Stay here," he urges. "I want to remember you just like this."

I bite my lip, holding in the tears, and nod. He's right. If I follow him to the door, if I see him leaving, I won't let him go gracefully.

"I can't say it," I whisper. I can't even think the word.

He nods in agreement, mashing his lips together. "Me neither," he replies. He kisses me one last time, and then he's gone.

TWENTY-NINE

To my surprise, I don't cry at all after he leaves. All I feel is a gaping emptiness, and as I methodically make my breakfast I'm glad Allie insisted I take the whole week off. I expect I'll go through a range of emotions as I process this. Not something I want to do in the office.

But at the same time, wallowing at home all day isn't going to help, either. Considering my predicament for a moment, my fingers hover over the address book on my phone. Given recent events, I decide to just go for it.

"Sera," Allie answers, sounding surprised. "Are you okay?"

"Not really," I admit. "But probably not for the reasons you think."

"I was waiting for you to need me, whatever the reasons," she assures me. "How can I help?"

"Take the afternoon off?" I ask tentatively.

"Sure thing, boss," she replies. "Retail therapy?"

"Retail therapy," I agree.

∾

LUNCH FINDS US AT A BURGERS AND BEERS ESTABLISHMENT AT the mall. Allie is surrounded by half a dozen shopping bags to my one lonely bag holding a sweater I thought my mom would like. Evidence of my lack of enthusiasm for anything right now. As we wait for our order, Allie sits silently, waiting for me to talk.

"So, Bryce told you what happened on Friday?" I put forth.

She nods. "You don't have to talk about it if you don't want to," she offers. "But I'm happy to listen. I hate to see you so devastated, Sera. I'm so sorry you had to go through that."

I run my finger lightly over my nose. The deep purpling had started to turn to a sickly green yellow since the day before, with a smattering of bluish patches remaining. But while the physical trauma is already fading, the emotional trauma has been usurped by Alessandro's departure.

"I was pretty upset about it when I came to on Saturday," I admit. "But it's almost like a distant memory now." I sigh heavily, not really knowing where to start.

Allie looks at me, concerned. "Bryce told me Alessandro took you home yesterday," she admits. "You didn't sleep with him, did you?"

I don't know whether to be annoyed at Bryce for sharing

that with her, or thankful that I don't have to explain why he was even there in the first place. In either case, I choose not to be annoyed by the inherent judgment in her question.

"Yes, but only because he's not married anymore," I confess and inform her all at once.

She gasps in shock. "Sera! Omigod," she gushes. "He got divorced?"

"Yep," I confirm.

"Well, that's a nice surprise?" she hazards. But then she looks confused. "So why do you look so distraught?"

The waiter delivers our salads, and I pick forlornly at mine for a minute. She eats quietly, clearly on the edge of her seat waiting for my answer but unwilling to be anything but perfectly accommodating for fear of scaring me away.

"He left," I say finally. "Went back to Italy. For good, it seems."

She drops her fork on her plate in shock. "What? How? Doesn't he own a company here?" she asks, my answer bringing her only more confusion.

I shrug. "He wouldn't explain himself, Allie," I reply gloomily. "He just gave everything up and left, just like that. I have no idea why."

"So, he tells you he's not married anymore but is leaving the country, so you have sex with him?" Allie is not normally this judgmental, so I'm surprised by the distinctly critical edge to her tone.

But I don't blame her. It was a hell of a way to torture

myself. "I can't explain it," I reply tiredly. "I love him." *I'm drawn to him. I can't stay away from him. I need him.* I keep those thoughts to myself, as I know they won't help the conversation any.

She huffs lowly. "Clearly, he doesn't give two shits about you," she fumes. Her words cut through my numbness and tears spring to my eyes.

I put my fork down and push my plate away. "He loves me, Allie," I insist. "He clearly thought he was sparing me some great pain. I wanted to talk him out of it, but he's even more stubborn than I am."

"Well, that's saying something," she replies. She regards me for a moment. "I'm sorry, Sera, I just see how much you're hurting, and I hate that he did that to you. Especially after everything he's already put you through, and everything else that's been happening."

"When it rains, it pours," I respond dully. It's quickly becoming my favorite idiom.

"Well, I hate to say this, but maybe you should come back to work," Allie suggests. "I think everyone is pretty freaked out, and seeing you in one piece wouldn't hurt. I know how much you like burying your emotions in work."

I smile wryly. "True story," I admit. "Maybe tomorrow." It would be good to have a distraction, and a sense of normalcy. The only other thing I could think to do this week was to visit my mother, but I don't think I could handle the inevitable inquisition that would unleash.

"Good, then maybe you can personally tell Charles Sutton to back off and wait for you to call him when you're ready," she responds. "Because he won't listen to me."

My ears perk up. "Mr. Sutton keeps calling?" I ask.

"That's an understatement," she replies. "I have no idea what's got his knickers in a twist. I told him you wouldn't be in today, and I wasn't sure when you would. It kind of set him off and he called Ellie, Jackson, and Maggie, fishing for an explanation."

"I met with him on Friday and told him about the arrests, but mentioned we hadn't caught the mole yet," I explain. "And then he offered me a job."

"Really?" Allie's eyebrows shoot up. "What did you say?"

"Well, it was more of an open-ended invitation to hire me," I add. "I told him I'd think about it. I imagine the recent drama followed by silence has him concerned."

"What would happen to ERS?" Allie asks, worried.

"Don't worry, Allie, you're not going to lose your job," I assure her.

She looks guilty. "I'm not just worried about me. I'm worried about everyone, you included. That company is your life," she says.

Her wording stops me cold in my tracks. I'm extremely proud of my accomplishments, but hearing ERS referred to as "my life" disturbs me in a way I can't quite put my finger on right away.

We eat in silence as I attempt to name my concern. And then it hits me.

"Allie, have you ever heard that saying, 'No one ever said on their deathbed, 'I wish I'd spent more time at the office''?" I ask.

"Of course," she replies slowly. "What are you getting at, Sera?"

I study her for a moment, contemplating Charles Sutton's offer.

"I think it's time I spent a little less time working," I reply frankly. "I need to meet with Mr. Sutton."

"Now?" Allie asks, looking wistfully at her half-finished salad.

I chuckle. "No, Allie, let's finish eating our lunch first," I reply, pulling my plate back toward myself. "And then maybe something with chocolate in it while we're at it." My mind has kicked into high gear again, finally, and it's made me ravenous.

Mr. Sutton arrives at my apartment the following morning at ten a.m. as agreed. I show him in and offer him a seat in the living room.

"Can I get you anything to drink, Mr. Sutton?" I ask kindly.

He waves me off. "No, I'm fine, thank you," he replies, and I settle on the couch across from him. "And I think you can start calling me Charles."

I'm a little surprised but happy that he still seems keen on forming a bond. "Of course, Charles," I reply. "I imagine you want to know what's going on."

"Direct as ever, young lady," he says approvingly. "I was highly concerned when I couldn't get ahold of you yesterday after last week's events."

"Naturally," I allow. "And I wanted to share the tale in person, as it is rather unbelievable."

"I assumed as much from the shiner on your face," he replies blandly, and I can't help but laugh. "Well, I trust all is well, since you seem to be in decent spirits."

"Indeed," I agree. "The events of the last few days have thrown a few things sharply into contrast for me."

"Oh?" he asks curiously. "Do tell."

"All right," I reply agreeably. I choose my words carefully so as not to alarm him. "As I was leaving work on Friday, the leak made herself known to me."

"Speak plainly, Sera," he encourages me. "You're not going to give me a heart attack if that's what you're worried about. I'm made of tough stuff."

I laugh appreciatively. "Okay, then," I reply. "One of my employees kidnapped me at gunpoint and tied me to a chair in the penthouse of our building, where she proceeded to explain why she has been sabotaging me, and why she was about to kill me." I pause, appreciating his shocked expression. "Thankfully, I was able to stall her long enough for the cavalry to show up and stop her, but unfortunately not before she punched me in the face for being impertinent. I spent a little more than a day in the hospital, mostly for shock. She didn't even manage to break my nose properly." I shrug nonchalantly.

Charles guffaws and slaps his knee. "You're a robust woman," he chortles. "That's quite a tale, and I'm glad to hear you are relatively unscathed. Why was she after you?"

"In one of my early deals, I bought the apartment building she lived in and terminated all the leases to renovate and re-rent at a higher price point," I explain. "The paperwork clued her deployed fiancé that she was living with another man. Apparently, they had some serious domestic issues come from it, and as a result, in her anger, she destroyed my car and set fire to her apartment attempting to stop my greedy, heartless, money-grubbing ways. When that didn't work, she came after me after she'd been dishonorably discharged from the military and served her time, orchestrating the events of the past few months to take me and my company down."

He ruminates on that for a bit, then asks thoughtfully, "The words 'greedy,' 'heartless,' and 'money-grubbing' — your word choice or hers?"

I have to think about that, and I'm not quite sure. "I can't honestly remember," I admit. "If I chose them, it's paraphrasing her accusations against me."

"Do you consider yourself to be those things?"

"I'm not the most socially aware person at times," I admit. "And her words affected me deeply at first. But other events since have made me acutely aware that I am none of those things."

He smiles, clearly satisfied with my answer. "I'm glad to hear you've once again taken a negative and found the positive in it."

"Oh, I have, sir," I agree. I begin to weigh my next words but stop myself. If I can be blunt with anyone, it's Charles Sutton, and I'm about to lay all of my cards on the table, so there's no point in being coy about it. "Are you married, Charles? Do you have a family?"

"Of course," he replies, bemused. "I've been married nearly thirty-five years. My Marcia and I have three wonderful sons."

"Has your career ever gotten in the way of being a family man?" I press.

"There have been difficult times," he admits. "And goodness knows I'm something of a workaholic. But I chose wisely, and I love my wife and my children. I know where my priorities are, even if I've walked the line on occasion."

I'd asked to set up my lead-in, but his answer honestly touches me. And it makes me confident that I'm placing my trust in good hands.

"Charles, I want to work for you," I state simply. "But I'm at a crossroads, and my service would come at a fairly steep price."

He regards me attentively. "I'm listening."

"I currently have forty-three employees. Seven business support function employees, a project management team of fourteen, a property management team of nineteen, and our general brokerage of three. Are you willing to absorb those employees?"

He considers carefully for a few minutes before replying, "We can take everyone except the property management team," he says slowly. "It's not a business I've ever been interested in." He pauses. "However, we can create a subsidiary company for property management services if you have someone willing to run it. If they produce results, we'll keep them. If it's more trouble than it's worth, we'll cut them loose."

I ponder his counter offer. "I'll check with my property management lead. If she's amenable, I think that would be better than having to drop hundreds of units and cut all those jobs," I agree. "But I want at least a ninety-day trial."

"Reasonable," he replies. "And what of you?"

I hesitate, knowing he'll like this next part less. "I need to take time off," I respond. "I'll be leaving the country for an indefinite period. When I return, I'm all yours."

As expected, his eyebrows shoot up and his jaw drops. "That's quite an ask," he admits. "Any idea exactly how indefinite we're talking?"

"A few months, maybe?" I hazard. "I wish I knew. I'm sorry. I know it's a lot to expect."

"A few months is nothing," he says, surprising me. "I thought we might be talking about years." He looks closely at me for a few minutes and smiles kindly. "He must be quite a young man."

And I must wear my heart on my sleeve more than I thought.

"I think so," I reply. "But that's what I need to find out."

"You don't trust easily, do you, Sera?" he asks shrewdly.

"No, sir," I agree. I've always kept my heart under lock and key, safeguarded from the world.

"Good," he commends me. "We have an agreement, then." He stands, offering his hand.

I scramble to my feet and shake it in disbelief. "Thank you, Charles," I respond.

∽

As soon as he's gone, I call Bryce.

"Hey, gorgeous," he greets me, sunshine-smile in his voice.

"Hey, Bryce," I return. "I need your help."

"Anything for you, Sera," he says. "What is it?"

"It's Alessandro," I respond. "He's gone back to Italy. And I need you to help me find him."

There's silence on the other end for a beat. "Am I allowed to ask why?"

"Because I love him," I say simply. "And I'm going after him."

∽

Thank you so much for reading! Please take a minute to leave a review on any retailer, goodreads, and/or BookBub. Even if it's just a couple of sentences, your opinion is important to potential readers and to me. Thank you!

∾

Want to know what happens to Sera and Alessandro? Get *All of Me* (Book 2) now at https://melanieasmithauthor.com/books-all-of-me.html

∾

Sign up for Melanie A. Smith's newsletter to get a FREE book plus all the latest news and more
https://melanieasmithauthor.com/newsletter.html

ACKNOWLEDGMENTS

I've always wanted to write a novel. Since I was seven or eight maybe? But time and life got away from me until I was finally able to eke out a corner of my life to write again more than thirty years later (eep, my age is showing!). In any event, it absolutely would not have been possible without, well a LOT of people really, but first and foremost my husband. Without everything from his formidable child-distracting skills to his patience with my never-ending rumination over possible plot lines to his input on, well, all of it — from character development to web design. His surprising tolerance (and dare I say, enjoyment?) of this process has been a huge blessing. So, thank you, darling, for your patience and encouragement.

Likewise, several of my closest friends have been an inestimable source of support as I've embarked on this journey in reading drafts, providing feedback, and just generally being ridiculously positive and encouraging. A huge thanks to all the lovely ladies who've lifted me up through this. Jenny Gardner, I'm especially lookin' at you, babe. You're not just my best friend of two decades — your wisdom, advice, and insight have been amazing always, but especially throughout this adventure. Besides which you're also one badass copy editor whose services make this book all the better.

I'll refrain from listing the dozens of authors who have generally inspired me over the years, but I do want to thank two recent authors that specifically reignited my writing spark. Firstly, E L James, for demonstrating that something as humble in origins as fan fiction can become something so widely enjoyed, and something as simple as one amazing and complex character can absolutely make a book. Secondly, Sabaa Tahir, who while a friend-of-a-friend with whom I was barely acquainted while we both attended the same university, has inspired me with her wild success since and with her spectacular work. Even with such a tenuous connection she really hit the idea home that writing a good book isn't just for the mysterious authors on the best-seller list — it's people I know. People like me. So, a huge thank you to both these extraordinary women.

And lastly, the thought of bringing the kind of enjoyment I get from books to others is hands-down my biggest motivator in writing. So, a huge thank you to everyone who read this book. Truly, I hope you enjoyed reading this as much as I enjoyed writing it.

ABOUT THE AUTHOR

Melanie A. Smith is a former engineer turned stay-at-home mom and award-winning, international best-selling author of steamy contemporary romance. She crafts strong book boyfriends with hearts of gold and smart, self-sufficient heroines. When she's not lost in the world of books, you'll find her spending time with family, cooking, and driving with the windows down and the stereo cranked up loud.

facebook.com/MelanieASmithAuthor
twitter.com/MelASmithAuthor
instagram.com/melanieasmithauthor

BOOKS BY MELANIE A. SMITH

The Safeguarded Heart Series

The Safeguarded Heart

All of Me

Never Forget

Her Dirty Secret

Recipes from the Heart: A Companion to the Safeguarded Heart Series

The Safeguarded Heart Complete Series: All Five Books and Exclusive Bonus Material

Life Lessons

Never Date a Doctor

Bad Boys Don't Make Good Boyfriends

You Can't Buy Love

The Heart of Rutherford: Life Lessons Novels 1 – 3

Stand-alones

Everybody Lies

Last Kiss Under the Mistletoe

Tough Love

Finding His Redemption

Vegas Baby (Hot Vegas Nights)

Pompous Paramedic (A Hero Club Novel)

Short Stories

Cruising for Love

Hot for Santa